Tetons by Morning

by

Lucy Naylor Kubash

North Star Legacy, book 2

Tetons by Morning

Cover Art by *Tina Lynn Stout*

The Wild Rose Press, Inc.
PO Box 708
Adams Basin, NY 14410-0708
Visit us at www.thewildrosepress.com

Publishing History
First Edition, 2026
Trade Paperback Print ISBN 978-1-5092-6419-3
Digital ISBN 978-1-5092-6420-9

North Star Legacy
Published in the United States of America

Dedication

Dedicated to my family for giving me the gift of time.
To Emily, for sitting beside me for hours with your
little picture books, while I scribbled in my notebooks.
To Chris, for ten years of visits to Wyoming and a
reason to travel there.
To Tom, for fifty-three years of taking me where I
needed to go. To a writer, time is golden.

Chapter 1

This is it. This is the place. It really exists.

Hunching his shoulders in the early morning chill, Chance McCord watched the sunlight spread in golden waves across the land and glint off the Grand Teton Mountains. The rays shone in his eyes, and he shifted in the saddle and tipped his hat lower to get a better glimpse of the view. Below him, the Buffalo Fork of the Snake River meandered through the valley still dressed in the fading fall colors of the high country. A biting wind swept across the ridge, telling of winter storms soon to come and a river that would be bound fast in ice and snow.

Today, a lone moose struggled to cross the river, slipping awkwardly on its tall skinny legs.

The wind blew over the hillside, and Smoky whickered when he caught the wild scent. The big gray Appaloosa shook his head and stamped his hoof.

"Whoa, son. It's all right." Chance stroked the gelding's neck until Smoky calmed, then swung his leg over the saddle and dismounted. Holding the reins in one gloved hand, he walked a little closer to the ridge's edge and watched in silence as the light turned an even more shimmering pink.

In the last few weeks, he had ridden the hills and ridges, searching for the place that in past years was so often a part of his dreams. Storms had kept him from riding to the farthest reaches of the valley, but a break in the weather provided an opportunity to continue the quest. Of all the places he stopped to consider, none had reached into his soul nor spoken with the voice he recalled from long ago. Not until this morning had the strange sense of peace and belonging suddenly filled him, as if he'd left a part of himself here as a child and not found it until now.

Smoky head-butted him, telling him it was time to go back to his warm stall and a bucket of sweet feed. Chance always rewarded his horse for venturing out on such a frigid day.

"Okay, fella, I get the message. Just give me another minute." Chance turned to imprint the scene on his mind and memorize the landmarks, so he could find the place again without riding for days. An aspen, its nearly bare branches stretching to the pewter sky, stood perhaps ten feet away. He tugged a blue bandanna from around his neck and strode over to the tree. Dropping the reins for a moment, he carefully tied the bandanna to one of the lowest hanging branches—not too tight, but enough so the wind could not dislodge it. "Okay." He directed his words to whatever had finally brought him to this place. "I'll be back. I need to bring Casey here."

The wind picked up as he stepped into the saddle, and a soft sigh whispered through the pines. It sounded like someone calling his name.

****

In the ranch house kitchen, Casey stood at the counter and wound the cord of the old wall phone around her fingers. Her mother rattled on. Why couldn't they have a better conversation? Even after three months, Mom's advice remained the same.

"Come home, Casey. It's okay to admit you made a mistake. Daddy and I understand, and we'll be glad to let you and Jamie stay here until you get yourself straightened out."

Mom pleaded like that every time they spoke. "I've told you before. I made no mistake." Casey kept her voice steady. "I married Chance because I love him, and I'm not leaving him, no matter if what you think I've done is wrong."

"But it happened so fast. How could you even know him? You were just confused and maybe infatuated, and he took advantage of that. Now you've had a few months to think about it, surely you know—"

Anger bubbled inside, but she tamped it down and fought to stay calm. "What I know is that Chance is my husband. He's Jamie's stepfather, and we're a family now. You need to believe I'm happy." *Why can't she respect my decision?*

Seconds of silence passed. "Well, your daddy and I aren't. We miss you, and it's not right you've taken our grandson so far away. Thanksgiving won't be the same without the two of you, and then Christmas is coming. We won't always be around, you know, so it wouldn't hurt for you to consider our feelings."

Casey held her tongue for a span of three breaths. Her parents had her best interests at heart. They just couldn't understand the impulsive trip to Wyoming that last summer had led to a whirlwind romance and marriage. "Then come out for a visit. We'd all love to have you." *Not sure this is a good idea, but I'll offer.*

"To Wyoming? Now you know it's just too far for us to drive this time of year. With your father's arthritis, he isn't up to traveling."

"You could fly into Jackson."

"You know we hate to fly, but if you need money to come home, well, of course, we'd be willing to send you some."

"I don't need your money." Casey's voice trembled now, both from the too-familiar argument and her own inability to convince her mother she was happy.

"I have to think you do. With an itinerant rodeo cowboy for a husband, you certainly can't have much. You left a perfectly good job here, and you've probably gone through the money from Matthew's insurance. It's a real shame, you giving it to someone like that. It should have belonged to Jamie."

Casey wouldn't even go there. Chance would take nothing from her, and she'd started a college fund for Jamie with that money. Tired of the distressing issue, she let Mom rattle on for another moment, said she had to go, and hung up. She sagged against the wall behind her and bit her lip to hold back a wealth of crazy emotions. Talking to her mother these days made her sad.

A moment later, Chance and the wind burst through the kitchen door. As always happened, his presence filled the room, and this morning, the pungent scent of lodgepole pine and saddle leather clung to his rugged physique. His broad shoulders filled out the fleece-lined denim jacket as well as the faded jeans fit his long legs.

At the sight of her handsome, dark-haired husband, Casey's heart beat a little faster. She'd wondered where he'd gotten off to so early today. Now she knew. He was out riding.

"Casey, you won't believe what I found." He crossed the kitchen, his boot steps heavy on the floor. He stopped, pivoted, and saw her. His jaw tensed. "Casey, honey, what's wrong?" He moved to stand in front of her and, with one chilly hand, lifted her chin. His gaze flicked to the wall phone. "You were talking to your parents, weren't you? Isn't it a little early?" He pushed back his cowboy hat and scanned her face.

No sense in avoiding his question. In his uncanny way, Chance recognized the problem. She lifted her gaze to meet his deep-blue eyes. "You forget it's two hours later in Michigan. Daddy still goes out to oversee the milking. I just thought…I'd see how they're doing."

"So you called them?"

Casey nodded. "Last time we talked, he wasn't feeling well. I got…worried." Tears welled in her eyes. She struggled not to let them fall.

Chance sighed and drew her against his chest, holding her close.

She slipped her arms around his middle and pressed her face into his jacket, breathing in the scent of autumn and the mountains. The scent soothed her a little, but a raw sadness still dwelled in her heart.

He stroked her hair with one hand. "I thought you decided not to talk to them for a while."

"They're my parents and my son's grandparents." She muffled her voice against his jacket. "I can't just pretend they don't exist."

"Nor should you, but I don't like seeing my wife cry, which seems to happen whenever you have a conversation with them." He hesitated, took in a deep breath, and let it out slowly. His hand stilled in her hair. "*Are* you sorry?"

Puzzled, Casey lifted her face. "For what?"

"Marrying me. Not taking more time to think about it. Do you wish…?"

She leaned back, taking in his rugged appearance. The past months had been an adjustment in learning to live with Chance and his family. The long Wyoming winter still stretched ahead, but the love that dwelled in her heart only grew stronger every day. "Not for a minute. This is my life now. You're my life. Never doubt that." To prove what she said, Casey drew his head down and kissed him. She played her lips over his, evoking his soft groan. He tasted cold, like the wind, but his lips warmed as she deepened the kiss. His embrace could drive out every sensible thought from her head. They stood together, his hands tangled in her hair. She vaguely heard voices, and then his father and brother Kyle walked into the kitchen.

"You need to start thinking about moving those cattle soon. It's November, and any day now another storm will blow out of those mountains." Justin broke off his tirade. "Okay, you two, isn't it a little early for this nonsense? We've got work to do around here."

Chance broke off the kiss but kept his back toward Justin and Kyle. "I'm taking a trip to Rock Springs in a few days to pick up a couple of young colts." He kept his voice low so only she could hear. "Want to come? We can get away from here for the day."

She would welcome a day to escape, too, and gave him one more quick kiss. "You bet, cowboy. Just tell me when, and I'll be there."

"We'll talk tonight." He squeezed her hand before letting her go and facing the other McCord men, who were already back to talking about ranch business.

She stepped away and then they were gone from the kitchen, leaving Casey alone. *What to do with the rest of the morning?* Jamie wouldn't arrive home from school for hours, and Billie, who cooked for the ranch, went to her cabin until lunch time. Perhaps the hardest change when she married Chance was deciding where she fit in with his family and learning a new way of life. She still struggled to figure it out.

Back in Michigan, she'd worked at a large public library and loved her job. She was widowed three years ago, and her work and Jamie were the saving graces in some very dark days. She went on without Matt and was doing all right, and then his Aunt Billie invited Casey and Jamie to come to Wyoming for the summer. What started out as an opportunity to get away from it all for a few weeks turned into a whole new adventure and chapter in her life. Who would have thought she'd fall so completely in love with Chance McCord, ex-rodeo champ and prodigal son of the North Star Ranch? Leaving the security of her job and family to live in such a wild place was a huge decision.

But she left that life and never regretted it for a minute. That didn't mean coping was always easy. She fixed herself another cup of tea, her third since rising, and sat in front of the fireplace in the ranch house living room. Popping open her laptop, she hoped the Wi-Fi was working. At least, she could check email and work on the website she was building for the North Star. With luck, they'd have some new reservations for the dude ranch next spring.

Chapter 2

A few days later, Casey stood beside the horse trailer and listened to a metallic clanging echo across the holding pens. She pulled her blue knit hat over her ears and hugged herself against the biting wind whipping around her. Chance had said to wait here while he spoke with the government agent, but the more she listened to the sound of the wind rushing by and the haunting *clang-clang*, the more she shivered in the late morning air. Still, she didn't climb inside the truck. Soon enough, they'd start the long trip back.

On the drive south to Rock Springs early this morning, a few snow flurries had followed them. She worried about Jamie, back at the North Star in the care of Billie and Justin. Billie promised the boy would be fine, and Ed, the wrangler, would meet him at the bus stop in the afternoon. But what if snow fell harder in the valley?

The clanging increased, sending a touch of melancholy rippling through Casey's heart. What was that sound?

Chance returned to the pickup truck, his shoulders hunched against the piercing wind. The temperature had dropped another ten degrees. He drew on his worn leather gloves and noticed Casey standing outside. He shook his head. "You didn't have to stay out here. The weather's turning bitter. C'mon, get in. We have to pull around the back. The colts are separated from the rest of the herd." He opened the door to the truck cab.

She turned to climb inside, but that metallic sound echoed again. *Clang-clang-clang.* She hesitated. "What is that sound?" She looked past him to the pens, where a hundred horses huddled together in groups of a half-dozen or so.

"They're banging on the metal fence." He cupped her elbow in one hand to hurry her inside.

Casey still hesitated. "Why are they doing it?"

He blew out an impatient sigh. "I reckon they want out."

She watched the captured horses. "That sounds so…sad." A glimpse of understanding shone in his blue eyes. He knew how she felt about animals.

A few moments later, he parked behind the big holding corrals to load the two colts—one, a fine-looking roan Appaloosa, and the other, a dark chestnut with a white blaze. Brought in off the range a month ago, the young mustangs were only in a trailer once, right after the roundup.

Chance peeled off the quilted vest he wore and, in spite of the cold, rolled up the sleeves of his flannel shirt, revealing sinewy arms still brown from last summer. He pushed back his hat and approached the colts. In turn, he held each colt around the neck and sweet-talked the young horse into wearing a halter and lead rope. That accomplished, he motioned Casey toward the hay in the truck bed. "Grab a couple of handfuls and stand outside the front of the trailer. Let them see it."

Casey scooped up the hay and stuck one hand through the trailer window to entice the colts.

Chance led them forward, speaking quietly but not allowing a lot of room to revolt.

I'm glad he knows what he's doing. She'd watched Chance work with other mustangs. He possessed strong arms, but convincing these two colts that they had to load into another conveyance like the one that ended their freedom took the better part of an hour. The process involved Casey holding out more than a few handfuls of hay. She understood Chance's plan but didn't blame the colts for resisting.

Back home, Kyle didn't support the idea of bringing mustangs to the ranch. He didn't believe training wild horses was worth the time and effort.

But Chance was determined. He'd worked with wild horses away from the ranch and wanted to do it again. They'd make fine trail horses, he said, and eventually, maybe he could train more to sell to the National Park Service.

Roy, the head wrangler at the ranch, had a way with the wild ones and had agreed to help Chance.

Casey wouldn't argue with the plan, but she never once considered the mustang holding pens were such a desolate place. Seeing the wild horses that were used to roaming the range, but were now confined to pens, about broke her heart.

The agent finally came out and helped Chance finish locking up the trailer. They talked for a few minutes.

Casey wandered over to a smaller corral where a single horse stood off by herself, away from the other huddles.

The blue roan mare nosed lackadaisically at the hay strewn on the ground but flicked her ears forward when she caught sight of Casey.

"Hey, girl, how come you're over here alone?" she spoke in a low, soft voice. "Are you an outcast?"

The mare whickered but didn't approach the fence to investigate. The horses at the North Star were curious sorts, always on the watch for some human to give them a treat, and Casey had made friends with most. They often met her at the fence for a head scratch and a carrot or two. Not this one.

She stood her ground and eyed the trailer.

Casey read fear and perhaps even anger on the mare's wise face.

The mare turned her gaze back to the human.

A strange jolt shot through Casey, as if some connection had suddenly formed.

She turned to leave but heard the sound again— *clang-clang*—and another low whicker. She glanced back.

The mare had approached the gate and hit it with her shoulder.

"Casey, honey, let's go. We gotta beat the storm brewing over the mountains." Chance stood next to the truck and waited.

Casey's stomach clenched in a fearsome ache, and a flash of emotion anchored her to the spot.

He moved alongside her and touched her arm. "What is it? We need to go—"

"We can't leave her. She needs to go with us, too." She checked his puzzled frown. "Can we take her? Please? I have the money. I'll pay her adoption fee."

"She's a mare, and they just brought her in a few days ago. She has an injury, and they thought—"

"Injury?" Alarm flared through Casey. "So, what

does that mean? What will happen if no one wants her?" Too often, a useless horse came to a bad end.

Chance opened his mouth, closed it, and finally just shook his head. "We'll take the blue roan mare, too," he said over his shoulder to the agent. "Get the papers ready for me to sign."

The agent returned to the office.

Casey grabbed Chance's arm and stretched on tiptoe to kiss his stubbled cheek. "Thank you," she whispered.

Behind them, the mare clanged against the gate.

Chance rummaged in the truck bed for another lead rope.

Casey approached the gate but made no attempt to touch the mustang. "Don't worry, Blue Lady. You'll like the North Star. It's a good place and a good home. You'll see."

Distrust lurked deep in the mare's sable eyes. In answer to Casey's soft and reassuring words, she turned away to gaze toward the wide-open range.

A bittersweet sadness pricked at Casey. *I'm not sure we'll win this horse over, but we have to try.*

****

Inside the office, Chance signed the adoption papers and handed over the fee.

The agent, a young guy who, with his smooth chin and too-big shirt, didn't look old enough to work for the government, eyed him. "Surprised you want that one. She's lame and won't be an easy keeper. Mind my asking what you've got in mind for her?"

Chance shrugged and took the papers the agent held out. "My wife likes her," he spoke the only explanation necessary. As he left the building, he met someone coming in. He stood aside and waited for the older man to pass. While he glanced out at the threatening weather, he noticed the cowboy stop and do an about-face.

"That you, Chance?"

The vaguely familiar voice rang a bell. He hadn't seen Lane Harris in over five years, and in that time, the man had aged. His white hair matched his drooping mustache, and his shoulders were bent. A well-worn cowboy hat hid his eyes.

He tipped the brim back to stare. "We heard you went back to the valley. That true?"

A stinging jolt ran through Chance. He said nothing but took a step away from a man he'd hoped to never see again.

"Yeah, you probably don't recognize me," the old guy went on in a raspy voice. "I didn't look so old back then."

Familiar pain and regret burned like acid in his throat. "I know you," Chance finally spoke. "How goes it, Lane?"

"Tough, but we're managing." A strained silence yawned between them. Lane shifted from one bowleg to the other. "Heard you quit the rodeo and got a new wife. That true?"

"Yes, to both." Let him just get away.

"She from Wyoming?"

Chance folded the papers in his hand. "No, Lane, she's not. Casey moved here from Michigan this past summer. We've only been married a few months."

The older man adjusted his battered hat and smirked. "Did you move as fast on her as you did on Angela?"

13

Chance smacked the folded papers against one hand and refrained from offering a sharp retort. What would harsh words gain him? Lane Harris had suffered enough. If taking a stab at him made the man feel better, so be it. "I'll pretend I didn't hear that. Good day to you." He slammed out the door and strode over to the truck where Casey sat inside.

She looked back through the rearview window at the horses in the trailer and watched him load the surprisingly docile mare.

He secured the trailer gate and climbed inside the truck cab.

"What's wrong?" Casey asked. "You look upset. Is it about the mare?"

He chewed on the silence for a few seconds. "The mare is fine. Let's get on the road. The storm will be hot on our heels all the way to Jackson, but if we're lucky, we'll have a tailwind." *And the farther I get away from Lane Harris, the better I'll feel.*

Chapter 3

A week later, another big storm hit and besides blanketing the Tetons and the valley in another layer of white, the snow drove a pack of wolves to hunt closer to the ranches. Bison moved into the cattle pastures, forcing Chance to saddle up every day and chase them away. Accompanied by the Great Pyrenees dog, Mariah, he rode along the perimeter of the winter pastures, checking for any signs the wolves stalked nearby. The predators normally stayed to the north in Yellowstone, but hunger forced animals, as well as humans, to leave their comfort zone.

The wind stung like needles against his face, and he flexed his shoulders to ward off the rawness that sank into his bones. After a day spent in the saddle, his body always reacted to the cold and refused to move the way he wished it still could. Blame it on old rodeo injuries. Blame it on just plain getting older. Whatever, he simply wasn't the man he used to be—the one who rode the meanest broncs across the Divide. Chance McCord, Top Bronc Rider at the Cody Night Rodeo. Chance McCord, Best All-Around Cowboy at the Cheyenne Rodeo Days for three years running. He owned the belt buckles to prove the wins, and the memories of more nights spent in the back of his truck than he cared to count. In a way, the memories kind of ate at his soul. Because today, Chance McCord rode along the edge of the Bridger-Teton wilderness and looked for tracks in the snow.

He should have worn the scarf Casey tried to tie around his hat to keep it from blowing off. Should have listened to the woman who loved him in spite of everything. She and the boy were the people who made his life worth living right now and kept him from just going back on the road. Dealing with his father and brother was still a work in progress. Would he ever feel a part of the family he had once left behind? Ever fit in? Probably not, because in all his thirty-four years, he never had.

Smoky stopped and snorted, blowing steam from his flaring nostrils.

Not far away, a young bison did the same. Snow and frost covered the shaggy face as the bull lifted his head from the hay roll and eyed Chance and the huge white dog racing toward him.

Mariah had grown up on the ranch and knew how to avoid kicking hooves and sharp horns that could snag a hundred and fifty-pound wolf and toss it yards away. She'd played this game with many a bison, and they usually saw things her way and moved on. This fellow had found an easy dinner and had no intention of moving.

Chance watched the dog dart and dash for a few minutes. He urged Smoky to move closer. The Appaloosa balked at the request, but as any good cow horse, he listened to his rider.

Seeing them approach, the young bison pawed at the snow-covered ground and grunted.

Mariah barked and went in from the side, snapping but backing off in time to avoid the swing of his massive head. She dove in again, this time narrowly missing the tip of a horn.

To the herd dog, chasing off the bison was a game and all in a day's work. But even if she didn't know it, Mariah wasn't getting any younger, and the last thing Chance wanted was for her to get hurt. He nudged Smoky with his heels, and they broke into a lope. "Heeh-ahh. Get moving now!" He pulled off his hat to wave it over his head. "Get outta here!" Smoky carried Chance in wide circles around the bull, while he continued to wave his hat and shout. He reined in a short distance away and waited.

For one second, the bison stood his ground, lowering his head and snorting but finally deciding it was much easier to just leave. With one last grunt, he kicked out a hind hoof and headed back to the snowy wilderness beyond the North Star.

Chance patted the gelding's gray neck. Mariah joined them, and he tossed her a liver treat he'd stuck in his pocket this morning. "Nice job, guys. Guess we showed him who's boss around here."

Mariah's tongue hung out, and she wagged her plumy tail.

No doubt the old girl was ready for another go-around, but they'd had enough fun for one day. Chance reached inside his fleece-lined coat and pulled from his flannel shirt pocket the phone Casey had insisted he carry now while riding the ranch. He checked the time. Jamie would get off the school bus in half an hour. Texting Casey, he let her know he'd bring Jamie home.

Waiting for the yellow bus to arrive, Chance watched an eagle soar overhead. Last summer, he'd taken Casey to Jenny Lake. They'd seen an eagle dip over the water and snatch a trout, and she was so amazed at the sight. Seeing the wonder in her gray eyes had made the sight all new for him, and he'd known then he could never leave this woman behind. No matter how much he missed the rodeo, no matter how much he struggled to adapt back into his family and this life, Casey was reason enough to stay. She and the child he had quickly come to think of as his son.

The bus lumbered down the valley road and braked noisily to a stop in front of the North Star's entrance.

Jamie, his backpack straining against his thin shoulders, disembarked and stood for a second looking about for the familiar truck. A slight kid for eight years old, Jamie looked like the next stiff wind could knock him over. Unruly blond hair stuck out from a red stocking cap, and his winter coat hung open. The knees of his jeans looked wet. From playing in the snow? Casey would have fits when she saw him.

Chance rode Smoky forward and waved to the bus driver to go ahead.

Mariah greeted the boy and led him to where Chance waited.

Jamie squinted into the wind that swept between them. "Hi, Chance. How come you're here today?"

"Just out checking for intruders and thought we'd ride back together. If you're okay with that."

"Heck yeah, you know I am." A grin lit his ruddy-cheeked face.

Chance reached for the backpack and stuck it in front of him. He held his arm down to Jamie.

The boy latched on.

He swung him up behind him. "You hangin' on?"

Jamie nodded against his back and wrapped his

small arms around Chance's middle.

Chance turned the Appaloosa toward home. They'd only done this once, in the early fall right after school started, but spending more time together seemed like a good idea and gave them an opportunity to connect without Casey hovering about. His wife was a sweetheart—he'd always be the first to admit—but sometimes, she suffocated the kid with her concerns. He waited until they got a little way along the ranch road. "How is school going? Teacher giving you a lot of homework?"

"Mostly math. I'm not too good at it. I hope Mom can help me."

Chance had hated school but was pretty good with that subject. Of course, who knew how they were teaching math to kids nowadays. "Maybe I can take a look tonight, and we'll figure it out together," he offered. "Believe it or not, I got *A*s in math." So far, he'd held back on taking over any parenting duties, but if he and Jamie were to build a father-son relationship, they had to start somewhere.

"That'd be great. Thanks."

"No problem." The boy shuddered against his back, and Chance, with a nudge of his heels, asked Smoky to pick up his pace. The temperature had dropped a few more degrees, and as the winter sky turned to early dusk, he drew Jamie's arms tighter. "Let's get on home. Snow will hit soon." He nodded toward the clouds building over the mountains. "Your mom wouldn't like if we got stuck out here."

Chapter 4

Casey lifted the pot of boiling potatoes from the stove and carried it to the sink to drain. Here at the ranch, five meals out of six required mashed potatoes with a pound of butter and a gallon of gravy for them to swim in to keep the men happy. She tried to convince Billie some healthier choices might not be a bad idea, especially with the heart-friendly diet Justin's doctor prescribed.

They attempted to make some changes but had a hard time explaining healthy eating to guys who worked outside most of the day and came in to dinner hungry as the pack of wolves that threatened the cattle.

She worried about Jamie getting started on a lifetime of bad food choices, but tonight, Casey wouldn't argue. She dumped the butter into the pot and stirred the huge frying pan full of brown gravy. While waiting for the butter to melt, she glanced at the kitchen clock above the sink. What was taking so long for Chance and Jamie to get home from the bus stop? Had they gotten waylaid somewhere?

"Don't worry so much." Chance's motto echoed in her head. Yet, she couldn't help it. She was a natural-born worrier. Leaving the gravy to simmer, she covered the potatoes and went to look out the back door. When they arrived at the barn, she would see Chance and Jamie from here. The deep indigo sky to the west promised more snow, and a few flakes fell now in lazy but ever thickening circles. Casey pulled her phone from her jeans pocket to send Chance a text when she saw Mariah come bounding into the ranch yard. Just behind her rode the man and boy, slightly snow-covered but none the worse for wear.

Chance lowered Jamie to the ground and handed him his backpack, motioning him toward the house.

The boy trudged through the snow.

Dismounting, Chance led his horse into the barn. He wouldn't make it inside the house for probably an hour. He always dried Smoky and fed him before taking care of himself. Just one of the things she loved about the man.

Dinner now was a far-less hectic time than during the summer or the fall roundup, when they fed more ranch hands plus whatever guests ate with them. Casey had even convinced the family to eat dinner in the seldom-used dining room for the winter. She loved the room with its long table and tall windows that framed an amazing view of the mountains. And the murals on the walls that Chance's mother had painted once upon a time lent a pleasant warmth.

Easily her favorite time of day, Casey enjoyed sitting with Chance and Jamie and hearing about what they'd done in their hours away. Yet, the ranch talk that constantly went on among the McCord men and Roy and Ed, the wranglers who stayed over the winter, overwhelmed their conversations. Sometimes, she wished they'd give it a rest and talk about something else.

Once they were all seated, the men dug into the food and began asking Chance if he'd seen any signs of the wolves today.

"No wolves," he assured them. "Just an ornery little bison helping himself to our hay. Mariah and I sent him packing." He winked at Jamie. "You all would've been proud of the old girl."

First, wolves stalking the cows and now, a bison in the pasture. Casey twisted her napkin and debated asking a question. On the farm, they never had to deal with wild buffalo coming in to steal feed from the cows. Would her question show her ignorance about the difference in ranch life? Too bad. She'd ask anyway. "Isn't there a risk a bison will charge when you chase it off?"

Silence followed for a few seconds. "Of course, there's a risk," Justin spoke, "but we face a lot of risks out here. We just learn to live with them. You will, too, Casey."

Much as she cared about her father-in-law, he could be a bit of a bear. Still a darn handsome man at seventy-one, with snow-white hair and a rugged build he'd passed on to his older son, Justin sat at the head of the table. He fixed Casey with his piercing silver-blue gaze. Grumpiness had become part of his demeanor since the heart attacks and following surgery left him unable to work outside, as he'd spent his life doing. Then there were the mustangs and Justin's growing disapproval of their presence. He'd agreed to Chance bringing them to the ranch last summer, but lately, his attitude had changed.

She tried to tolerate his gruff comments, but tonight what he said rubbed against her edgy nerves. After another conversation with her mother earlier in the day, she couldn't cope with anyone else telling her what she needed to do. She finished eating quickly and hurried her dishes into the kitchen.

After everyone made fast work of the mashed potatoes and roast beef, Billie carried in a pile of plates. She set them on the counter and pushed a small hand through her short, gray hair. "Fellas were really hungry tonight. I guess the cold weather does that to a body." Glancing at the stove with its dirty pots and pans, she heaved a sigh. "I'll get busy here. You take care of Jamie. I'm sure he's got homework." Billie rubbed at her back and grimaced.

Casey patted the wiry little woman's shoulder. "I'll clean up. Why don't you head to your cabin before the full force of the storm blows over the valley? Roy can walk with you. And enjoy a day off tomorrow. I'll cook the meals."

She sent Casey a weary smile. "You're a doll for offering, but I can't leave you with all the work. Anyway, it's the first of the month, and we need to take kitchen inventory and make our shopping list, plus with the holidays coming—"

"I can handle it." Casey tried to keep the frustration from her voice. "I live here now, and if I don't learn how to do all this, I might as well go back home." She hadn't meant for her words to come out so harshly. Worried Billie might take offense, she turned and gave her a quick hug. "I'm sorry. What I meant is I have to learn how to fit in with this family. I'm not trying to take over your work. I just want to do my share."

"You do more than your share, believe me, and don't listen to what Justin says. He's just taking his frustration out on the world, and since we're the closest, we get to bear the brunt." Billie squeezed Casey's arm.

"But you're right. I need a day off, so I accept your offer. I've got some emails to reply to, anyway, and a book to finish reading."

In the last month, Casey had helped Billie join an online book club that met for discussion once a week. Taking part in the group had encouraged Billie to reach out beyond her small circle of friends, and she admitted the discussions kept her mind active. Without any more protests, the older woman shrugged into a heavy parka that dwarfed her petite frame and started out the back door. Perhaps Billie had also tired of Justin's foul moods.

Roy entered the kitchen. "Thanks for the dinner, ladies. You all keep us pretty well fed." He patted his flat stomach beneath his flannel shirt and winked at Casey. His coal-dark gaze stayed fixed on her for a moment. "The apple pie really hit the spot. If we're not careful, we'll all put on ten pounds this winter."

Casey shook her head. The lean, broad-shouldered wrangler would never gain weight. Not quite as tall as Chance, Roy was all hard muscle and well-honed from spending hours in the saddle. She nodded toward Billie. "Make sure she gets inside okay." She didn't want to offend Billie's independent nature, but who knew what lurked in the winter twilight?

"Will do. You have a good night." He plucked his jacket from a hook by the door and hurried out after Billie.

Roy always did anything she asked. She and the young Arapaho wrangler had become friends when he'd taught her to drive the ranch truck last summer, because she didn't know how to drive a stick shift. Chance had once said Roy had a thing for Casey, but she still didn't believe it. They were just good friends. He was a hard worker dedicated to the North Star, even to helping with the mustangs' training, and Casey thought a lot of him. She was certain Chance did, too. "Reading sounds like a good way to spend a snowy day," Casey tossed after their departing figures and shut the door behind them.

Chance came into the kitchen carrying a stack of dishes. "Billie leave already?" He stood at the counter and peered out the window above the sink.

"She needed to call it an early evening." Casey took the dishes and set them near the dishwasher. "I gave her the day off tomorrow. She deserves a break, and I assured her I can handle all the meals with no problem." She turned to loading the dishes. "Although you all might eat something other than mashed potatoes for a change." She straightened to grab another plate.

Chance sidled alongside and put his arm around her waist, turning her. "Whatever you do will be fine with everyone. One thing you learn on a ranch is not to mess with the cook or make him mad."

Casey stared at his chest. "Or her."

He tipped her chin. "Or especially not her." He kissed her lightly.

She enjoyed the moment but still couldn't get the idea out of her head that since she and Chance were married, she somehow needed to prove herself. She waited until he lifted his face.

"Did that convince you?"

"Of?"

"The fact you belong here." He gave her a half-smile and tucked stray stands of her hair behind her ear, his fingers lingering.

Could he read her mind? She toyed with a button on his shirt. "I just feel like Justin doesn't think I'm measuring up, and I know he's especially upset we brought Blue Lady home. I thought he and I were good friends, but now…" Glancing into Chance's face, she saw his eyes darken.

"What my father thinks is really of no consequence." His gaze searched her own. "You need to believe that."

"But—"

"There are no buts, Casey. I might have to deal with him, but you don't, and I won't have you feeling you need to be anyone but who you are. I love you, just the way you are." He paused for a second. "Does that make any kind of sense?"

Standing on tiptoe, she leaned in and returned his kiss. "Absolutely."

Jamie entered the kitchen, carrying the gravy boat and potato bowl. "Here, Mom, I brought you these. Can I go do my homework now? Chance said he'd help me with my math."

Casey lifted her brows at this discovery and poked Chance in the ribs. "You're good at math?"

He shrugged. "I am. Is that so hard to believe? I know you think I'm just a dumb cowboy."

"All I can say is better you than me." What a relief. She really hated math. She shooed them from the kitchen, noting how Jamie tried to match Chance's manly swagger. Her husband might limp now and then from his bum knee, but he could still turn a woman's head. He would always turn hers.

Later, in their room, Casey put on her favorite pink-flowered flannel pajamas. The first time she'd worn them this winter, she had to put up with Chance's teasing. He said she looked like a little kid, and yes, the old house grew chilly at night, but she didn't need flannel to keep her warm anymore. She had him. His comments sometimes made her blush, but the passion they shared was enough to make any woman shed those pajamas in a hurry.

She sat at the antique dressing table she'd inherited from her grandmother, one of the few items she shipped from Michigan to Wyoming. Loosening her hair from the tieback, she sat for a moment and tried to empty her head of all stress, rubbing her temples and flexing her shoulders. She heard the door open.

Chance entered the room and stood behind her. "Feeling better?" He rested his hands on her shoulders and massaged them gently.

"Mmm hmmm." She let the day's tension flow out of her body. "How did the math homework go?"

He chuckled. "Nothing like what I ever learned, but we got through it all right."

She couldn't stifle a yawn. "I should get Jamie tucked in."

"I took care of that, too. He fell asleep before I left his room."

She leaned back against Chance, savoring his warmth. Even with all the family conflict and adjustments, she never doubted how he felt. But was their love enough to make him stay? The question still haunted her. Sliding a hand over one of his, she curled her fingers around its roughness. "Jamie worships you, you know."

He kissed the top of her head and then drew her up for a proper kiss.

His embrace drove away her fears, and she melted against him. Running her hands up and down his back, she enjoyed how good his hard muscles felt beneath her fingers. The kissing and touching could easily lead to more, but fatigue tugged at her body tonight. "Go take your shower." She gave him a little push and went to turn down the quilt.

He undressed and sat on the edge of the bed, a small frown forming between his brows. "It's not what I really want from Jamie, you know. I don't need worship. I just want to have mutual respect between us."

Like you didn't—still don't have—with Justin. She wouldn't speak the hurtful words out loud, even though they were true. "You'll have it, Chance. Jamie will always respect you."

Yawning again and thinking about the long day she faced tomorrow, Casey climbed into bed and sank into her pillows. Exhaustion tempted her to fall fast asleep, but she sensed something else troubled Chance tonight. She forced herself to stay awake and waited until he turned out the light and settled on his side of the bed. She reached out to touch his arm. Questions were always easier to ask in the dark. "What's bothering you? Did anything happen while you were out riding today? I mean, besides chasing bison."

He hesitated a moment, then covered her hand with his, lacing their fingers together. "Do you think of this as home?"

Not what she expected to hear. "I'm…not sure what you mean. This house? Wyoming?"

"Just here." He lifted her hand and kissed it. "With me. Does the North Star mean home to you now?"

Casey leaned on one elbow and peered into her husband's face. Even in the shadows, she saw an uncertainty lurking in his eyes. Hadn't they put those doubts to rest when they took their marriage vows? "Why would you ask me that? Wherever you and Jamie are is where I want to be."

His gaze held hers. "Earlier tonight, I overheard you tell Billie if you can't fit in, you might as well go home. So, is home still in Michigan?"

She sighed and rested her cheek against his warm, bare chest. He always carried the scent of the outdoors, the pine trees and the mountains, that soothed her. But tonight, her heart ached. Why did they both still have so many doubts and uncertainties? "I know what I said, but remember when we married, we promised to always tell each other the truth? Well, here's my truth. Some part of me will forever belong to the place where I grew up. It's just a fact. Probably like the rodeo is part of you, but I'm also saying I don't want to live anywhere without you. You are my home." She stroked his whiskery jaw with light fingers.

Had she answered his question? In the months since they'd married, Casey often worried that Chance missed his life on the road. Would he even tell her if he did? Everything had happened so fast. Their whirlwind romance over the summer, the decision to marry, vows taken in front of a judge instead of the wedding in the chapel she'd envisioned. Sometimes, in the morning, when she awoke in this room, she took a moment to orient herself, especially to the man beside her. She had to remind herself he wasn't Matt. But then she remembered, and she wasn't sorry. Not for one minute. Deep down inside, was he?

Chance ran his hands across her back and then beneath the flannel top, skimming along her spine.

Casey sighed and moved on top of him. Her pulse racing, she kissed him deeply and felt his response swell against her. Sleepiness disappeared in a cloud of rising desire. The incredible connection they shared seared through her body.

"I thought you said you were tired," he whispered against her lips and unbuttoned her pajama top.

She smiled and helped him remove the flannels. "There's tired, and then there's tired. I might've gotten my second wind, so how 'bout you wear me out?"

He gladly obliged, and, in a moment, her flannel pajamas and his briefs disappeared onto the floor.

Casey rolled over and tugged him to cover her, wrapping her arms around his neck and tangling her hands in his already rumpled hair. Even in the shadows of the room, she saw the blue fire of desire glowing in his eyes and felt the need to have him inside her. "Have I ever told you how much you turn me on, cowboy?"

He braced his elbows on either side of her shoulders. "Not recently, but let's see if I do." He dipped his head and pressed featherlight kisses along her jaw, teasing her until she shivered.

The warmth of his skin on hers and the searing kisses he traced on her throat left little need to talk. Casey sank into the bliss of their lovemaking, running her hands over his strong arms and gripping them to keep from spiraling over the edge. No matter what other doubts they had, no matter what tribulations they might face, this powerful need would hold them together.

He brushed his whiskery chin across her breasts, teasing them.

Casey gasped and urged him closer.

He sought and touched her most intimate places, his fingers working some incredible magic until she felt wet and begged for more.

"So, do I?" He stroked her lightly.

His touch sent shock waves of pleasure racing along every nerve ending, and desire pulsed low in her belly. "Absolutely," she breathed as wave after wave of sensual sensation brought her to the edge. Then, because she couldn't wait any longer, she insisted, "Now."

He cupped her bottom in his work-roughened hands and lifted her.

Her breaths racing, Casey arched against him and welcomed him inside. His rhythm matched hers, and like a rushing train, she raced with him to a shattering climax that left her limp as a rag doll but still reluctant to let Chance go. She held him for a moment longer, waiting until her heartbeat slowed but reveling in knowing she'd satisfied him, too.

He groaned, rolled off, and flopped on his pillow. "That was pretty fantastic, Casey McCord. Is my mission accomplished? Did I turn you on?"

Feeling more secure in his love, she snuggled against his shoulder. "You always do. But do you believe me now when I say I'm home?"

He traced a finger over her face. "Truth is, Casey, we're both home. Believe that with your whole heart."

Casey sighed and relaxed into his warmth. Any doubts she felt drifted away, and that was enough. At least for now.

****

Chance lay awake and thought about the place he'd

found on the mountain last week, the one that spoke with such a haunting voice. He still hadn't told her about it. Never the right time. His wife felt awkward and out-of-place living in the ranch house with Justin and Kyle. He ached to find some way to ease the transition. Moving out of the bunkhouse, where he'd lived over the summer, had been hard enough. They had no other choice for now, but someday, he hoped they'd have a place of their own. *A home.* With so little to offer her, he had to hold on to the dream. More than anything, he wanted to make Casey happy. That's all that really mattered in his life right now.

Chapter 5

On an early December afternoon, Chance carried a saddle to the tack room in the back of the century-old barn. He found an empty rack and dragged it to the farthest corner, perching the saddle atop, then looking around for something to cover it. He spied an old striped saddle blanket. *That'll do the trick.* Jamie wouldn't come in here before Christmas anyway.

He'd bought the saddle from a local maker, paying partly in true barter fashion by promising to work with the guy's young horses come spring. He also planned, in the spring, to get Jamie riding another horse besides the pony, Buckwheat. The pony was nearing thirty. Time to retire the old fella and for Jamie to learn about handling a cutting horse.

Mighty fine piece of craftmanship. He ran his hands over the smooth leather and admired the saddle, hoping the kid would appreciate it. Whether Casey would agree, he wasn't sure, but the saddle might convince her.

Footsteps sounded outside the tack room, and he jerked the blanket over the saddle.

Kyle walked in seconds later and halted. "I thought you were going into town today. Back already?" He studied some papers in his hand; a frown creased his forehead.

Chance moved from the saddle rack. "I just had

some business with Aaron Bishop." What had his brother looking so concerned?

Kyle glanced from the papers. "At the saddlery? You were always good at doing your own repairs. What's up?" He folded and tucked the papers inside his coat.

Chance debated letting his brother in on the secret. The tension over bringing the mustangs to the ranch still lay between them, but Kyle had complained little of late. Maybe ranch business kept him too busy, or maybe it was simply time for the two of them to build a new relationship. He pulled the blanket back to show him the saddle.

Kyle gave a low whistle. "Very nice. Looks a little small for you, though. Don't tell me Casey wants to learn cutting and roping skills."

"Ha! Not hardly. The saddle is for Jamie, for Christmas. Do you think he'll like it?" He adjusted the saddle on the rack and imagined his stepson sitting in it for the first time.

"I'm sure he will, but what about your wife? Does she even know?"

Chance grinned. "I'll find a way to convince her it's a good idea."

Kyle shook his head and leaned against a stall door. "Yeah, I'm sure you will. You're a pretty smooth talker."

Glad for the opportunity to spend a little time with his brother without Justin's interference, Chance covered the saddle again and tried to think of some way to prolong the moment. An estrangement between the brothers had kept them apart for far too long. "Speaking of Christmas, have you heard from Marianne? Is she coming home?"

Kyle's girlfriend had accepted a teaching position in Spokane, and they'd not seen each other for several months. At the mention of Marianne, his kid brother pretended to check out some bridles hanging on their hooks. "I called her last night. She's decided to stay in the city over the holidays. Her parents are flying there for a few days."

"And you're not going?" *Doesn't sound promising for you guys.* "You know we can handle things."

Kyle shrugged. "Winter isn't a good time to leave the ranch with only Roy and Ed here, and I don't want Dad out doing things he shouldn't. Marianne understands."

Chance pushed the saddle rack farther out of sight, then faced Kyle. "Maybe she does, but don't let go so easily. I acted like a fool, being afraid to commit, and I almost lost Casey. I'm lucky she kept after me."

Kyle took off his hat, his unruly brown hair falling forward. He pushed it back in a nervous gesture. "It's okay. We'll work things out, sooner or later."

Chance noted Kyle's downcast gaze. His brother was twenty-five, but to him, Kyle would always be a kid. One who, with his soft brown eyes and gentle ways, reminded him so much of their mother, it sometimes hurt to look at him.

He went to Kyle's side and clapped a reassuring hand on his shoulder. "Better make it sooner, brother. Trust me on this." He took advantage of their closeness to reach inside Kyle's coat and pull out the papers, stepping away so he couldn't grab them back. "What's this?" Chance stared at the figures on the pages.

Kyle jammed his hat on and grimaced. "The feed

bill. Has to be paid by next week. Not sure there's enough cash right now to cover it. I've got some vet bills, and Dad's hospital bill is coming due, what the insurance didn't pay. And we've got the extra horses to feed over the winter. That's another reason I can't leave here. I took a part-time job in town, at the hardware."

And you're just now telling me this? His brother's refusal to talk about ranch problems rankled Chance, but since coming back to the North Star early last summer, he hadn't asked a lot of questions about the finances. Running the ranch was a struggle, but they did all right. Didn't they? He needed to pay more attention. In the meantime, he had some emergency money stashed from a job he'd worked in Colorado before coming home. Enough to cover the feed bill and have some left over for the special gift he wanted to buy for Casey. Maybe he'd have to look for some extra work himself. "I'll take care of this," he told Kyle.

"But—"

"The ranch is my responsibility now, too. At least, it is if you believe I'm part of the North Star." He met Kyle's raised brows. "But let's keep it between us and for sure not let Justin in on it. Deal?" He held out one hand.

Kyle nodded and shook on it, though he still seemed reluctant.

Considering his own track record of disappearing over the years, Chance couldn't blame Kyle. This time, he wouldn't let them down. "Come on, let's get inside for dinner. I heard Casey's making something besides mashed potatoes. We better see what's cooking and pretend we like it. And remember, the saddle's a secret."

On the walk to the ranch house, Chance considered just how would he explain the saddle to Casey? By the time they reached the warm kitchen, the December twilight had gathered, and more snow began to fall, but he still didn't have an idea.

****

"Wow, this is so cool!" Jamie clamored behind the tall Christmas tree to reach the western saddle "Santa" had left in the McCord living room. "I didn't even ask for it, either. Isn't it great, Mom?"

"Beautiful, but isn't it a little too big for Buckwheat?" Casey glanced at Chance.

Chance avoided Casey's question and pulled the saddle out so Jamie could get a better look at his gift. "It's a cutting saddle." He pointed out the tall horn and flat seat that made the saddle worthy of a well-trained cow horse. "Later, we'll take it out to the barn. You can sit in it on the rack and see how it feels."

Jamie continued to check out the saddle and admire its engravings.

Chance returned to sit beside his wife on the sofa. Her glare, sharp as a knife, cut through him.

"Care to explain?" she whispered.

He didn't. He'd kept the saddle a secret and hidden in the barn until bringing it inside early this morning, before anyone else stirred. Of course, she wondered what plans he had up his sleeve, and he would tell her later. Right now, he just wanted to watch the boy and enjoy Christmas morning. He hadn't done that in a long time. "We'll talk," he promised and slipped a small, sparkly silver box into her hands. "Merry Christmas to my best girl." While everyone else was busy digging into Billie's fresh-from-the-oven cinnamon rolls, he stole a kiss.

Casey gave him a rueful smile and slid open the box. "I hope your only one—" She gasped at the jade pendant in the shape of a turtle nestled inside. She'd seen the necklace in a jewelry store in Jackson last month and fallen in love with its simple elegance. She plucked the gold chain from the box and glanced at Chance, her eyes filling with tears. "How did you know?"

"I have my ways." He took the pendant and, moving her hair aside, fastened the chain around her neck. "It's Wyoming jade. I knew you would like it, and for the record, Mrs. McCord, you are the only one…forever."

She gazed at the pendant. "I love the jade, but does the turtle have a special meaning?"

He touched the pendant where it lay against Casey's throat. "A turtle is like a woman, always carrying home on her back. She can make a home anywhere."

She gave him a small smile. "That's lovely. I like that."

In the afternoon, Chance convinced Casey to trudge through the snow to the barn. As promised, he set the saddle on a rack and lifted Jamie to sit on it. "How does it feel? Think you'd be able to spend the day riding?" He adjusted the stirrups and stood back to observe the boy. Saddles were an essential part of ranch work, and one had to fit right, if you were riding for hours.

"Feels super. Is it like the one you use?" Jamie glanced from one side to the other.

The kid was taking measure of himself—an

important step in growing into his place on the ranch. "It's a cutting saddle, yes. It might seem a little big, but you'll grow into it."

Bundled in her puffy parka and knit hat, Casey huddled on a trunk in the tack room and eyed the saddle. "It also seems a little big for a pony. Won't it fall off Buckwheat?"

She wouldn't like his answer, but they'd promised each other the truth…always. "It'll fall off the old guy, but it should fit a horse just fine." He cast a glance her way.

"Which one?" Her voice held a suspicious tone. "I suppose Chester might be okay for him to ride." She pressed her lips together.

"Chester's a trail horse," he said of the older gelding they often put inexperienced riders on. "And this isn't a trail saddle. It's a—"

"Cutting saddle," Jamie finished.

Chance heard her quiet "*hmmmm*" but ignored it and pretended to adjust the stirrups again.

"Do I get a cutting horse?" Jamie asked. "Like you and Kyle?"

"We'll have to find one that fits you, like the saddle fits, and then you'll need to practice a lot. You can't go out on a roundup until you learn how to handle your horse. But there's plenty of time for that come spring."

Casey's disapproval hung in the air, but he was glad she said nothing to dampen the kid's enthusiasm or spoil the enjoyment of the gift.

She waited until evening when everyone else went off to bed and just the two of them sat in front of the fire. "You should have asked me first before you got the saddle. I don't know if Jamie is ready for such a big step…riding a horse. The pony is one thing but—"

"I was riding with Justin at Jamie's age. It's not like I plan on taking him on any roundups right off the bat, so stop worrying." Chance leaned back on the cushions and tugged her arm.

She resisted. "It was different for you. You were born to this. You grew up around horses and ranch life. Jamie and I didn't."

"You lived on a farm. *Is* that so different?"

She didn't answer but stared off to a far corner of the room.

In her silence, he read the reluctance to let this go. He moved closer and touched her arm.

Casey shrugged him away. "I lived in Michigan, and we didn't have grizzly bears and wolves and bison to deal with. Maybe an occasional coyote."

He chuckled and tried to put his arm around her.

She scooted forward on the cushion.

Okay, she had put on her stubborn mood now. The same one that had her following him to the cabin last summer and insisting he not ignore her. The one that led him to asking her to marry him. Everything seemed so right then. Now, they were facing everyday problems and needed to navigate their way through them…without losing the love that brought them together.

Rubbing his hand across her stiffened back, he sighed. "But you live here now, and you're the one who wants to fit in. If Jamie doesn't learn to ride with the rest of us, he'll never do that."

A moment of tense silence crackled between them.

"He's my son, and I won't let him do something

dangerous. It's my responsibility to keep him safe and not let him do things he's not ready to do." Her voice held an unusual chill.

Chance reached for one of her hands.

She tucked them beneath her.

How did he make her understand? "But you don't know if he's ready until you let him try."

"But—"

"Casey, I know I'm not Jamie's father, but if you want us to build a relationship, then give us the opportunity to do it. I would never put that boy in danger, and you know it. Do you want me to be a father to him?"

Her shoulders drooped. "Of course, I do. I just can't risk losing him."

He heard the tremor in her voice and sat forward to dip his head and peer into her face. "Neither can I. I lost one child, and it's something I live with every day. But we need to let Jamie grow and learn things. We can't protect him from all of life's dangers and risks. But you have my word, I won't put him on a horse until I'm sure he's ready. You trusted me once. Do you trust me now?" Her gaze met his, and he saw the worry she still harbored. "Come here."

She slid closer and into the curve of his shoulder. "I do trust you, but let's not talk about it anymore."

The subject was far from closed, but Chance let it drop as they watched the fire flicker and die. They'd promised to never lie to each other, but what Casey said didn't convince him.

Chapter 6

The last of the Christmas decorations were packed into plastic totes and stacked by the staircase. Chance would haul them to the attic later. Hard to believe the holidays were past. School was back in session, and Casey gave Jamie the last two Santa cookies in his lunch box before Roy took him to the bus stop. Thank goodness for the wrangler's help, especially when Chance left early, as he'd done the past few days. Whether her husband was out chasing bison, or wolves, or looking for wayward steers, she wasn't sure and didn't ask. But on a morning like this, with January snow falling, a sudden stab of loneliness drifted over her…and maybe just a touch of melancholy.

After-Christmas blues, her mother would say. Post-holiday letdown the self-help gurus called it. Whatever, she missed her library job and doing something a little more useful than struggling to drag a spent spruce tree out the back door while it shed needles like green rain. Giving the tree one final tug, she made it to the steps where the wind whipped the spruce out of her hands and rolled it halfway across the snow-covered yard. Muttering, she pulled on her boots and went after the tree. Where the heck did they want this darn thing, anyway? She wrestled the tree back to the porch.

Roy came trudging through the snow. "Here, I can take it, Ms. Casey." He hurried to the steps and took them two at a time. "We'll put it through the wood chipper. Boss says no dry brush left around the buildings. It's not fire season, but we've still got to be careful." He hoisted the tree on his broad shoulder just as another gust of wind blew through the porch. "Looks like another storm's brewing." He nodded toward the mountains, shrouded today in a cloud of mist.

Glad to turn over the wayward spruce, Casey hunched her shoulders against the cold. "Thanks, Roy. I really appreciate your help." She waited a moment. Did she dare ask where Chance had gotten off to so early? But the last thing she wanted to sound like was a nagging wife. "Lunch is at twelve thirty," she reminded him and went back inside, grateful for the warmth of the friendly kitchen. Putting the tea kettle to boil, she spied the bunch of bananas turning brown. Jamie would only eat so many bananas in a week. *I'll make banana bread and a pot of soup for lunch. That'll warm the guys up.*

Billie had gone into town with a friend, and once again, Casey had offered to take charge of the day's meals. Working as the ranch cook might not sound like the most glamorous job, but the position was important, and they'd all come to appreciate the variety in meals she now provided.

After hauling out the giant soup kettle, she set to sautéing chicken and chopping vegetables. The aroma of the meal filled the room, reminding her of how, as a girl, she'd helped her mother in the farm kitchen at home. Back then, she couldn't wait to escape into her world of books. Arnette Madison had a hard time understanding her daughter's interests.

The only things important to Mom were church,

hard work, and family, and in that order.

Going off to college several hours away was a welcome relief to Casey, something else her mother didn't approve of. Mom and Daddy had wanted her to attend community college so she could remain at home, but the scholarship she won gave her the freedom she longed for then. In a way, not so different from the young Chance, who at eighteen was so desperate to leave the ranch. Now, she was back in the kitchen. *How the heck did that happen?* Oh yeah, she came to Wyoming for the summer and fell in love with a handsome cowboy.

With the soup simmering and two pans of banana bread in the oven, she had time to curl up in front of the fire and read. She'd missed that luxury these past few months. Her books shipped from Michigan were still packed away, but maybe she could find something of interest in Justin's study with its many shelves of books.

She intended to just slip in, choose a book, and leave, but Justin rested in the leather chair behind his desk. She thought he'd gone somewhere with Kyle. Pausing in the doorway, she steeled herself to deal with his moodiness.

"Casey, come on in. I won't bite." He didn't turn around.

She hesitated. "I didn't mean to bother you."

"You're not. I'm only sitting here looking at the mountains. Well, what you can see of them today."

She ventured into the masculine room with its magnificent view of the Tetons. In the summer, the craggy peaks were glorious against the immense sky. Today, barely visible, they stood enclosed in swirls of snowy white clouds.

Justin fastened his gaze on them, anyway.

For a second, the Grand peeked out from behind winter's curtain. She heard Justin sigh.

"What's up?" He turned his chair to face her. Tall with silver hair and piercing blue eyes, Justin was still a ruggedly handsome man, but finely drawn lines were etched deeper around his mouth and at the corners of his eyes.

"I just need a book to read. I got all the decorations put away and lunch started, so I thought I'd take a break." She walked to the shelves that reached the ceiling. Justin owned an amazing collection, and Casey took only a moment to find something of interest. A mystery set in the Wind River country caught her eye.

"The author writes a good story." He nodded to the novel. "Knows her subject and the country she writes of well. My wife enjoyed those books."

The sudden hitch in his voice touched Casey. He seldom mentioned the woman who had died sixteen years ago, but she sensed he still missed her mightily, as did her two sons. "I hope you don't mind if I borrow it then. My books are still in storage." She saw him smile, something else he seldom did anymore.

"Casey, my dear girl, you are welcome to anything in this house. I thought you knew that."

Truthfully, she didn't. Last summer, she and Justin had struck up an unlikely friendship. Together, they worked on *The North Star Legacy*, a book he was writing about the McCord family's history in the valley. Reading an old journal, she learned about Garrett and Martha McCord, early settlers in Jackson Hole, and all the hardships they faced. She'd enjoyed the time spent with Justin, but that all halted when he had open heart surgery and then faced a long recovery. He showed no interest in returning to the book, and his curt remarks kept Casey at a distance. "I do, it's just…" She took a deep breath. "I know you're upset we brought the mustang mare home. You think she won't ever be useful. Just so you know, it was my idea, not Chance's. I…couldn't stand to see her…in that awful pen."

Justin pursed his lips and nodded. "I've been a bear lately, about a lot of things. Billie has let me know that in no uncertain terms. The woman never minces words. She said I need to apologize."

"You don't." Casey turned the book over in her hands and avoided eye contact. "I realize you've had a hard time since the surgery."

"True, but it's no excuse for treating my daughter rudely. I do think of you as the daughter I never had. My son and I might still have our issues, but you are not one of them. Having you and Jamie living in this empty house is a real welcome."

Casey summoned a smile. "I can't imagine living anywhere else now."

He sat straighter in the desk chair and motioned to the leather sofa.

She perched on the corner of the cushion and watched him gather his thoughts.

He steepled his fingers in front of his face. "When Alicia came to the North Star, she had a hard time adjusting. She was an accomplished artist but a city girl at heart, and life out here can be lonely. She eventually found a way to fit in. We were married for twenty years when she died. My life has never been the same."

His voice held a contemplative note that tugged at

Casey's heart. She knew how it felt to lose someone so young and still so full of life. "The loss was hard for Chance and Kyle, too," she reminded him.

He nodded and clasped his hands together. "Chance left us the first time, a month after she passed. Even then he and I were always at loggerheads, and with Alicia gone I guess he saw no reason to stay."

The McCord men never really recovered from that loss, but what followed years later was an even greater tragedy. After the loss of Chance's first wife, Angela, and their small son, Scottie, in a car accident, Chance had left the ranch for a second time and not returned until last summer.

"But enough of that." Justin leaned back in his chair. "How are you and Chance doing? My son a good husband?"

Her cheeks grew warm. She shifted on the sofa. "The best."

"What's this about the saddle being a bone of contention?"

Why are secrets so darn hard to keep around here? She sighed. "We're working it out. I'm just concerned Jamie isn't ready for such a big step. He only started riding last summer and—"

"Alicia felt the same way with Chance. I had to fight her tooth and nail to let him on a horse. Then we couldn't keep him off. I guess we still can't. I will tell you, there's no one better than Chance to teach that boy everything he needs to know about horses. How to handle them, how to ride them, and how to read their every mood. He's quite the man when it comes to horses."

She jerked her chin at this admittance coming from

Justin. "Please tell him that. He needs to hear it from you." Why was it so hard for the father and son to communicate?

Justin waved away the suggestion. "Wouldn't matter. Chance and I have come to an understanding, but we'll never be close enough to talk like that."

Such stubborn men! "Just tell him what you said to me. It might make a world of difference in how you two get along." *And maybe things could be more peaceful around here.* "And, while you're at it, you should stop feeling sorry for yourself."

Justin's heavy brows shot up an inch. "Sorry for myself! You think I—"

"I do, and you're mad because you're not able to get out and do the things you once did. You should be thankful for what you can do and for just being alive." Before he could comment, she jumped up and headed for the doorway. "I have to check the bread. Lunch is at twelve thirty." She left Justin to mull over her words. Maybe she was too harsh, but somebody had to jolt him out of his doldrums and make him realize the truth.

In the kitchen, she stirred the soup and glanced out the window. Within the hour, the men should come in for lunch. Would Chance be with them?

Chapter 7

In town, Chance paid for the newspaper ad he placed for the following week. Settling his hat on his head, he stepped out onto the snowy street. That much was done. Now, he just needed to work on this new idea. They hadn't taken the old sleigh out of the barn in years, and the conveyance needed a lot of repairs. But this was early January, and snow would hang around for months yet. He'd start working on the sleigh tomorrow. How would Justin and Kyle feel about his plan? He hadn't talked to them yet, because he wanted this to be his own project and a way to bring in a little more income.

Along the street, skiers milled about on this late afternoon. Most looked for places to eat. Would they drive out to the ranch after a day spent on the slopes? Would winter visitors to the valley welcome the opportunity to take an old-fashioned horse-drawn sleigh ride in view of the Tetons? The success of his venture depended on it.

The sun slipped behind the mountains, and shadows crept across the town. Frost hung in the late afternoon air. He should get home for dinner but needed some time to think about the project. He usually avoided coming into town, but he hadn't seen the inside of the local watering holes since way before he returned to the valley last summer. In spite of the nip in the air, a cold one sounded good. Buttoning his coat, he turned and headed for the Silver Buck Saloon.

He avoided the saddle-shaped barstools and stood in an empty spot at the end of the bar. With the flick of a wrist, he downed a shot of whiskey. The fiery liquid burned but warmed him from the inside out. The longneck he would nurse. Holding the beer, he turned sideways and observed the mix of tourists and locals filling the establishment.

Nearby, several girls—a cute blonde and two brunettes in tight jeans and short puffy jackets that left their midriffs bare—studied the murals of western scenes behind the bar and chattered and giggled. Maybe in their early twenties, the girls glanced from him to the murals. He heard one say, "Are there still real cowboys out West?"

He itched to say *hell yeah* but just drank his beer and ignored their stares. Word traveled around the valley fast, and he couldn't afford to piss off somebody when he was looking to bring more paying visitors to the ranch. He finished the beer, thought about having another, but paid before he could change his mind. When he turned away from the bar, he nearly bumped into one of the girls.

"Can I take your pic?" She didn't wait but held up her phone to focus with the western murals in the background.

Her boldness rankled him, but he forced himself to smile and tip his hat. Next thing he knew, they were asking to take a selfie with him. Flashing back to his rodeo days, he shrugged and obliged. Seemed buckle bunnies were always hanging around, wanting a photo—and sometimes more. These were snow bunnies, who had maybe, or maybe not, spent the day on the slopes and were now out for a good time.

The girl with the phone slipped her arm around his middle and leaned in close. Her two friends snuggled in on the other side. She held out her selfie-stick and did a rapid-fire series of photos. "How about we take some photos here?" The blonde tugged him toward the saddle stools.

"Nope, sorry, ladies." He pulled one arm away.

"C'mon. We want to prove we really saw a cowboy," the blonde purred. "Then you can buy us a round."

Chance was pretty sure they'd already had a few rounds and were past tipsy. "You ladies have a good time. I'm on my way out." He tried to move past them. The taller brunette flung one arm around his neck and kissed him full on the mouth. Then she wiggled her hips against him.

Growling deep in his throat, he backed away.

The other brunette made a grab for his hat.

Chance was faster and side-stepped her reach. He lifted a warning hand. "One thing you need to learn about us cowboys, you never go for the hat."

"Are all you guys so grouchy?" The hat-grabber blocked his way. "How about you give me a kiss?" She puckered bright-red lips.

He wanted to pick up the tease and set her aside, but keeping his hands to himself was the better choice. Last thing he needed was a drunk girl calling foul.

Someone yelled at the girls from the other end of the bar. They turned to wave.

Taking advantage, Chance extricated himself from the three and escaped out the door to the tune of their giggling protests. Outside, he exhaled a sigh of relief. At one time in his life, he would've appreciated all the female attention. Now, he just wanted to get away.

At home, he stopped in the main barn. Far in the back, he pulled aside the tarp that had covered the sleigh for so long. Faded red with faint yellow designs on the wooden sides, the old conveyance seriously needed painting. Maybe he'd have to wait on that until the recent bitter cold snap ended. *Yeah right, like that'll happen soon.* The sleigh, an original from his grandparents' day, should appeal to those who came to Jackson Hole to have a real western experience. At least, that was the plan. He needed to start the refurbish right away to have the sleigh ready in time.

For the rest of the week, after helping Jamie with his homework, he headed to the barn and stayed late, sanding the runners smooth and cleaning the leather seats that were cracked with age. At one time, a few mice had made themselves at home. He hoped folks riding in the sleigh wouldn't notice. Maybe they could hide the holes with blankets.

He paused in sanding the runners to straighten and work out a kink in his back. A squeaking sound reached to the far corner of the barn—the big door sliding open and closed. Muffled footsteps echoed in the center aisle. He listened to their pace. *None of the wranglers or even Kyle.*

"Chance, are you in here?"

Casey's soft voice reached him. He didn't want her to know about the project until the sleigh was ready. But now was as good a time as any to explain why he'd spent the last week in the barn until long after she'd gone to sleep. "Back here." He kept his voice low so as not to frighten the horses. "Watch your step, though."

She picked her way through the obstacles of old tools and bales of straw. "What are you doing in here? It's freezing cold and—" She saw Chance standing in front of the sleigh. Her eyes grew wide. "What is this?" She walked around the sleigh as much as the space would allow, stopped, and lifted her gaze. "How old is it? Where did it come from?" She held out a travel mug. "Here, I thought you could use something warm, since you've been out here for hours."

He took the mug gratefully and wrapped his stiff fingers around it. "It's from my grandparents' time. I remember they used to take Kyle and me for rides around the ranch. I know it's old, but it's still in workable shape. I've almost got it ready to pull out."

Casey studied the sleigh. "Sounds fun, but what inspired this? I couldn't help but wonder all week what you're doing out here."

Lifting the mug to his mouth, he drank the strong coffee that was sure to keep him awake tonight, He savored the kick and thought about how to explain the plan. First, maybe he should apologize. "I forget to check in, you know? I've lived too long with only myself to think about."

She closed her eyes, pressing her lips together. "You don't have to *check in* with me. It's not what I expect."

Her gray eyes focused on him again, reminding Chance of the winter sky or the deep misty clouds that covered the mountains this time of year. He could so easily get lost in Casey's eyes.

"I just…I miss you…and those flannel pajamas only keep me so warm." Her cheeks flushed.

He chuckled at her honesty, but then, she did ride up a mountain after him. He reached for her mitten-enclosed hand. "Come on, sit with me." Setting the coffee mug on a tack box, he placed his hands on her waist. He could barely feel her slim body through the parka and lifted her easily into the old conveyance. He climbed in beside her and put an arm around her slender shoulders. "Now, what do you think?" He eased them back against the sleigh's seat with its cracked and worn leather. "Isn't this nice?"

For an answer, Casey shivered in the January cold.

He reached behind them and grabbed the fleece-lined coat he'd shed earlier. Drawing it over her, he settled her against him. "Better?"

She nodded. Slowly, her shivers stopped.

"Okay, then imagine this. The Belgian team, Mac and Red, hitched to the sleigh and pulling us through the valley, with the mountains in view." He stretched out one hand and swept it across the imaginary scene. "A full moon rising above their peaks. A few clouds swirling around the Grand and Mount Moran. Maybe the Milky Way out on the horizon. Or maybe the northern lights. How does that sound?"

"Sounds lovely." She leaned into his shoulder. "Where did you learn to paint such a picture?"

He frowned in pretended offense. "What, you still think I'm just an itinerant old cowboy with no sense of romance?"

Casey sighed. "You know that's not what I think." She slipped one hand from beneath his coat and touched his five o'clock-shadowed-face. "In fact, you can tell me more."

He would, except everything he wanted to say went

right out of his head. Only one thing played on his mind when he leaned in to kiss her—that nothing better in the world existed than kissing Casey...unless it was removing her flannel pajamas.

Unzipping her coat, he slipped his hand inside and beneath her sweater, cupping one breast and rubbing his thumb over her nipple until she moaned softly and snuggled closer. He pulled off her hat and trailed kisses across her face and down her throat, nibbling at the soft skin just behind her ear.

She giggled.

"You like that?" He brushed his stubbly chin against her neck, Casey's most vulnerable spot.

"Yes, but stop...we can't do this out here." She tried to push his hand away.

"Why not? There's nobody around. The horses won't tell." He kept kissing her just below her ear, then followed its shell with his tongue.

She let out a quick breath. "It's too cold...it's too..."

He lowered her to the seat and silenced her protests with a long, deep kiss. They didn't talk again until a long time later. He barely heard the door slide open again and footsteps come closer.

Casey put her hand against his mouth to ward off another kiss. "Somebody's here," she whispered.

Chance sat up and pulled Casey with him. She kept his jacket over her and quickly adjusted her sweater.

"Ah, hey. Sorry, guys," Roy said. "Didn't mean to interrupt. I just saw the light on and thought maybe you had a sick horse...or something."

Chance winked at Casey. "No sick horse. Just looking for a little privacy. Hard to come by around here, you know?"

Roy looked away. "Yeah, I can imagine. I'll leave you two alone, then."

"It's okay. We're just getting ready to head to the house, anyway. But while you're here, I guess I'll let you both in on my plan, since I'll probably need your help and Casey's approval." He moved away and looked over the side of the sleigh. "What would you think if we drag this thing outside tomorrow and take it for a spin?"

Roy took off his hat and scratched his head. "Hitch it to the team, you mean?"

"Sure, Mac and Red could do with a little exercise. But you might as well know, I've run a newspaper ad offering sleigh rides here at the ranch. It's something winter visitors to the valley might like. Even skiers when they're done for the day. They can go on rides through the elk refuge, but this would be on our side of the river. Not sure what we'll charge, but a couple of the other guest ranches do it to pretty good success. No reason we shouldn't try." He waited to hear their thoughts. Was the idea crazy? Could they pull it off? How would Casey react? She sat forward, unaware of her tousled hair where he'd pulled off her hat.

"We can even offer refreshments after the ride, and how about the old shed we don't use? We could fix it into a warming shed. Folks could stop in after the ride." She pushed back her hair and glanced between the men, her eyes sparkling. "I'll make hot chocolate. It wouldn't be hard. I know we can do it. I'll get started on the shed tomorrow. It's Saturday, so Jamie can help. We'll just need to plow the snow out of the way. I'll ask Ed. I'll update the ranch website and post something on our social media page." She ticked off the items on her fingers, then pulled Chance close and kissed him hard. "I think it's a grand idea! Don't you, Roy?"

The wrangler plunked his hat on his head and shrugged. "Sure, why not?"

Thankful he had their support, Chance climbed from the sleigh and helped Casey step down. "You're really something, Mrs. McCord," he whispered in her ear.

"I just need you to promise me something." She slipped her arm through his as they followed Roy out of the barn.

He waggled his brows. "Finish what we started?"

She nudged his arm. "Hush."

He glanced at the vast midnight-blue sky above. "The moon and the stars?"

She stopped walking. "Well, sort of. I want that ride you described with the moon rising and a million stars shining above us."

Chance exhaled into the frosty night air. He was a damn lucky man. Having Casey's support meant a lot, and her idea about serving hot chocolate would add extra appeal to the endeavor. His wife truly was a gem. He hugged her close. "I'll put that order in pronto."

Chapter 8

"I'm so happy Chance thought of this idea." Casey dumped another bag of chocolate chips into the mixing bowl and lowered the beaters into the double batch of batter. "It's given him something to think about besides chasing bison and wolves."

During the first week of sleigh rides, Chance was out five nights in a row, taking winter visitors across the snow-covered fields.

Casey and Billie spent hours in the kitchen, baking cookies, with Jamie as a willing helper after school. The weather cooperated by bringing plenty of snow. By the end of the second week, the phone rang constantly with people calling to make reservations. She checked the website almost every hour.

"Other than you two getting hitched, it's the best thing that's happened here in years." Billie stooped to remove two pans of oatmeal cookies from the oven. "You don't know how good it makes me feel. Of course, you're still the best thing." She slid in two more pans of cookies.

"I think Chance coming home is the best thing, but you're right about this whole idea putting him in a different frame of mind. He's having a good time." *Plus, it gives us something to work at together.* She'd even painted the flower designs on the sides of the sleigh. Casey scooped spoonfuls of chocolate chip dough onto another two sheets. *Good thing I bought extra pans.* The refreshments served in the warming shed were a big hit after a frosty sleigh ride across the valley. The couples and families went through dozens of cookies and gallons of hot chocolate.

Casey watched Jamie learn to harness the two Belgians and lead the gentle giants from the barn.

Justin even helped Billie pack the cookies each night.

The only one who didn't take part in the new venture was Kyle, who made himself scarce on sleigh-ride nights. Not even the sweet aroma of baking brown sugar and chocolate drifting through the house enticed him to join the rest of the family.

She filled the last cookie sheet and set aside the empty bowl. "What's with Kyle, do you think? He's certainly quiet and keeping to himself lately."

Billie perched on a tall stool while the cookies baked. "I'm guessing it's got something to do with Marianne living in Spokane. He went to the Double Diamond for a video visit with her and her parents, but you know yourself virtual is a poor second to being with the one you love."

Casey nodded. "We tried to convince him to take a few days off and go see her. He said business is slow at the hardware store, and we can certainly hold down the fort here. I'm not sure why he won't go."

Billie shrugged and reached for her coffee cup. "Might be he's afraid she doesn't really care about him so much. Seems all the McCord men have had issues with women."

Thoughts of what Justin had told her about his struggles ran through her mind, as well as her own rocky beginning with Chance…and the doubts she still had sometimes about not fitting in. The past weeks working together had brought them closer, and she hoped strengthened their marriage. Now, if only Kyle and Marianne could work things out.

"Maybe I'll talk to Kyle, see if I can encourage him to take a trip to Spokane." Casey measured out flour to start another batch of cookie dough. "Getting away from the ranch for a bit would probably do him good." But that conversation would have to wait. Tonight, she had scheduled six groups for sleigh rides, and then she needed to talk to Chance about doing something special for Valentine's Day, only two weeks away. *If we advertise taking a sleigh ride as a romantic way to spend the evening, I'm certain it'll go over as a big hit.*

****

On Valentine's Day, Chance brought the team to the barn after the last sleigh ride of the evening. The teenagers had sung loudly and had a great time. They weren't nearly ready to quit just yet. He, on the other hand, was more than ready to call it a night. He stepped from the driver's seat just in time to see one boy—probably about seventeen—grab a girl and kiss her.

The girl yanked her arm away and took off for the shed.

Chance waited until they all disembarked from the sleigh, then moved over to the kid and leaned in close. "Your girlfriend might appreciate it if you were a little less forceful."

The kid glared. "What business is it of yours, man?"

Chance lifted a brow. "My sleigh, my rules. But trust me, girls don't like guys who force themselves."

Although, some girls liked to force themselves…like the ones in the bar.

The kid just shook his head and took off after the others.

Chance watched him go. He'd probably acted a lot like him at the same age.

Roy stood next to the team. "Offering romantic advice now, boss?" Without hesitation, he took hold of the harness, ready to lead Mac and Red to the barn.

"Remembering what it's like to be seventeen and in a big hurry." Chance stared at the wrangler. How did he always appear so quietly and at the right moment? He'd gotten used to Roy calling him *boss* the last few weeks. Not sure the title fit, but the wrangler worked hard and had a good hand with horses, especially the mustangs. He respected Roy for that.

"I can put the fellas away for you tonight." Roy scratched Mac's head as the Belgian nuzzled his shoulder.

Chance glanced toward Casey where she welcomed the teens into the warming shed and handed them mugs of hot chocolate. She and Jamie had decorated the shed this week with red and white lights and cutout hearts. She'd stayed out every night until the last guest left, then spent another hour cleaning up. His wife had thrown herself into the events wholeheartedly, with no complaints. She enjoyed doing it, but he still had a promise to keep. "You can leave Mac and Red. I'll tend to them."

"You sure, boss?" Roy lifted his chin and scanned the yard. "I don't expect we'll get anymore folks now."

Chance nodded toward the shed. "I'm sure, but you can go finish for Casey and send her on over here.

We've got one more ride to take tonight."

Roy just nodded. "Sure, boss-man." He ambled away toward the shed.

Chance stroked the Belgians' heads and slipped them each an apple from his pocket. "I know you boys are ready for the barn, but we've got a special run to make. Think you can do that?"

They snorted and blew on his gloved hands, their breath steaming around them.

He rubbed their cheeks. He lived by the code to never ask more of a horse than he was ready to give. If he asked them to work in the hot sun, then he stayed until they cooled off. Ask them to go one more mile in the cold, and he'd give them extra sweet feed. He'd made sure the wild broncs he rode received kind treatment. For a minute, he leaned into the warmth of Red's big shoulder and scratched between the Belgian's furry ears.

"Roy said you wanted me." Casey spoke from behind him. "Did something happen?"

He turned. How was it she'd agreed to marry him? A Midwestern librarian—a woman of courage, a woman of heart—had married a man who'd been on the road more years than he cared to count. Her wistful smile sent a familiar emotion rushing through him. As happened every time, he fell all over again for the misty gray eyes that always enchanted him. "Well, since the stars are just beginning to come out, I thought we might take the ride I promised you. If you're game, that is."

She hesitated. "Okay, but I should make sure Jamie gets ready for bed first." She started to turn back.

"You can only see the stars before the moon rises. Billie will take care of the boy."

She faced him. Her eyes brightened. "Is it just as I ordered?"

He tipped his hat back to get a better view. Seeing the sweet smile that touched her mouth, he felt his heart race in anticipation. "Close as I could get." Stepping nearer, he lifted the hood of her parka over her head, then helped her into the driver's seat and climbed in beside her. He reached into the back seat for a plaid wool blanket. "It gets plenty cold out there." He nodded toward the path he took across the valley. "Better bundle up." He gathered the reins and clicked to the Belgians.

They moved away from the ranch yard, and in a few moments, Mac and Red pulled them briskly toward the snow-covered fields that sparkled in the night. The bells on the harness jingled in the frosty air, as the sleigh flew over the frozen ground.

The icy wind made talking difficult, so Casey inched closer to Chance and tucked one hand beneath his arm.

Soon the house lay far behind them, and darkness closed in like a silent curtain.

Chance drew the horses to a stop beside a grove of cottonwood trees, where winter-bare branches reached to a sky now peppered with a million stars. Far out on the horizon, the Milky Way glimmered in a cloud of silver-white. Did Casey notice? He heard her soft sigh.

"A magical sky," she whispered. "Don't you think so?"

Knowing the Belgians wouldn't go anywhere without his command, he dropped the reins and drank in the display. The silence was so loud and the cold so fierce, they brought a strange kind of peace to a man's soul, and maybe even to a woman's.

Casey turned to him. "It's just how I imagined. Thank you for bringing me out here."

He lifted his hat from his head, setting it on his knee. "I made a promise, but tonight, I had my own reasons. We've been so busy these past few weeks, we've hardly had time to say *hello*."

"I know, but giving the sleigh rides has been a wonderful time. Your idea turned into a great success."

"Much of the success is due to you. So, thank you, Mrs. McCord, for making it work with all the promotions and for handling the business side. You have great organizational skills." He moved closer. "But enough about business. How about we start out with that *hello?*" He saw a little confusion but also wonderment in her eyes.

"I don't—"

He leaned closer and felt the mist from her breath on his face. "I just think a man ought to say *hello* before he kisses a lady." He kissed her then, their lips cold but soon warming. He encircled her in his arms with an urgency he sensed took her breath away. The bitter temperature, the night's low wind, and the brightness of the stars faded away into a cloud of only the two of them alone in the shadow of the Tetons. "I thought about doing that all week," he murmured. "It's been a long wait."

"Let's not wait so long again." She kissed him this time, wrapping her arms around his neck.

Once again, the incredible passion and love that existed between them flared like a wildfire.

Casey opened her eyes.

An amazing display of green and white lights

shimmered in the sky over the mountains.

"Oh my, cowboy, you sure know how to win a girl over." She sighed and snuggled against his shoulder.

For a few long moments, the northern lights sent pillars of startling colors streaking above them.

"How did you know?" she asked.

He gave a low chuckle. "Haven't you learned by now? I have my ways."

Soon, the Belgians' impatient stomps thumped in the snow.

She laughed. "I think they want to go home."

"Hmm, I think I do, too." Chance jammed his hat on and drew away just enough to pick up the reins. This time, he handed them to Casey. "How about you do the driving? I've done my share tonight." He leaned back in the seat and waited.

She hesitated a moment, straightened, and gathered the reins. "What makes you think I can drive the team?" She tossed him a teasing glance.

Did she think he didn't know that the past week Roy had taken her out with the team and taught her to drive? "I don't know. Just a hunch. How about you show me?"

The cold wrapped around them, and she shivered without the warmth of the blanket. But she lifted her stubborn chin and glanced back at Chance. "You hangin' on?"

"Yes, ma'am."

The Belgians snorted, their breath blowing clouds into the frosty night.

She flicked the reins over their rumps.

With a lurch, the sleigh sped over the snow.

This time, they left all thoughts of stars and the

northern lights behind them.

Near the ranch yard, Chance leaned forward and motioned for Casey to urge the horses past the barn and on toward the circle of guest cabins. They were closed for the winter, but the windows in the one that sat on a small hill glowed with a soft yellow light. Hazy smoke curled from the woodstove's chimney. "Pull the team close by."

The team halted outside the cabin.

Casey dropped the reins on her knees and stared at the cabin. "What's this? Did we open the cabin for someone?"

"In fact, we did." He reached for the reins.

"For who? And why didn't I hear anything about it? I don't remember seeing a reservation."

He tipped his hat to hide a grin. "Only two other people knew, and they were sworn to secrecy." Stepping from the driver's seat, he turned and lifted Casey after him. "Go inside. Should've warmed up by now."

Her eyes widened. "So we're—"

He kissed her quickly on her cold nose. "We are. Get inside before you freeze. As soon as I settle the team for the night, I'll be back." Halfway to leading Mac and Red to unhitch them from the sleigh, he saw Roy move from the shadows.

The wrangler took the Belgians' harness in hand. "Go on, boss-man," he said. "I got it."

Chance relented but paused before walking away. "*Boss-man*. Why do you call me that?"

Roy shrugged and turned away. "Don't see anyone else worthy of the name right now."

****

Inside the cabin, Casey glanced around. How had this happened without her knowing? No doubt, Billie had a hand in it, and maybe even Justin, but they'd kept the secret.

The woodstove threw a cozy circle of light and warmth around the main room. She gravitated toward the heat, pulling off her mittens and holding her hands out. In a few moments, she shed the parka and knit hat and hung them on the hooks by the door. A blue granite coffeepot, already filled with grounds and water, sat on the small propane stove. She turned on the burner. Chance could use a cup after caring for the team.

While she waited for the pot to perk, Casey sat on the sofa with its green-and-brown pine cone print and spotted a heart-shaped box of candy on the end table. So, her cowboy had remembered Valentine's Day after all. *And here I thought he didn't notice the decorations I hung in the shed or even paid attention to the red velvet cookies we baked for the sleigh riders tonight.* Touching the satin bow on the candy box, she thought about the incredible ride they'd taken beneath the stars and the northern lights. Yep, rodeo man Chance McCord could charm a girl's socks off—or her flannel pajamas—but she'd known that from the moment they met.

The coffeepot started to perk, sending the rich aroma of coffee into the air.

Chance entered the cabin, stomping snow from his boots and bringing in the frosty night air. "Wow, feels pretty good in here." He shrugged off his fleece-lined coat, hanging it and his hat next to Casey's parka. Blowing into his cupped hands, he ambled to the counter. "And that smells great. How'd you know it was just what I needed after getting half frozen out there tonight?"

"I have my ways." She poured coffee into two mugs. "Now, take off your boots and let's sit on the sofa so you can get warm. Look, here's some cookies I made today. I wonder how they got here?" She chuckled softly and balanced the plate on top of one mug while carrying everything to the end table. She kicked off her boots, tucked her feet under her on the sofa, and waited for him to join her. The hitch in his step and the halt in his usual swagger said the old injuries plagued him, and winter only made them worse. "How's the knee? Cold get to it today?" She handed him his coffee.

He eased himself onto the sofa and heaved a ragged sigh. "Price you pay for youthful foolishness." He cradled the mug in his hands and sipped the hot brew.

Somehow, even that simple gesture set her heart to skipping. She studied his hands for a moment. How worn they were from the cold and the hard work, and yet how gentle they felt when he touched her.

He ate two cookies and finished the coffee.

Casey took his mug and set it beside hers on the end table. Pulling his hands to her face, she rubbed her cheek against them. His skin was rough from honest work, but she appreciated that and sighed. "This is nice, you know? Just you and me. But what gave you the idea?"

His dark blue gaze met hers. "We've never had this. You've put up with me and my family, and my crazy ideas with no complaints, but for this one night, it's just about us."

Casey leaned in closer and kneeled, taking his beard-stubbled face in her hands. "Thank you, Chance, for the ride under the stars." She kissed him gently. "And for the northern lights and the candy." Another kiss. "And for this." The next kiss lasted a long minute. "But mostly just for being my favorite cowboy."

He put his arms around her and all thoughts of the cold outside slipped away as kisses grew hotter, and a succession of sighs escaped into the night.

Leaning over backward on the sofa, Casey pulled him with her, exploring the width of his chest, undoing a few snaps of his flannel shirt, and relishing the feel of warm skin and hard muscles.

"Not much room here," he murmured against her throat.

"Do we care?" She snuggled against him and undid another snap. "Besides, we're nice and cozy here. The bedroom might be cold."

He slid one hand beneath her sweater and skimmed over her silky bra before he unhooked it.

Casey shivered in delight as his rough skin met hers.

"I guess you don't have your flannels, but I lit the water heater in the cabin. Should be hot by now."

Her eyes flew open. "Meaning?"

He grinned. "We can get plenty warm in the shower."

"Are you suggesting what I think you're suggesting?" She met his gaze that shone as dark-blue as a midnight sky and brushed his lips with her own.

"I am. We need to conserve water out here in the West, and I can't think of a better way right now." Chance drew her up, and a draft of cool air drifted between them. "So, get rid of this." He drew her sweater over her head and tossed it onto the arm of the sofa. "And this." Her bra joined it. "Now hustle on in there." He patted her bottom. "I'll join you in a minute after I check the stove and make sure the door's locked."

Casey crossed her arms over her breasts against the sudden loss of his body heat and made a beeline for the bathroom. She found new towels, hair pins, and her favorite shower gel. Did her cowboy do this, too? No, probably Billie. Everybody on the ranch must know she and Chance were in the cabin tonight, but at least, they had some privacy. She twisted her hair into a knot and pinned it, quickly finished undressing, and turned on the water in the shower. Thank goodness, it gushed out hot. She stood beneath the spray and let it beat on her neck and shoulders, washing away the stress of the day and warming her body.

Yet, none of it warmed her as much as when Chance joined her. She slid her arms around him and sidled in close. The water showered over them. *He feels so good.* She rubbed her cheek against his bare chest. Thank goodness, his skin was smooth, with only a small patch of rough hair. She'd never cared for hairy-chested guys, but she did like how hard his body was…everywhere. Running her hands over his arms and across his shoulders, she sank eager fingers into his taut muscles and reveled in his strength. In her time on the ranch, she'd seen Chance handle the craziest horses without flinching, swing an ax to chop wood, and chase a bison out of the pasture. And yet, with her, he was as gentle as the Belgians. "Who would've thought you'd do this?" She pressed closer until not even the water could come between them.

"Now do you believe that I'm not such a rambling rover after all?" He trailed his hands over her back, then pulled loose the hair pins and tangled his fingers in her hair.

She lifted her face. His kiss drove out all thoughts except what was happening, and Casey gave in to the magic of his mouth and hands traveling over her body. Her pulse pounded in her head as he cupped her breasts in both hands and massaged them until her legs went weak. Feeling him slide one hand between her thighs and reach her soft, sensitive core, Casey relished his exploring touch, but before ecstasy claimed her, she eased away. "Not yet," she murmured. "It's your turn, cowboy."

After five months of marriage, she knew what he liked and skimmed her hands over his slick skin, following their path with kisses and strokes that soon had him dragging in eager breaths and groaning. Hearing his response set her own body to humming in anticipation.

"Hell, woman, you're out to torture me."

She laughed. "I like the sound of that." After a few more slow caresses, she slid her way back up his body to latch her arms around his neck.

Leaning against the shower wall, Chance lifted her against him and grasped her bottom. "Let's see who can hold out the longest," he challenged.

Like a thousand caressing hands, the shower rained over them. Feeling every inch of the water and Chance on her body, Casey reached for his arousal and guided him in, tossing her head back. She most liked to feel his raspy face brushing against her throat.

He kissed her pounding pulse and dragged his whiskery chin across her soft skin, then traced his tongue across her breasts, teasing them with gentle nips. "You had enough?" he growled and shifted her higher.

For her answer, Casey pushed him in farther until pleasure, like a fast-moving river, ripped through her. She didn't hold back, reaching her climax in a long exquisite moment that burned like a raging fire in her blood and rivaled the peak of the northern lights.

He followed a second after with a fierce shudder of release, then pressed his face into her wet and tangled hair. "I love you, Casey," he finally whispered. "You are amazing."

She buried her face against his neck and savored the glow of the aftermath while he still stayed inside her.

With a long sigh, Chance eased her along his body but held her close and cradled her head until their heartbeats slowed and the water cooled.

"Enough of this." Casey shivered and reached for the faucet, flipping it off. "Race you to bed." She slid away from the chilling shower. Grabbing the thick towels, she tossed him one and set to drying herself off.

He drew her close and took the towel away, rubbing it briskly over her skin and pausing for a few quick kisses. He spent a moment towel-drying her hair.

Casey escaped and sprinted for the bed. Shivering, she slipped beneath the flannel sheets and pulled Chance in. "You better keep me warm tonight, cowboy. You forgot my flannel jammies."

He drew the sheet and quilt over them. "Then come here."

She snuggled her head into the curve of his

shoulder and sighed. "Do you remember our first time? How hard the floor was, even with the sleeping bag?"

"I didn't notice. I was too busy discovering other things." He kissed the top of her head. "I still am." He slid a hand down her spine and rested it on her hip.

"Do you like what you discovered?" She trailed her fingers over his chest, stopping to tease his nipples until they tightened.

"Yes, ma'am," he groaned. "And I'm still discovering. Like if you like this." He pulled her close and rubbed his erection against her.

Casey didn't hold back her sigh of desire, building again so quickly. "You know I do." She propped herself just enough to gaze into his face and see the dark blue fire burning in his eyes. Truth was, she could never get enough of him, and no matter what anyone might say or think about their whirlwind romance, it would last a lifetime.

This time, they went slower with long deliberate caresses and featherlight kisses that teased and promised. She wanted to draw out the waves of intense pleasure far into the night, but the man had magic hands and played her like a fine instrument, trailing his fingers across the hollow of her back, then lightly up and down her legs and arms and everywhere until her heart pounded and she thought the growing fire inside would consume her. "You do know how to tease a girl," she gave a desperate whisper.

He pulled her on top of him where reaching the peak this time became a journey of new discovery until neither could hold back any longer. For a moment, Casey sailed to the top of the mountains and took Chance with her.

Lying back against his arm, Casey waited for her heart to slow its wild rhythm. The man left her well-loved and full to the brim. But with one hunger satisfied, another took over. "I'm hungry. Are you hungry? Too bad there aren't more cookies." She remembered the Valentine candy and scrambled over him to bring the box of chocolates into the bedroom. Slipping back under the covers, Casey lifted the red satiny lid. "What do you prefer? Nuts? Caramel? I actually don't mind the crème ones myself." To prove it, she popped one in her mouth and relished the chocolaty sweetness on her tongue. Teasingly, she licked her lips.

Propped on the pillows, Chance watched her, his gaze lingering on her mouth. He leaned on one elbow and traced a thumb over her lips. "Actually, I just prefer you."

Casey held out the box of candy. "And you shall have me, but you better eat one to keep your strength."

He laughed, ate one, and let her eat two more. Taking the box, he set it on the nightstand and leaned over. He kissed her, tasting her lips. "I guess I prefer the chocolate crème, too."

Casey rested her arms on his shoulders. "Then you'll have to fight me for them, cowboy."

"I'd rather just do this." Easing Casey onto the rumpled sheets, he left a trail of kisses as his hands found all the right places that made her sigh.

Later, she listened to his soft, even breathing, and a deep sense of belonging filled her heart. This was home. This was where she needed to be. Nowhere else. Could she tell him that? Would he understand? She flattened one hand on his chest.

He opened one eye. "Aren't you tired yet? Duty calls in the morning, you know."

"I just want…to tell you something." She didn't resist the urge to trace her fingers over his whiskery chin.

"That you're crazy about me and think I'm the best all-around cowboy in the valley when it comes to pleasing a lady?"

"There is that, but…" She let her voice trail off, deciding not to mar the precious moment with a serious conversation. Who knew when they'd have a night like this again? Saying no more, she kissed him and soon forgot what she had even wanted to say.

All through the night, Casey imagined the northern lights dancing above the mountains and heard the wind sweeping through the canyons, bringing more snow to the valley. Somewhere in the distance, wolves howled, but inside the tiny cabin, love glowed in her heart with a fire all its own.

Chapter 9

March settled in, and the snowmelt began, leaving wide swaths of wet, muddy earth exposed and bringing an end to the sleigh rides. A warm wind blew through the valley, and the temperature climbed, breaking up the ice in the rivers.

Chinook wind, Roy called it. "Soon the mountains will send snowmelt down and make the rivers rise," he told Casey.

"I can't wait until the mountain flowers bloom again," she remarked at breakfast one morning. She'd caught the scent of spring in the air. *Soon, it'll be a year since I came out to visit Billie.* If someone had told her she would stay, she would have laughed in disbelief. *And yet, here I am.*

"Well, don't get too used to it," Justin warned. "We'll have another big snowfall or two or three, but at this point, you know the cold won't last forever. Though it sometimes snows in June."

Casey set his plate of pancakes in front of him. "Please don't tell me that. I just need to believe it will get warm again someday soon." She turned toward the stove but had second thoughts about eating breakfast.

She spent the morning updating the ranch website and checking for early reservations. Five families had reserved cabins. The season would get off to a good start. When she finished, her head ached, and she had a crick in her neck. Stretching, Casey closed her laptop and headed for the porch, where a balmy wind whistled through the pines. Except for that sound, everything else lay quiet. Where had everyone gone off to? Even no Mariah in sight. Ah yes, Chance had told the wranglers, since the spring roundup was only a week away, they could take the afternoon off. Billie had driven Justin to a doctor's appointment in Idaho Falls and left sandwiches in the kitchen for lunch. Who knew where Chance and Kyle were at the moment.

Guess I have the afternoon off, too. Rubbing her neck, she sauntered to the pasture to visit Blue Lady, who was due to foal soon. The mustang mare had surprised them when her belly rounded out. A little bonus, Chance remarked. Casey stood at the fence and tried to entice Blue Lady with a carrot, but even though they'd brought the mustangs to the ranch months ago, this one still did not trust anyone. "I hope you learn to like us before your baby arrives," she spoke softly to the mare. "All new mamas need help now and then."

For an answer, Blue Lady turned away and wandered to the far end of the corral. She stared at the mountains.

A wave of sadness swept over Casey. Did Blue Lady still miss her freedom and the other horses on the range? *I guess I understand.* Not ready to return to the house yet, she sat on a bale of straw and pulled out her phone to check for missed messages. Maybe she'd see one from Chance. Nothing. But since she could get a signal out here, she tapped a social media app and scrolled through the feed. Her life on the ranch had been too full the past few months to check any videos, and few interested her. Today, she noticed one titled *A*

Real Cowboy and clicked on it.

She saw girls dancing and having a good time at one of the local bars. In a time long gone, she was part of such a group, before she met Matt Girard. The video switched its focus and settled on a tall cowboy standing at the bar, downing a beer.

He turned.

Casey felt her heart lurch. *Chance.* She bit her lip and watched, compelled to see what happened next. The girls approached him and asked to take a photo. Fully expecting Chance to refuse, she felt sucker-punched when he let the giggling girls gather in close and hang on his arms while one held up her selfie-stick.

He smiled for the photo, the same smile that always won her over, even when they disagreed. Casey swallowed hard.

The girls begged him to buy them a drink. One grabbed Chance and kissed him. He broke away. Another reached for his hat. He warned her.

Casey clicked off the video and sighed. When had this happened? Not recently; the girls were dressed in winter gear. Surprising Chance didn't mention the incident. Was that what she got for having a handsome cowboy for a husband now? *Don't get upset. It's just a bunch of silly girls out for a good time. They mean nothing.* Somehow, she couldn't quite convince herself.

As she walked back to the house, Casey saw a small brown truck bump up the drive. She didn't recognize the vehicle. Who might be the visitor? She waited at the steps.

The truck stopped in the drive, and a woman got out and waved. Their closest neighbor, Jeannie Hanson from the Double Diamond Ranch, came striding toward her. Jeannie and her husband, Morly, were longtime residents of the valley, and they'd welcomed Casey when she first came to the North Star.

Ten years older than Casey's own thirty-three, Jeannie looked as young as her daughter, Marianne, with a clear complexion free of lines. Undoubtedly, she guarded her skin well against the dry western air. Jeannie had let her hair grow out over the winter and clasped it back with a leather barrette. Her faded jeans and pink shirt fit her slim figure like a teenager's.

Glad to see her friend, Casey waved back. Maybe Jeannie's company would pull her out of the doldrums, especially after seeing that video.

"Hi there," Jeannie called out and joined Casey. "I hope it's okay I stopped by. I've been meaning to do that since the weather broke, but you know how ranch life is. Something always needs tending."

"Of course, it's fine." Casey motioned toward the door. "Please come inside. I'll start a fresh pot of coffee."

Jeannie hugged her. "Everything okay?" She studied Casey's face.

"Sure. I'm fine. But I think I'm the only one here right now. Even Mariah seems to have gone off for the day." Casey noticed Jeannie's sideways glance and suspected she didn't believe the "I'm fine" part, but they went inside and sat at the kitchen table while the coffeepot perked.

"So, how are things going here at the North Star? I heard about the sleigh ride excursions this winter. Sounds like a great success."

"It was, and we're already making plans for how we can expand the event next year. I think if we advertise sooner, we'll have even more folks. Kyle's not so keen on the idea, but maybe it's just not his thing. Chance and I handled it, and the guys helped. Roy taught me how to drive the team. Jamie had a blast, and he and I even took the sleigh out by ourselves a few times."

"I saw that boy of yours with Chance in town last week. He sure sprouted this winter. If you don't mind my asking, how is the father-son relationship going?"

Casey considered the saddle she and Chance had disagreed about and the horse she'd heard him and Jamie talking about last week. She leaned her elbows on the table and weighed her words before speaking. "It's going…fine. Jamie thinks the world of Chance. I guess I'm the one having issues."

Jeannie lifted a neatly shaped brow. "About?"

Casey fiddled with the napkin holder on the table. "Just worried about Jamie getting on a horse and riding on the roundups." *Like the one starting soon.*

Jeannie gave her a reassuring smile. "You don't have to worry about that, sweetie. Chance won't let him do anything until he's very sure Jamie is ready."

She puffed out a sigh. "So everyone has told me."

The coffeemaker emitted a final hiss, cutting off further questions on the subject. Casey rose and went to the cupboard. She took down a single mug to fill for Jeannie, having second thoughts about drinking any coffee herself. She put a few slices of pumpkin bread on a plate and brought it all to the table.

"Mmmm, this looks wonderful." Jeannie helped herself to the bread, spreading a slice generously with butter. "Aren't you having any?"

"I had a big breakfast," she fibbed.

"You said Kyle wasn't too excited about the sleigh rides. Do you think he's maybe a little jealous of Chance taking part in running the ranch now?" Her friend sipped coffee and bit into the bread.

"That might be part of the problem, but what I really think is bothering Kyle is his girlfriend lives so far away now." She waited for Jeannie's reaction. Indeed, how did Jeannie feel about her daughter, her only child, moving to Spokane?

Jeannie set her cup on the table. "You're probably right, and the truth is I miss Marianne myself. As much as I'd like to keep my baby on the ranch, I know she needs to live on her own. She loves her teaching job, and she's getting used to life in the city."

Casey nodded. "We've tried to talk Kyle into visiting her, but I guess it's something they'll have to work out on their own."

"As you well know, the path to true love is strewn with more thorns than rose petals." Jeannie finished her bread and took a few sips of coffee. "Now, if you can stand one more nosy question, how are things going with you and Chance?"

The question jolted her. Stalling, Casey stared out the window. How did she answer her friend's question or explain her recent seesaw emotions? Even now, the memory of the sleigh ride she and Chance had taken under the stars and the intimate night spent in the cabin filled her heart with amazement. The depth of her love for the man surprised even her. She'd loved Matt, but, somehow, loving Chance was totally different and went beyond anything she had imagined she could feel. She simply had no words for the overwhelming passion they shared, at least none she would say to Jeannie.

And yet, some days, a sense of loneliness engulfed her. Now, after seeing the video, she had a million questions about whether Chance was truly happy with their life. She had to say something. "We're good. Although, sometimes, it's hard to deal with family, you know? My parents are convinced I was just infatuated with Chance and that I should be ready to come home by now. I love living here, but it's so different. There's so much…so many…"

"Men." Jeannie chuckled. "Believe me, Casey, I know. I'm sure testosterone runs off the walls here. I tell you what, we have a women's service group that meets twice a month. We do a potluck, sometimes we have a speaker, but, usually, we just yack and work on community projects. We're sewing quilts to sell to fund them. I think it'd be a nice opportunity for you to get away from the ranch. In case no one has told you, loneliness is a big problem out here, and you're still adjusting. I'll let you know when we meet next, and you can even ride with me. It'll do you good." Jeannie reached across the table and patted Casey's arm.

"I'll think about it." She appreciated Jeannie's concern, but right now, a nap sounded very appealing.

A short time later, Jeannie rose to leave.

Casey walked her outside. The spring-like weather had turned a few degrees cooler, and a line of dark clouds banked over the mountains. An uneasy shiver crept across her skin.

"Sure you're all right?" Jeannie touched her arm. "I hate to leave you alone."

Casey snuck a quick look at her phone. The text she'd sent Chance earlier had gone unanswered. Not unusual. Depending on where he was, signals were often nonexistent and messages sometimes got lost for hours. Still…

"I'm just a little worried." She stuck the phone in her jeans back pocket. "Chance gave the guys the afternoon off, and then he sort of disappeared. He does that sometimes. Only today, I'm feeling a little off about it. He says I worry too much." Maybe he was in town…doing what?

Jeannie thought for a minute, then glanced off to the west and the storm that undoubtedly would hit by evening. "Come on." She motioned for Casey to follow her. "I think I know where he might be today."

Casey hung back. "I need to meet Jamie at the bus stop."

Jeannie held up a hand. "The school bus isn't due for a couple of hours. You'll be back in time."

Casey hesitated only a second longer. "I'll get my jacket."

A short time later, Jeannie turned her truck onto a dirt road that led into the hills behind the ranch house. The drive reminded Casey of the place where she'd found Chance last summer, when she followed him to the old cabin and confronted him and the doubts he had about coming home. Only, in this place, she saw no cabin, no other buildings, only a windy hilltop with stone markers enclosed by a black iron fence.

At the bottom of the hill, Jeannie stopped and pulled in next to Chance's pickup.

A sharp chill rippled along Casey's spine. "I don't understand. What is this place?"

"The McCord family cemetery. Jeannie peered through the windshield to the top of the hill. "Alicia is buried here and a set of grandparents…and Angela and

Scottie. The accident happened about this time of the year, and I'm betting it's the first time Chance has visited their graves since they died."

Because he left the valley for five years. Casey bit her lip and shook her head. "He should have told me. I would have gone with him."

Jeannie tapped a finger on the steering wheel. "Maybe he's still not sure how to do that."

"Do you think he even wants me here?" Casey frowned. "Maybe he'd rather be alone with them."

"I think you should go find out." Jeannie reached across the seat and grasped Casey's hand. "You won't know what's in the man's heart if you don't ask, but I have a pretty good hunch you are the only person he'd want with him today."

She hoped that was true, but a peculiar ache filled her chest and tripped her heartbeat. She squeezed Jeannie's hand. "Thanks, Jeannie, for everything. I think I've got it from here." She shrugged off the nagging fatigue and left the truck to trudge up the hill.

Chapter 10

At the top, she met with a gust of wind that blew her hair across her face and sent old dry leaves from last fall to twirling around her feet. She pushed her hair aside and paused at the wrought-iron gate to the little cemetery. Should she interfere?

Head bowed, Chance stood in front of two markers, one with an angel engraved on its face. He hunched his shoulders forward and gripped his hat in his hands. Two yellow roses peeked out from the front of his coat.

Casey's breath caught in her throat. Last summer, Billie had told her about the car accident that had taken the lives of Chance's first wife and their young son. Shortly after the accident, Chance left the North Star the second time and stayed away for five years. Even now, this must be so painful. The first time he'd visited the graves since they died, Jeannie said.

What can I do to help him? What should I say? She lifted the gate latch and let herself in, trusting she would find the right words.

A few clumps of snow remained on the ground, but the dry leaves crunched beneath her boots.

Chance turned slightly.

She said nothing but went to his side and slipped her hand through the crook of his elbow. *Please don't let him move away.* She sighed and pressed her cheek to his jacket. As always, the denim held the wild scent of the mountains she so loved, almost as much as she loved him.

He didn't move away but nodded toward the gravesites. "I had to fight to bring them here."

She glanced up. "Fight who? And why?"

He didn't meet her gaze. "Lane and Delia Harris, Angie's parents. They wanted Scottie and Angie buried closer to their place in Pinedale."

This took Casey aback. "But you were her husband and Scottie's father. Why shouldn't you be the one to decide where they were laid to rest?"

Another gust of wind hit them. He squinted into it, staring off toward the vast wilderness that stretched far beyond the small family cemetery. "They were in pain, too. They thought this country was too wild…and that I didn't care about my wife and child to put them some place like this. That wasn't true."

"Of course, it wasn't." *Though they were right about one thing. This is a wild place, remote and lonely.* But Chance had buried a piece of his heart here, just as she'd left a part of her heart in Michigan. "It was a terrible time for all of you, but at least, you could put them to rest. Jamie and I never had that opportunity."

He slanted his dark-blue gaze at her.

She glanced away so he wouldn't see her tears brimming.

"What do you mean, Casey?" His voice turned low and husky.

She swiped at a tear that escaped. "They never found the wreckage…or Matt's body. His plane crashed somewhere in Lake Michigan during a storm. He's still there. That was probably the hardest thing, not knowing where he was and hoping that somehow, someday, he'd come back. For months, I listened for the sound of the door opening and his footsteps in the hall. After a year, I knew Matt was never coming home, and I had him declared legally dead. I had to sell the house. My family didn't agree with my decision, but we needed to go on."

He hugged her hand closer. "Casey, honey, I'm sorry you went through that. We've both traveled some pretty rough roads. Maybe that's why we found each other, and we're such a good fit."

She sniffed and dared to meet his midnight eyes. "You think? But we are a good fit."

He broke away for a moment and crouched to lay his hand against each headstone. The wind tugged at the small bouquets of flowers he'd placed on the graves. He straightened and drew her over to the other markers on the hill. One stone was for the grandparents he'd known as a child; the other stone read, *Alicia Mary McCord, Beloved Wife of Justin.* "This is my mom. I gave her a hell of a time as a kid, but she never criticized me. When she was gone, I had to go, too. Nobody understood that." He placed the yellow roses on her grave. "They were her favorite flowers."

Casey leaned against his arm and cried a little more.

Chance stroked her hair and handed her his bandanna.

She buried her face in it and let the tears flow for all they'd lost.

He turned and pulled her against him. "I thought I'd learned how not to make you cry. But I've still got some learning to do. I'm sorry if my coming here upset you."

His voice vibrated in her ear. "No," she denied and shook her head against his jacket. "It's not that. I'm just feeling a little…oh, I don't know, emotional. Maybe it's spring fever?" *Or seeing someone else kiss you.*

He tipped her face and brushed his lips across her forehead. "Comes with the Chinook wind."

Casey pressed her face into his chest for a moment and composed herself.

Chance stuck his hat on his head and, tucking her against his side, led her to the gate.

Without looking back, they left the little cemetery to the surrounding wilderness.

They met Jamie at the bus stop, and a short time later, the temperature plummeted, and rain slanted in icy sheets across the valley.

When they pulled into the ranch yard, Casey knew something wasn't right.

Roy and Ed stood just inside the open barn. Roy held the reins to Scout and looked ready to ride out.

But in this storm? She turned to Chance. "What do you think's going on?"

He growled low in his throat. "I'm sure I'm about to find out." He shoved the truck in Park, turned the key off, and opened his door into the driving rain.

Jamie watched Chance through the windshield. "Is something wrong, Mom?"

Chance sprinted across the space to the barn.

Casey tamped down the fear rising in her throat. "I'm not sure, but let's go inside. The rain's getting worse." She hastened Jamie into the house. "Go change your clothes, and I'll make hot chocolate." This morning, she was thinking about iced tea. How quickly the day went from spring-like back to winter's clutches.

A message on the answering machine said Justin and Billie were staying in Idaho Falls, rather than driving back in the storm. *A wise decision.*

She poured milk into a pan and waited for it to heat, then stirred in the cocoa. Peering out the window, she could barely see across the yard. When the door burst open, she jumped. Anticipating Chance, she turned to see Ed enter the kitchen, followed by a rain-soaked gust of wind.

He slammed the door behind him and turned to Casey.

She didn't care for the look on his face. The wrangler's frown sent ripples of queasiness surging over her.

"Sorry, Ms. Casey." He glanced at the water puddling beneath him on the floor. "Chance asked me to get his duster."

Without questioning, she went to the mudroom off the kitchen and returned carrying the long waterproof coat she'd seen Chance wear only once. "What's going on, Ed?" She gripped the duster and refused to let go until he explained.

He hesitated for a second. "We gotta find Kyle. Before the storm, he and Mariah went looking for a crazy heifer that broke out of the fence. They haven't come back."

Casey put a hand over her pounding heart. "And you're riding out there? Can't you take Roy's Juanita?"

"Horses can go places even a four-wheel drive can't, ma'am, and no telling where that heifer got off to." Ed held out one hand.

She relinquished the duster. How far would they have to ride to find Kyle?

Ed nodded and disappeared into the storm again.

As an afterthought, she turned off the burner under the hot chocolate and grabbed her own rain slicker.

Sheets of gray swept across the valley, powered by a mountain wind.

Casey flew down the steps and raced to the barn. The sleet stung her face like tiny needles. She skidded to a stop where Chance sat astride Smoky and put her hand on the duster, where it covered his knee. Looking into his face, she struggled for what to say. "Do you have your phone?" she managed.

He leaned down and cupped a gloved hand over her cheek. "I do. Roy's going with me. I asked Ed to stay here."

"What if we don't hear anything?" She grasped his hand.

"You will. I promise." He let go and pulled his hat low, shadowing his face.

"Please ride safely." She watched as the two men took off at a lope and then a gallop across the rain-soaked pastures.

Ed closed the barn and came to stand beside her.

They watched until the men and horses rode out of sight.

"How will they know where to look for them?" Casey asked.

Ed swiped at the rivulets that dripped from the brim of his hat. "If anyone can find Kyle, it'll be Roy Silver Wolf."

Behind them, Jamie shouted from the doorway. "Mom, what's happening? Can I come out?"

Casey looked at Ed. "Please come into the house. You need to dry off and get warm, and we can use the company. I'll make coffee."

He nodded and followed her to the house. For the next hour, Ed sat in the kitchen and kept Jamie occupied playing gin rummy.

She checked her phone for messages and kept watch out the window. When the house phone rang, jangling already raw nerves, they all jumped. Casey snatched it from the hook.

"Casey, it's Jeannie. What's going on? Morly was heading back from town a while ago and thought he saw Chance and Roy tearing out toward the creek. He figured, in this weather, it must not be anything good."

Casey fought to keep her voice calm, but in the last hour, she'd grown more anxious as a thousand scenarios of what could happen played in her head. Briefly, she explained.

"Are you alone? Do you want us to come over?" Jeannie asked.

Casey wound the phone cord around her hand. "No, I'm okay. Ed's here. I think we can handle it, but thanks anyway."

"Well, call if you need help, you hear?"

"I will. Thanks, Jeannie." Casey hung up and went back to staring out the window. *Where are they?*

Another half hour passed with no word from Chance.

Ed sat at the table, drinking his third cup of coffee.

Jamie bent his head over his homework.

She slid onto the bench beside Jamie.

Ed set his cup on the table and gave her a half-smile. "Are you doing okay, Ms. Casey?"

"Not so good," she admitted. A strange sense of unbalance made her queasy again. "Ed, be honest. Do you think they're okay?"

He shrugged. "They're pretty tough. I wouldn't worry too much."

To Casey, the Texan didn't sound very convincing. "It's a harsh country, isn't it? I guess maybe I didn't realize how harsh until today." She folded her hands together to keep them from trembling. Memories of another night of waiting still haunted her. That night had changed her life forever. *I can't go through this again. I just can't.*

Jamie set his pencil down and reached out to grab her hands with his small one. "They're gonna come back, Mom. I know they are. Chance promised to help me with my math again, and he won't break his promise. He and Roy will be okay."

Tears stung her eyes, and she looked away. Was staying in Wyoming a bad idea? Had she caused Jamie more pain than his young life needed? But no. In truth, her son had changed these past few months, from a timid little boy to one who now comforted his mother as best he could. She stood, pressed a kiss to the top of his head, and was grateful he didn't protest.

"Thank you, Jamie and Ed. I appreciate you both. Now, I better put together something for dinner." If she made dinner, they had to come home. *Right?*

Chapter 11

As they entered a rocky gully, Chance pulled Smoky alongside Roy and Scout and squinted in the same direction as the wrangler's gaze. They'd ridden for well over an hour along the rising creek. The rain had eased some, but they were both feeling the bite of a raw wind. For a short time, they'd followed tracks, but now the rain had washed away any signs of which way Kyle had ridden.

"Hell, I don't know which way to go," Chance admitted. A sense of desperation took hold of him. "I doubt he's getting any of the messages I've sent, if he's even out here."

"We need to keep following the creek," Roy insisted. "He's out here."

"What if he—"

Roy stood in his stirrups and lifted one hand for silence, then closed his eyes and appeared to just listen.

At first, Chance heard nothing but the rushing water that flowed faster by the moment. In such a short time, Antler Creek had gone from a meandering tributary of the Snake River to a treacherous beast threatening to overflow its banks.

"There!" Roy swung his head to face toward the creek's headwaters.

Somewhere ahead, a faint sound floated to them on the wind. A sharp, staccato sound that broke through again…and again.

Smoky tossed his head and answered the alarm with a loud whinny.

Chance recognized the sound. "It's Mariah," he shouted over the wind. "Ed said she was with Kyle!" He urged the Appaloosa ahead.

Roy and Scout followed.

The sure-footed horses navigated a gully, but even Smoky and Scout slipped on the precarious, rain-slick ground.

A quarter-mile ahead, the heifer stumbled away from the creek, hightailing it back to the herd.

Somewhere in the rain, another horse whinnied.

Ranger! Kyle's buckskin.

Smoky whinnied again.

Chance spotted Ranger tied to a bush and the Great Pyrenees dashing back and forth on the bank. He kicked Smoky into a fast lope.

Seeing them, Mariah stopped and barked but did not leave her post.

Vaulting from his saddle before they came to a halt, Chance slid on the half-frozen mud and joined the soaking-wet herd dog.

She whined but jerked away, panting and staring out at the wild creek.

He followed her gaze, and his stomach clenched.

In the churning water, Kyle clung to a downed tree, his head barely visible above the rushing torrent.

Damn fool kid. "Hang on!" He yanked off the duster, his coat and hat, and pulled his phone from his pocket to toss them all on the riverbank.

Roy rode Scout in front of him. "Boss, wait! Here!" He flung one end of the rope coiled on his saddle. "Put this around you before you go in."

Giving no argument, Chance pulled the lariat over his head and tight around his middle.

Roy let the rope out enough for him to wade into the creek but kept it taut.

As if they were roping a steer, Scout planted his rear hooves in the wet ground.

Roy wrapped his end of the rope around the saddle horn and held it tight.

The shock of the freezing water nearly took his breath away, but Chance waded in, the creek swirling around him, first knee-deep, then waist-high, and then nearly to his chest when he reached the tree. He felt a searing ache. Soon numbness would set in.

Caught between two branches, Kyle's grip on the tree slipped, as he tried desperately to keep water from rushing into his mouth. He choked and gasped for air.

Chance wasted no time and worked his way in beside him, sliding an arm around his brother and lifting him as much as the tree would allow. "Take it easy. We'll get you out of here." He tried to reassure Kyle, even though the fury of the water sucked them down. "Can you move closer?"

"Can't move," Kyle rasped. "Foot's caught." He coughed and spit out water. "Heifer fell in. Got her out, but I slipped. It wasn't so deep, then it rose…"

"It's okay, man, save your strength." To escape the water, Chance shoved them both against the trunk of the tree.

"Do you need help?" Roy's shout echoed above Mariah's barking.

"His foot's caught on something," Chance yelled back. "I'm going to have a look." He lifted his brother's arm over the stub of a branch. "Hold on to that, you hear? Hold on!" He watched Kyle's eyes glaze over. *Hypothermia*. If he didn't work fast, it would set in quickly. His own teeth chattered.

Holding his breath, Chance ducked under the water and felt along his brother's leg. Kyle's foot was caught all right, wedged between a rock and a thicker branch of the tree. He tried pulling at the rock, but the tree didn't move. *What do I do?* He came up for air. The rush of the creek grew stronger.

Kyle had slipped from the branch. He focused his eyes unsteadily on his older brother.

Chance moved behind him and hooked his arm beneath Kyle's chin, lifting his head out of the water as much as he could.

"I…don't want…to die," Kyle gasped.

"You won't," Chance promised.

The water rose higher.

"It's…o-k-kay." Kyle's teeth chattered. "Just don't leave m-me…'t-'til it's over."

The plea ripped into Chance with the same force of the rushing creek and echoed in his brain like a voice from the past. *Don't leave me!* They were the same words Kyle had cried the day Chance first left the ranch sixteen years ago. His kid brother had begged and pleaded for him not to go, because their mother had died, and he was afraid. If Chance didn't move fast today, then Kyle would drown in this creek. He waved one arm toward Roy. "I'll put the rope around the tree, and you pull it, so I can free him."

"I hear you," Roy called. "Just say when, boss-man."

His icy fingers were getting stiff, but he willed

them to move. With one hand, he loosened the lariat from around his body and tugged the rope over his head. He gave Kyle a brutal shake. "I gotta let go. But you hang on, dammit! You hang on!" He took a breath to duck under the water again. The raging creek filled his nose. In his head, he heard a voice that gave him a sudden burst of strength, a voice from long ago. *Take care of your brother.* He searched for a part of the tree he could slip the lariat over that would give the rope enough purchase so Roy and Scout could pull it away from the rock. He had to find it. *He had to.*

As if another hand guided him, he found the solid branch and slipped the lariat around the broken tree. He tightened the rope twice before bursting back out of the water and giving Roy a fist-up. "Pull it! Now!"

He lunged for Kyle and, grabbing his brother's upper body, lifted his face out of the water. At first, the tree, imbedded for too many years in the rocky creek bottom, didn't budge. "Keep pulling!" As the water flowed over Kyle's face, Chance hooked one arm beneath his chin. Planting his own foot against the tree, he gave a mighty shove.

Scout pulled.

The tree shifted.

Again! That voice in his head commanded, and he obeyed.

Ripped from its watery prison, the tree rolled upward with the lariat still attached.

Chance pulled Kyle away from the tree's grasp and hung onto him in the creek's swift current. He yanked the rope from the branch and slid the lariat over and under Kyle's shoulders. "Okay, let's go!"

Roy and Scout backed away and eased them both

from the water.

On the bank, Chance collapsed beside his brother but only for seconds. Dragging himself to his knees, he saw Roy bent over Kyle, straddling him and pumping his chest.

"Breathe, Kyle. Come on, man, breathe," Roy issued a stern command, then added something Chance didn't understand. *Arapaho words.*

A sound gurgled from Kyle's throat, and water suddenly gushed from his mouth.

Roy turned him on his side and held him, muttering another phrase.

Chance still kneeled, hands on his knees, coughing up his own share of creek water. When he could speak, he looked at Roy. "Thanks, man. Good job."

Roy just nodded. "You, too, boss-man. We better get you guys back before you both freeze to death."

Mariah bumped against Chance. She whined and licked his face.

Leaning on her for support, he staggered to his feet and stumbled to where his brother lay. He grasped Kyle's one hand while Roy grabbed the other.

They got Kyle standing, but his right leg flopped awkwardly.

"Think something's broken." Roy slid one arm around Kyle's waist. "Come on, man. Let's get you on your horse."

Chance helped Roy drag Kyle onto Ranger and prop him in the saddle.

His brother immediately folded and began to slide off.

He gave Kyle a rough shove. "You stay there!" he commanded. "You stay on your horse."

How many times as kids had he yelled at his brother? Told him to cowboy up and act like a man? He'd ignored the scared little boy begging him not to leave and owed Kyle big time for that. He wasn't even sure saving his brother from the flooding creek paid the debt.

Roy rode beside him. "I've got him, boss. You go on and get your horse. We better clear out. There's more storm behind this one."

Chance grabbed everything he'd left on the riverbank. He shrugged into the duster and brought the coat back to the horses. He tugged it around Kyle, whose own jacket was lost to the creek. "Get him back," he rasped out. "I'll be right behind you. I just gotta let Casey know what's happened."

The two rode off and disappeared into the gray mist.

For warmth, Chance leaned against the patient Smoky and stared at his phone. He could barely see the numbers. The wind cut through his wet clothes, and, even beneath the duster, he shivered. He clenched his teeth to stop their chattering. One bar of signal strength blinked in and out, but he forced his fingers to press the buttons on the phone. He had to let Casey know what to expect.

Chapter 12

"Time for bed." For the last hour, they'd sat on the sofa reading, but Casey marked the page and closed the book.

"Can't I wait with you, Mom? Please?" Jamie didn't budge. Despite his insistence earlier that Chance and Kyle were all right, his back stiffened with tension, and fear shadowed his bright blue eyes.

"You need your rest, son. So, please, do as I ask." Casey leaned over and kissed his cheek. "I'll be there to tuck you in shortly."

He heaved a heavy sigh and dragged himself up the stairs.

Her own body ached with worry and fear, much like that night when she'd waited for word on a plane that would never come home. *Please don't let this be happening.* The phrase rolled over and over in her mind while she held tight to hope.

Ed went out to do barn chores.

No doubt, he was glad to get away from her fear that was by now palpable. Casey perched on the edge of the sofa in front of the fireplace. The strange sense of uneasiness that had plagued her today settled in the pit of her stomach and joined with the twinges of nausea she'd been fighting. She wrapped her arms around her middle and rocked slowly back and forth.

Outside, the wind gusted, soughing through the

pines.

Her phone vibrating against the coffee table jolted her. She snatched it and fumbled to see the text message.

—Ok but Kyle hurt. Need ambulance. Be there soon—

The weight of worry lifting left her suddenly drained, but she quickly tapped out a reply, then ran to the kitchen just in time to meet Ed at the door. "They're on the way back, but Kyle's hurt." Her hands shook as she showed him the text message. "Maybe we should drive out and meet them."

Ed nodded and patted her arm awkwardly. "We can't do that. We'd be stuck for sure in all this rain. But it'll be okay, Ms. Casey. I'm sure of it. I'll call for help and then go keep an eye out for the guys."

Casey sagged against the kitchen counter. Clutching her phone, she waited for another message. A flurry of questions raced through her mind. What had happened? Was Kyle badly injured? Should she call Billie and Justin? *No sense in alarming them until we know what's wrong.* She tried to calm her racing heart, but panic simmered just beneath the calm surface she was trying so hard to hang onto. The McCord men liked to handle things themselves, but she had never been above asking for help when she needed it. Walking to the wall phone, she checked the list of numbers hanging beside it. Hands still trembling, she punched in the number.

On the third ring, Jeannie answered.

"It's Casey. I'm…sorry to bother you." She fought to keep her voice from shaking.

"Oh, sweetie, that's okay. What is it?" Jeannie's

instant concern reached out through the phone lines.

Casey briefly explained. "I don't know how bad it is, but if I need someone to stay with Jamie—"

"We're heading there right now." Jeannie disconnected.

Replacing the receiver, Casey turned to see Jamie standing in the kitchen doorway in his super hero pajamas.

"Mom? What h-happened?" His small voice quivered. "Why isn't Chance back yet?"

She hurried and put her arms around him. He had grown so much lately—was nearly to her shoulder—and yet, despite his earlier bravado, Jamie was still a little boy. One who had gone through so much change in the past few years. "He's on his way, but Kyle's hurt. I don't know how badly. I've asked Jeannie Hanson to come over, in case I need to go to the hospital with them. Will you be okay?"

He gave a solemn nod. "Sure. I'm not such a little kid anymore. You don't have to worry about me."

She hugged him, and together, they waited for the men to get back. Nothing she imagined prepared Casey for what she saw when Roy rode into the ranch yard first, leading Kyle on Ranger.

Kyle lay draped over the buckskin's neck, his arms dangling.

Ed ran over to help ease a nearly unconscious Kyle off his horse just as the ambulance and the Hanson's pickup turned into the drive.

Her heart raced with dread as she watched the paramedics load Kyle on a stretcher and carry him to the waiting vehicle with the oscillating lights. Figuring they had that situation under control, Casey drew her sweater around her and went to stand at the end of the porch and wait for the other horse and rider to come in.

Jamie pulled on his hooded jacket and followed. "How come Chance isn't with them?" He stood beside her and stared into the darkness beyond the buildings. "What if he doesn't come home?"

Casey trembled at Jamie voicing the fear she'd secretly harbored all evening. "We can't think like that. We have to believe he's okay. Chance said he was okay." She did her best to control the tremor in her voice.

Roy strode to the edge of the yard, leading Scout and Ranger. He stared into the murky shadows where ten kinds of danger could arise at any moment.

Images of wolves and grizzlies rose in Casey's mind. She pushed them away. Why was Chance so far behind? What had happened out there? Drawing in a shaky breath, she willed the man to come home.

They appeared as ghostly figures—first Mariah leading the way, then Smoky and his rider.

Casey and Jamie fled the porch at the same moment, running across the slippery ground.

Chance dismounted and slumped against Smoky's side.

Jamie flung his arms around the man's middle in a fierce hug. "Chance! What took you so long?"

Casey stood back to give them a moment. Holding her own crazy emotions in check, she watched her husband bend over the boy and murmur something.

Then Chance lifted his head and met her gaze while he clung to Jamie.

His eyes held some unspoken emotion that sent a wave of relief flooding through Casey. She rushed into his embrace.

He held them both against him and shuddered.

The deep cold that emanated from his body chilled hers. She touched his face with gentle fingers. "Whatever happened?"

He pulled her up tight but didn't speak.

Jamie dashed away tears. "Mom was afraid you wouldn't come back."

"I'll always…come back," Chance rasped in a low, halting voice. "Always."

Roy appeared at Chance's side. "I'll take Smoky to the barn. You get some help, boss." He jerked his head toward the ambulance. "They're ready to take Kyle. You should go with them."

Slipping one hand beneath his duster, Casey touched Chance's chest. His flannel shirt was soaked and stiff from the cold. "Come on, Roy's right. You better see the paramedics, too." She tugged him toward the ambulance but only got resistance. She heard a car door slam and saw Jeannie heading their way. She leaned toward Jamie. "I want you to go with Jeannie. Will you do that for me?" The boy listened better than the man, but she refused to let Chance win this battle of wills. She slipped an insistent arm around his middle. "Don't argue with me, cowboy. You need to get checked out. Now, come on." She led him to the ambulance.

The paramedic took one look and nodded toward the back of the vehicle. "Think you best ride along with your brother. Going into the drink in this weather, it's a good bet you've got a few things going on. Let us find out."

Thank goodness, Chance didn't argue and climbed

into the ambulance.

The paramedic looked at Casey to see if she wanted to accompany them.

The medicinal smell from the interior reached her nose, and Casey's stomach lurched. She stepped back, her legs going weak. Someone gripped her elbow.

"We'll be right behind you," Morly Hanson spoke as the doors to the ambulance closed. "I'll drive you," he said to Casey. "You shouldn't go alone."

Her knees threatened to buckle, but the burly rancher held her upright. "On second thought, you best go on into the house with Jeannie. They'll take care of the men. C'mon, I'll help you."

She wanted to argue with Morly but heeded his advice. The fear and anxiety of the day caught up with her. "I can get inside okay." She attempted to shake away the woozy feeling. "But please follow them. I…have to call Justin and Billie." She bade Morly hurry and turned to make her way to the house.

The minute Jeannie saw her, she steered Casey straight to the sofa in front of the fireplace and made her lie down. "You just put your feet up, and I'll bring you a cup of tea."

She tried to avoid Jeannie. "I have to get Jamie to bed, and I need to call—"

"Already done. I got Jamie off to bed, and Morly called Justin soon as we got here." She left the room to get the tea.

Casey sank into the sofa pillows. She sought desperately to let the stress she'd harbored the entire day flow out of her, but pictures of what might have happened to Chance and Kyle paraded through her mind. How had they gotten so soaked? How badly was

Kyle hurt? She should have asked Roy. She should have gone to the hospital with Morly. She should have…

Jeannie's hand on her shoulder drew Casey from a murky dream where she searched for Chance in a rain-filled mist.

"Casey, wake up." Jeannie's voice broke through the mist. "You're dreaming, sweetie,"

Struggling to sit, Casey pushed her hair back with a shaking hand. She shook the dream away, but the haunting images didn't dissipate so easily.

"See if you can drink this and maybe eat a few crackers. I think you've probably not had much all day." Jeannie handed her a steaming mug of tea.

She took the cup offered but turned away the plate of soda crackers. Sipping at the hot liquid, she hoped it would stay down.

Jeannie sat in the big easy chair across from her. "Feeling better?"

Casey shook her head. "I was so afraid something terrible had happened."

"As well it might have. As it almost did. Roy gave me the rundown. Kyle would have drowned had they not found him when they did, and Chance not gone into Antler Creek after him. He saved his brother's life today."

Casey clutched the mug and absorbed Jeannie's words. "Do you ever get used to this? The everyday dangers? I don't know if I can live with the constant fear some unseen threat is waiting just around the corner. What I went through losing Matt, I just can't do that again."

Jeannie folded her hands and pressed them against

her lips. "Living here isn't easy by any means," she spoke over them. "It's hard enough for those of us born to it, and not everyone can adapt. Yet, you married Chance."

Casey rubbed her fingers against her temples. "I did, and I don't regret it for a minute. I love him with all my heart, but I'm scared…that I'll never fit in. Never measure up. That I can't cope with nights like this one."

Jeannie leaned forward in the big chair.

Her smile looked sympathetic, but her words didn't cut Casey any slack.

"Don't sell yourself short. You're stronger than you think you are, and now especially, you have every reason to stay and make this work."

"What do you mean?" Casey tried to sip the tea again, but her stomach said *no*. "What reason?"

"One that will tie you to the man even more than your love. You ought to know what I'm talking about. You did this before." Jeannie rose. "I'm going to call Marianne. She needs to know what happened to Kyle." She left the room.

Sitting alone with her own thoughts, Casey suddenly came to grips with the truth tumbling through her mind.

Chapter 13

In the morning, Casey sat in the rocking chair on the porch and watched the sunrise. As golden rays crept across the valley, a pallet of pink hues stained the sky above the mountains. The crisp, cool breeze rippled her hair where it lay across her shoulders. She wrapped her blanket more snugly about herself and pushed the rocker back and forth with one foot. Sleep had eluded her throughout the long night, and she'd finally come out here to escape an empty bed and sort out her jumbled emotions. Maybe Mom was right that her decision to stay in Wyoming was hasty and not well thought-out. Maybe, she should never have come out here at all. Would she ever figure out her place in this new life she'd chosen? After dealing with yesterday's events, she had her doubts.

Then she remembered the video. Watching it again went against her better judgment, but she turned her phone in her hand and opened the social media app, scrolling until she found *A Real Cowboy*.

She noted again how cute the girls were, how young, how bold, and how they pressed themselves against the real cowboy, who happened to be her husband. A slow ache grew in the pit of her stomach. *He could have pushed them away. He looks like he really didn't mind. He looks...* She fisted a hand against her mouth and held back a sob. The clunk of boots on the porch steps jolted her out of giving into the tears.

Roy stood by the railing and tipped his hat back. "You're awake early. Didn't sleep well?"

The touch of his black-as-night gaze was somehow comforting. Casey turned her phone over and brushed a hand over her face. "Not too. Last night…it was all such a nightmare."

"Yeah, I hear you." Roy glanced off toward the sunrise. "Did you get any word from the hospital?"

"Not yet. Do you think I should go there? I should have last night but—" She swallowed guilt for having backed away from the ambulance.

He moved closer and took off his hat. "Chance doesn't want you to do that. I'll go get him when he's ready."

The music on the video continued to play. Casey fumbled to turn her phone off.

Roy narrowed his gaze. "What have you got on there?"

She hesitated but after a second thought held out her phone.

Roy took it and watched the screen for a moment. He made a low sound and clicked off the video. "I was hoping you wouldn't see that." He handed the phone back to Casey.

Startled, she clutched the phone and bit her lower lip. "You already did? When?"

He shrugged. "Few days ago." He crouched in front of her, balancing on his heels. "It doesn't mean anything, Ms. Casey."

But it does! She wanted to shout, to throw the phone, to run fast somewhere and escape from what was maybe the worst decision of her life. Where was common sense when she needed it? Apparently, in short supply last summer. She rubbed a hand across her forehead. "I want to believe that, Roy. I know Chance would never do anything…to hurt me. But after yesterday, I'm just not sure I belong here." Except, like Jeannie said, something more important than her love for Chance might tie her to this place.

"You belong." Roy's dark gaze rested on her. "And this will all blow over. You just gotta have trust."

Trust. She and Chance had talked about it many times in the past months. So, why was trusting still so hard sometimes?

The sun inched over the mountains to the east, and the pale pink color in the sky faded away.

Casey leaned forward in the rocking chair. "Thank you, Roy. I appreciate your support."

His mouth lifted in a half grin. "I just came here to tell you not to bother with breakfast for Ed and me. We can take care of ourselves. You take care of you and the boy, and I'll drive him to the bus stop."

He stood then and left the porch.

Casey watched him go while the wind blew from the mountains. What would she do without Roy?

****

The medical center held Chance overnight for observation and treatment of hypothermia. He waited to leave until a helicopter airlifted Kyle to Denver for surgery on the compound fractured leg. Then he called Roy to bring him home. At the North Star, he motioned for the wrangler to let him out by the barns. He eased himself out of Juanita and glanced around the place. Snow lay patchy on the ground, but a group of young mustangs he'd yet to break kicked up their hooves and raced around the pasture. Farther on, the cows that would drop calves this year chewed their cuds and swished their tails. The ranch appeared a scene of contentment.

But what might've happened if he and Kyle hadn't made it out of the creek? Justin sure as hell couldn't run the North Star by himself anymore and hadn't been able to in a long time. Chance was just beginning to realize that truth. Now, without Kyle here, who would make the decisions and keep them afloat? Whose shoulders would carry the responsibility? The answer settled into his brain like the weight of a rock.

Roy parked and ambled over to Chance. "You okay, boss-man?" He stood beside Chance, his phone in his hand.

Chance shook away his concerns and glanced at Roy. "Yeah, just…reflecting. Casey in the house?"

Roy nodded and opened his mouth to say something but stopped and stared at his phone.

The wrangler had a concern. Chance stepped closer to see what held his attention. "Is there a problem I need to know about?" He didn't really want to know. He just wanted to talk to Casey and make sure she was all right. She was probably terrified last night.

Roy tipped back his hat and held out the phone. "I thought you should see this."

Chance took the phone and watched the video. A chill colder than the creek water smacked him hard. *A damn video*. He didn't know the girl had done that. He thought she'd only taken a few photos. "When did…how long—"

"It's making the rounds. Seems like a few folks recognized you." Roy dug one boot heel into the ground. "They left some nasty comments."

"Did Casey see it?"

"Yep."

Chance handed Roy's phone back and rubbed his neck. "It wasn't how it looks."

"Never is." Roy pocketed the phone. "Just thought you ought to know she's dealing with this...besides last night. She's pretty upset."

So, now a wrangler was telling him how his wife felt? Chance held back a sharp retort. He'd known for a while about the friendship between Roy and Casey—friendship on her part, but maybe something more for Roy. He blew out a heavy sigh. "Can you handle the work today? I need to spend some time with her."

"Sure, boss-man." Roy turned on his heel, then stopped. "You better let her know she belongs here." He said no more and headed for the big barn.

Chance watched him go. He'd trusted Roy with the horses and with his life. Now, with Kyle laid up, he'd have to trust Roy again. They had no choice. As he started for the house, his bum knee faltered, and he swore softly. He'd sure as hell made a mess of things. Would Casey forgive him?

****

Casey stood at the counter, kneading bread. Pushing on the lump of dough, folding it roughly back and forth and slapping it on the cutting board, she expressed all the frustration still churning inside her. She gave the dough a good whack and drew on the strength Jeannie was so sure she possessed.

"Guess I'm glad not to be the bread dough." Chance stepped into the ranch house kitchen and hung his hat on the hook by the door. He shuffled to the counter. "Or does it have my name on it?"

Casey shoved her hands into the floury mound again and gave the dough another smack.

He rested his hands on her shoulders and turned her to face him.

She couldn't—wouldn't—meet his gaze.

"Casey, honey, are you okay?" His voice sounded gravelly and raw.

"Are you?" she countered.

He gave a false laugh. "Other than feeling like somebody kicked me around in a flooded creek?"

She traced a finger over his chest and played with the pearl snaps on his shirt. "I'm sorry I didn't go to the hospital last night. I should have. I just—" Her chin quivered.

Chance touched her lips to silence the apology. "No need to say anything. I'm sorry you had to go through all that worry."

Strength and reserve rushed out of her. Casey smacked his arm this time, then grasped his shirt and shook him. "Don't ever scare me like that again." She pressed her face against the soft flannel and breathed in the scent of the mountains and sunshine that replaced the rain today. Damn, but she was glad he was here…and *alive*.

He backed up to the table bench and sat, pulling her, floury apron and all, onto his lap.

She felt him flinch and tried to stand. "You are hurt."

He kept her close. "Few bruises. They'll heal. Will we?"

They'd moved into another level of their marriage. Born in fear and uncertainty, an unfamiliar emotion rose inside Casey, one that said she would love this man, no matter what. "Roy said you saved Kyle's life. That if you hadn't gone into the creek, he would have died." She met his blue gaze and studied his face.

He rubbed his hands up and down her arms. "We can all thank Mariah. The old girl never left him, and Roy heard her barking. Another few minutes, and we might've been too late."

Casey buried her face in his shoulder. She hated that stupid video, but she still loved Chance and wanted to forget whatever happened.

He stroked her hair, and they sat that way for a few long moments.

"Something…something happened out there," Chance finally said. "Kyle got caught in a dead tree, and the water rose faster than I've ever seen it. I couldn't free him."

"Roy said you took the rope from yourself and put it around the tree," she spoke into his shirt. "He and Scout pulled it away." *What if Roy hadn't been there?*

"But…I couldn't find where to put the rope." His voice lowered. "We were both going to die. Someone…something guided my hand, and I heard…" He stilled his caress.

She felt him tremble. "What? What did you hear?"

"My…mother's voice. So clear in my head. And after all these years, I knew it. She sounded the same." He halted for a moment.

Casey straightened and peered into his face. "What did she say?'"

He stared at some far corner of the kitchen. "Take care of your brother. She said that to me before she died. *Take care of your brother.* But I didn't do that."

114

"You were young and grieving. You couldn't—"

"Kyle was a little boy, not much older than Jamie. He was scared, and I just left him."

Casey put her hand on his cheek and turned his face. Tears glistened in his midnight eyes. "Hearing your mother was a gift, Chance. Maybe even a miracle. Whatever we call it, I'm just thankful you came back, that you both did. I was scared half to death, and I don't want to feel like that again, but I guess living here, there are no guarantees."

He took a deep breath and exhaled slowly. "I leave for Denver tomorrow. Kyle needs surgery. Justin can't go, and I can't let Kyle be alone. I have to take care of him now. Morly's got a friend said he'd fly me there in the morning."

Casey remained silent for a moment. She didn't want him to go, didn't want to stay here without him, but maybe this was a moment of truth. She straightened her shoulders and drew on years of dealing with change. "Of course, you need to go. Somebody from his family should be there."

"I'll only stay as long as I have to. Roy and Ed will do anything for you. Whatever you need, just ask." He waited.

Casey nodded and stood to finish making the bread. "We'll be okay. We can handle whatever we have to." She started to walk away.

Chance caught her hand. "Will you be here when I get back?"

She read the fear in his eyes and the need to hear her answer. "Where else would I be?"

****

That night, Chance spent an hour on the phone

with Justin, reassuring his father that Kyle would be all right. After getting grilled about the extent of his brother's injuries, Chance listened while Justin reminded him to get ready for spring branding. Could Ed and Roy handle the work? Chance promised Roy would get some help from the Double Diamond, if necessary.

Justin finally stopped rambling and clicked off.

Exhausted after the conversation, he entered his and Casey's bedroom.

She lay propped in bed, reading. Her hair had grown longer over the winter, and, for sleeping, she wore the waves in a long braid over her shoulder.

The desire to release that tawny mass and bury his face in it right now sent a jag of need raking through him.

She didn't look up when he closed the door but only turned a page in her book.

He went into the bathroom and shed his clothes, taking a moment to inspect the evidence of the battering he'd taken in Antler Creek. Purple bruises had spread over his body, and his muscles ached. Letting the hot water beat over him helped a little, but he wished Casey would join him…like that night in the cabin.

She didn't.

He sank onto the bed and lay beside her.

She kept reading.

Did he dare mention the video? She didn't spend much time on social media, other than to promote the ranch. But the video was making the rounds, and she saw it. He was leaving in the morning and had to say something. "Casey, honey, can we talk?'

She marked her place in the book and set it aside,

but she didn't face him.

Maybe it was better this way, not looking her in the face. He took a deep breath and cleared his throat. "You might've seen something…something that looks one way…but it wasn't…that way. I—"

"Ssshh." Casey slid down and turned toward him. She ran her hand over his bare chest, stopping at the large bruise decorating his ribs. "Nothing's broken, right? They checked you out thoroughly?"

At her touch, he inhaled a quick breath. "Yeah, from head to toe. Like I said, a few bruises."

She leaned over and pressed a kiss to the largest bruise. Then she rested her cheek and slipped one arm around him. "What happened—what I saw—I don't want to talk about it. You're leaving in the morning, and I don't want to have any bad feelings between us while you're gone."

Could he blame her for wanting to let this incident lie? She'd lost her first husband after a quarrel. He trailed a hand over her arm where it pressed against him. "Do you still trust me?" He had to ask that.

"If we don't trust each other, then why are we here?"

Her breath whispered across his skin, stoking his need. Indeed. Why were they here if not for this? He eased her up and brought her face to his, capturing her mouth and playing his lips over hers with soft seductive kisses and trailing them down her throat.

After a moment, she sat and slowly removed the flannel pajamas—first the top, releasing one button at a time, then slipping free from the bottoms and tossing them aside.

Her perfect body enticed him until he could barely

wait. He reached for her. "Casey...come here—"

She brushed his hands aside. "Hush." Unwinding the braid, she shook her hair free and let it fall over her shoulders until the waves almost covered her breasts. Then, seductively, she leaned forward and grazed her lips across his. "Let's don't talk...about anything." She ran her hands over his shoulders and his stomach, lingering there before stroking him with featherlight touches.

"Casey, baby, you're killing me." He groaned and swelled to her teasing exploration.

She covered his mouth with one hand. "No words, cowboy. Just feel me."

Oh, he did. Every torturing fingertip she ran over his skin, every kiss she pressed to his aching body. He tried to just lie back and enjoy the sensations, the ripples of desire flooding through him, but he was hard, and he couldn't wait much longer.

He eased her over and slipped one hand between her thighs, stroking her soft skin just the way she liked. Up one side and down the other, and finally teasing the sweet spot that evoked a long sexy sigh.

"No fair," she murmured but moved in time with his caresses. "I thought I was orchestrating this."

"Honey, haven't you heard? All's fair in love." He kissed her deeply and then relished the sound of her shuddering climax. Before she could relax, he spanned her waist with his hands and, ignoring the bruises, lifted her on top of him. She didn't protest, but breathed out a deep sigh and took him inside.

He couldn't hold back any longer, and in a rush of release, he soared on the crest of his desire. When he drifted into half-sleep, he still held her close, her hair spilling over his chest. In the utter peace of the moment, Chance knew he could never live without this woman.

She let out a breathy sigh. "Not bad, cowboy."

He chuckled and brushed a kiss across her forehead. Keeping Casey safe and protected was all he wanted to do for the rest of his life. But would his leaving make a difference? Would the time apart change them? He hoped to hell not, because making love with Casey was the sweetest thing he'd ever known.

****

In the early morning, Chance dressed to leave for the airport. He leaned in and kissed Casey's cheek and lingered for just a moment, brushing one hand over her hair and tracing a finger along her cheek. He would've been happy to crawl back into bed, but the flight left in two hours. The magic they shared last night would have to last awhile.

She murmured something in her sleep, shivered, and curled her body.

He drew the quilt over her and watched her snuggle beneath its warmth. He hated leaving her like this. They'd made an incredible connection in the midnight hours, but doubt still lingered in his mind. Did she forgive him for the video? Would their love survive this separation? She'd gone through so much in the past few years—losing her first husband, traveling to Wyoming, marrying him—how could he expect her to deal with this latest hardship?

But he had no choice. Kyle needed him, and this time, he wouldn't fail his brother.

****

Casey pretended to be asleep and didn't open her

119

eyes until Chance was gone. In the thin sunlight that peeped through the bedroom windows, she lay still and mulled over the question haunting her. Was last night enough to make him forget the girls in the local bar, or any bar, or rodeo? She'd wanted to give him something to think about while they were apart. Something to bring him back. But Denver was a long way from the North Star with a lot of girls in between. And maybe once he was away, he would remember the freedom of the road. The freedom to do as he pleased. A lump of fear lodged in her throat, and she pressed her face into her pillow. Please let what they had together be a reason to come home.

A week later, she set the slim plastic case on the dresser top and waited for the test results. Within a minute, she had her answer. Sitting on the edge of the bed, she absorbed what the *yes* meant.

She had wanted to wait until Chance got home, but complications with Kyle's surgery required a second operation on his broken leg, and then pneumonia set in. Casey assured Chance he should stay in Denver. But she simply couldn't wait any longer to know for certain.

Yes. The test said a definite *yes*, with the added information of six weeks. She thought about Valentine's Day and the night in the cabin. That night, she'd realized how deep her feelings went for the cowboy she'd married. He'd become a part of her. And now, as a result, this happened. She placed her hands over her stomach. *How soon will I feel this baby stir? What will he or she look like?* Would he have his father's dark hair? Her own gray eyes? A long journey lay ahead, and she ached to share the news, but telling Chance over the phone or by text wasn't the way she wanted him to know he would be a father again next fall. Best she waited until he came home.

They'd not talked much about having more children, except to say maybe someday, but one night of lovemaking in a cozy cabin without taking any precautions had changed all that. What would Chance say when she told him?

Right now, she was just so tired. She lay on the bed and gave herself over to the relentless fatigue. She let her eyes drift shut. In her dream, she held a baby wrapped in a pink blanket and heard herself singing softly.

Chapter 14

Casey followed Jeannie as they made their way to the last open booth in the back of the bustling Hitching Post café and slid into the well-worn vinyl seats.

Jeannie passed a plastic-covered menu to Casey. "I don't know about you, but I'm hungry and dying for some caffeine." She turned her coffee cup over and nodded to the server, who came right over to fill it. "I make decaf at home, but sometimes I just need the real thing."

Casey ordered tea and only glanced at the menu. Nothing sounded good. She struggled with not just morning sickness but the all-day blahs.

The nurse practitioner at the women's health clinic today gave her a prescription for vitamins and offered suggestions for helping with the nausea, as well as providing her a due date of mid-November.

A lifetime away. She pushed the menu aside.

Jeannie shook her finger. "You need to eat something, Casey. Maybe soup and crackers?"

"Ugh. I think crackers are my least favorite food nowadays." She conceded, though, and when the server returned, she ordered the fruit plate. Glancing toward the lunch counter, Casey flashed back to last summer. She and Jamie had taken refuge in the café during a cloudburst…and met a dark-haired cowboy on his way home to the North Star Ranch. She asked him to please move over so they could sit at the counter. That day was engraved in her memory but now seemed a very long time ago. She twisted the silver wedding band on her finger.

"Earth to Casey." Jeannie waved her hand in front of her. "Are you okay, sweetie?"

A wistful cloud threatened to settle over her, but she shook it away. "Just remembering something and thinking about how I got to this place in my life."

Jeannie stirred cream into her coffee. "Well, that seems a little profound. Care to explain?"

She didn't and sipped her tea. "How did you know?" she asked after a moment. "About me, I mean. How did you know I was pregnant?"

Jeannie savored her coffee and smiled. "I have a nursing degree and worked at the women's clinic. Believe me, I can read all the signs, and you were showing plenty."

"That plain, huh?"

"Quite, but I'm curious. Didn't you feel any of this with Jamie?"

Casey set her teacup on the table. "I felt great then. Not a day of sickness, and I certainly don't remember dragging around half the day like a zombie." *But we were excited about having a child.*

"You were also nearly ten years younger. It makes a difference. As does having someone for moral and emotional support. Have you told Chance yet?"

"I can't. Not 'til he comes home." Casey fiddled with her silverware.

"Marianne says Kyle is improving every day. The trouble is, Chance feels obligated to stay with his brother. After their estrangement, I'm pretty sure he believes he owes this to Kyle."

"He does." Casey shrugged. "After their terrible rift, I don't want to come between them."

Jeannie unfolded her napkin. "I understand that, but you need your husband here, and he should know about this baby."

The server brought their food and placed a plate of cottage cheese and fruit in front of Casey. She attempted to at least pick at the fruit. More than anything, she wanted her baby to be born safe and healthy and wanted…as Jamie had been.

When she was dropped off at the North Star later Casey grasped her friend's arm. "Thank you for going with me to the clinic. I really appreciate it."

Jeannie patted her hand. "I'm more than happy to offer whatever support I can, even if I am a poor substitute for the person you really need."

"He'll be home soon," Casey assured Jeannie as much as herself.

****

"I wish Chance was here." Jamie shoved his math book aside and put his head on his arms. "I thought he'd come home this week."

Casey recognized his frustration. For the past hour, she'd sat at the kitchen table while he struggled to finish his homework. She did her best to keep him focused, but obviously, Jamie's mind had drifted somewhere else. Outside, a storm had blown about for most of the day, with the lights flickering more than once. The unsettled weather put everyone on edge.

She gave Jamie's shoulder a reassuring squeeze. "I know, I did, too, but Kyle's having a tough time, and Chance doesn't want to leave him in Denver without family around. You can imagine how Kyle must feel in the hospital, so far away from the ranch."

Jamie toyed with his pencil. "Yeah, I guess. But, at least, Chance can help me figure out my math. He's a lot better than you, Mom."

"Oh gee, thanks." She sighed. "Too bad it's not English or history. I'm much better at those subjects."

He sat up and grinned. "Yeah, I know, and anything to do with books, right?"

"Right." She patted his shoulder. *He's growing so fast, and I want to tell him he's going to be a big brother.* But that had to wait. Chance still deserved to know first. She remembered a trip she and Matt had taken when Jamie was probably four. They'd stopped at a museum, and Matt was so good about keeping Jamie occupied, while she walked around and looked at exhibits. "Do you remember…the time Daddy and I took you to that museum?"

Jamie tapped his pencil on his math book and frowned. "I think so. It was that really boring place."

She propped her chin on her hand, amused at his honesty. "You were pretty young. I guess you didn't have much fun."

"Yeah, but Dad told me funny stories so you could look at stuff. I can still remember that." His mouth twisted a little sideway.

Did the memory make him sad or bring him comfort? "I'm glad you remember that time. Your father was a very special man." *Even if we had our problems.*

The wind blew from the mountains and rattled the windows.

Jamie returned to his homework. A little while

later, he paused. "Can I ask you something, Mom?"

She noted the serious tone. "Of course you can. Anything. Well, unless it's how to solve those problems."

He shook his head. "It's not. It's…something I been thinking about, and I need to know what you think."

Casey scooted closer to Jamie. This "something" was of great importance.

He took a deep breath and let it out in a puff. "Would it be okay, I mean, do you think Chance would mind…if I called him Dad?" His gaze met hers.

She read the need for approval in her child's eyes but couldn't give him a straight answer. "I suppose it's something you need to ask Chance. I can't answer for him."

Jamie nodded but stared off into space for a few seconds. "Do you think my real dad would mind?"

A reply caught in Casey's throat. She swallowed hard. "He…your dad, Matthew Girard, would be very happy to have you call Chance dad." In her heart, she believed that, but would Chance accept Jamie's request? She hoped so. Before many months passed, another child would arrive—one who would forever call him by that name. *How much longer until he comes home?*

Chapter 15

Chance pushed the button on the coffee machine and waited for the foam cup to fill. In the past two weeks, he'd drunk enough coffee from this machine to float a damn ship. But like Casey's coffee, the potent brew did the job of keeping him going. After spending the last few hours wandering around the city streets outside the Denver hospital, he hated to come back inside, where the walls threatened to close in. Between the high-rise hotel where he bunked and the stifling hospital, he was hanging on the edge of stir-crazy.

How were they handling the work back home? Had Ed and Roy begun the spring roundup? Started the branding and vaccinating? Four more wranglers would return to work on the ranch for the summer, but they weren't due to start until mid-April. Roundup and branding presented a big job for the two men he trusted—one he'd trusted with his life…and his wife. But he didn't want to leave Denver until Kyle could come home. Even then, his brother faced weeks of recovery. He might not get back on his feet until the end of summer.

Coffee in hand, Chance turned from the machine. He left the small waiting room and almost collided with a nurse hurrying down the hall. "Pardon me." He took a quick step back to avoid spilling the coffee. Instead, the hot liquid sloshed over his hand, and a word he usually saved to swear at annoying cows slipped out. He recognized the nurse as one who'd taken care of Kyle most of the past week. In her efficient and no-nonsense manner, she'd become a regular force to be reckoned with.

She sidestepped the dripping coffee and frowned. Then laughing, she stuck her clipboard under her arm and snatched the cup. "Mr. McCord, you're not having a very good day, are you?"

He shook the hot liquid from his hand. "Doesn't seem any are too good lately." Earlier, she saw him texting and heard his choice words when he discovered the darn phone was out of juice. Then, yesterday, he had a mishap while helping Kyle with his dinner tray. The fact of the matter was, he and his kid brother were a little sick of each other's company and getting testy about it.

"Go run your hand under some cold water." She motioned toward the small sink next to the coffee machine.

He hesitated but blew on his hand. "It's okay. No bother."

She pulled on his sleeve and dragged him to the sink. Setting the cup aside, she grabbed his hand and stuck it under the faucet, turning on the cold water, and letting it wash over the burn. "I can get you something to put on it." She examined the bright-red spot on the back of his hand.

"It'll be fine." He tried to pull away, but she held fast to his hand.

"Oh, don't be such a cowboy, Cowboy," she admonished and yanked a paper towel from a nearby roll. She patted the water from the burn. "You guys are all the same. So scared to show a little weakness. It's pathetic."

And here he thought he'd shown plenty of that fault by running for so many years, unable to face what life threw at him. He slanted her a sideways glance and noticed again the clear light brown skin and silky black hair that hinted at Hispanic heritage—except for her crystal-blue eyes. She was perhaps a few years older than himself, a remarkably beautiful woman whose hands felt light and yet professional in their ministrations. Everything about her spoke of someone dedicated to her work, and yet, he detected a softer layer beneath the outward efficiency.

"Christina Truelove." He noted her name badge. "Nice name. And may I say thank you for taking good care of my brother. I hope he's not too much of a pain in the ass."

She smiled and shook her head. "You guys are all the same. He's as antsy as a springtime colt to get out of here. We've had to warn him more than once to take it one day at a time. Of course, with that pretty girlfriend he's got, I can understand his wanting to get sprung."

So, Marianne was back. She'd returned to Spokane for a few days, leaving a rather morose Kyle behind. Chance wished the two of them would settle whatever problem they had. He and Kyle had a ranch to run and getting home to do that had to be top priority. *Damn, that's something I never thought I would consider.*

"Yet, I take it all is not well in romance-land." The nurse finished patting dry his hand.

He drew away, and, this time, she let him go. "Yeah, they got their issues." As did he. He hadn't seen

Casey in almost three weeks and hadn't talked to her in two days. Missing her grated on him, as well as being cooped up in the city.

Christina Truelove paused.

He met with blue eyes that would never hide a single emotion she was feeling. Strange how something about the woman made him think he knew her...somehow...from somewhere. Even the name Truelove rang a distant bell.

"Do I know you from somewhere, Mr. McCord?" she asked.

"It's Chance. I don't know. Do you? I have the same feeling."

She studied him a second longer, then shrugged. "Well, I've seen more than a few of you rodeo boys in other hospitals where I've worked, so maybe that's it. Anyway, stay put, and I'll be back with something for that burn." She clutched the clipboard and hurried away.

Chance watched her go. How did she know he'd followed the rodeo? And was there more to the uneasy recognition than that?

Entering Kyle's room, he spotted Marianne sitting on the edge of the hospital bed.

A pretty young woman with long dark hair, she and Kyle held hands and talked softly.

Chance almost backed out but didn't move fast enough.

"Hey, bro, come on in," Kyle called out. "Try the cookies Marianne brought me. She made them herself." He held out a round tin heaped with some confections.

Marianne rolled her eyes. "You make it sound like I can't cook. Just wait 'til you get out of here, and I'll make you a four-course dinner you'll never forget. I took a gourmet cooking class."

That brightened Kyle's smile even more, and he helped himself to another cookie.

Chance crossed over to the window that looked out on the city. Holding his hat by the brim, he watched a line of dark clouds race across the gray April sky above the Front Range. More rain, maybe even snow, would move in by nightfall. He needed to get home.

"Have you talked to Casey?" Marianne spoke behind him. "Mom says they've had some pretty strong winds this week, and power went out overnight."

"I talked to Billie yesterday, but Casey wasn't home. She went somewhere with Jeannie, and she didn't pick up when I called her phone." Guilt for having left his wife to deal with the ranch and its problems, and the repercussions from the video, ate at him. But then, so did the obligation he felt to stick it out here until Kyle could come home. He hated being torn between two people he cared about so much. "I'm sure the guys have got everything under control, but I'll call again tonight."

"The storm played tricks with the cell service," Marianne added. "I had trouble getting ahold of the principal at my school to let him know when I'll be back."

"When will you leave?" Chance asked without turning around.

"Well, it looks like they're transferring me to a rehab center to get me back on my feet," Kyle mumbled around another cookie. "Probably spend three-four weeks, at least."

"And I'm planning to stay here in Denver. I have

some friends from college who're letting me crash with them 'til Kyle's released. I found a sub to fill in for me at school."

Surprised at this, he pivoted from the window.

Marianne snatched the cookie tin from Kyle and put it out of reach. She motioned for Chance to come closer. "Kyle has something he wants to say."

He moved to the side of the bed and stared at the brother he'd almost lost. Lying in the metal-framed bed, Kyle appeared vulnerable and visibly thinner, though perhaps the cookies would help take care of that.

Kyle raised his gaze and extended a hand.

Chance grasped it in his own.

Kyle gave him a firm shake. "I…just need…to say thank you." His voice shook. "For the risk you took in hauling me out of Antler Creek. I don't remember much, to be honest, but I guess I wouldn't be here if—"

"No need for this." Chance gripped his kid brother's hand, hoping the connection would transfer some emotions words could not. "You're my family, man. Just don't make a habit of doing crap like that. Another incident and I'll be white-haired like Justin."

"I sure don't plan on it." Kyle grinned. "What, you don't think Casey wants her cowboy looking old?"

He released Kyle's hand and rubbed his thumb across his stubbled chin. "Whether she wants that or not, I'm what she's got." He stepped back from the bed and tried to shrug off the feeling that had dogged him all day. The one saying he had to get home and make sure Casey still wanted him. She understood why he needed to be with Kyle, but the fear she regretted staying in Wyoming wouldn't leave him alone. Sex had been great before he left for Denver, but was that enough to make her stay?

"So, we think you should go home," Marianne announced. "Daddy even said he'd get Max to fly you tomorrow. We appreciate you've stayed this long, but it's okay now. Right, Kyle?" She gave him a nudge.

"Yep, we'll be fine, and I'll get there soon as I can." Kyle settled against the pillows she had plumped. "But somebody needs to be there now, making sure the guys get the work done."

He's worrying about the ranch, too. Good sign. "You know they will, and don't forget, you've got Silver Wolf to thank for dragging your sorry ass out of that creek." He wasn't sure leaving Denver was a good idea, but he wouldn't argue. Returning to the North Star was the best idea he'd heard in weeks.

****

Chance stared out the airplane window at the mountains far below. Cotton-white clouds swirled around the rocky peaks, making him long even more for the mountains that would welcome him home. He shifted in the cramped confines of the small plane and stretched his legs as much as the space allowed. He hated flying almost as much as he hated the city. But Max Pierson, Morly's friend, was an expert pilot, and it was decent of him to do this. During the flight, he learned Max was a ski instructor in Aspen in the winter and spent the warmer months shuttling business folks in his plane. His clipped-close, gray-flecked hair and fit and trim body made Chance feel rough and grubby—a cowboy in serious need of a haircut and a shirt that wasn't wrinkled.

Today, Max had brought his son along.

Quinn Pierson was a high-school kid excited to be

flying with his dad and Chance. Once they'd gained flying altitude, Quinn leaned forward from his seat behind Max. "Dad says you were in the rodeo, and you won a lot of buckles. Man, what was that like? What did you ride?" Quinn swiped a length of surfer blond hair off his forehead.

According to Max, the kid lived most of the year with his mother in California. But he was interested in the rodeo? Chance shifted his knee again to get comfortable. "I rode broncs. I only got stupid enough to ride a bull once." His life had flashed before his eyes. "Bull riders are a different breed, that's for sure."

"Yeah, but it's gotta take some nerve to ride a bucking bronc. Were you on the circuit a lot of years?"

"Enough." *Too many questions, kid.*

"But you don't ride anymore?" Quinn persisted.

"Nope. That's all part of the past." A past he'd rather not talk about.

"Chance got married recently." Max intervened. "With a new wife, not to mention a ranch to run, that's enough to keep any man busy, right?"

Chance caught the wink Max sent his way. "Yes, sir. Especially with spring roundup going on. Lots of work to do." But more than anything, he just wanted to go home and sleep with his wife.

Not a rancher himself, Max asked a few of his own questions and kept the conversation going much of the trip.

Near to the Jackson airport, Quinn turned to Chance again. "I bet you had a lot of good times on the rodeo circuit. Do you miss it?"

"It was fun, while it lasted." If he were honest, he still missed the rush of adrenaline that accompanied the chute opening, but that was all in the past, and he intended for it to stay there.

"I'd like to ride in the rodeo." Quinn threw his father a glance. "Instead of going to college."

Max let out a loud guffaw. "Don't let your mother hear you say that. You know she plans for you to apply to her alma mater."

"Yeah, and I don't even have anything to say about it." The kid flopped back and slumped in his seat. "Wonder what she'd do if I just didn't go?"

"Don't even consider it," Max warned.

"But it's not what I want!"

"College isn't a bad idea, Quinn." To stop an argument, Chance offered his own advice. "Fact is, I kind of wish I'd gone myself." Had Alicia lived, that might have happened, but he and Justin had never talked about college. He wasn't much older than Quinn when he went out on his own. "If you want to get a taste of the cowboy life, have your dad bring you to the ranch this summer. The wranglers will be glad to show you the ropes. They even hold a rodeo in town once a week. We'll take you."

"Really? Hey, you hear that, Dad? Think we can do it?"

Max leaned toward Chance. "Just don't get me in trouble with my ex." He glanced back at Quinn. "Sure, son. Sounds like a good time."

He'd never encourage the kid to skip college, but Chance understood his wish to have some say about his future. He also figured once Quinn got a taste of rodeo life, he'd be less enamored.

"Thanks for the offer, Chance. Mighty nice of you." Max started the descent into the valley and the airport alongside the Tetons.

"Least I can do for you flying me home." *Home and Casey.* Chance's heartbeat quickened. Damn, but he'd missed them both!

Chapter 16

"Thank goodness, that awful wind let up." Casey helped Roy tend to chores in the barn. "It's a good day for flying." In a few hours, Chance would be home.

"But we'll have snow tonight. The calendar might say spring, but by Wyoming standards, it's still winter." Roy leaned on his barn rake and watched Casey bottle-feed a small calf. "You're doing a good job there, Ms. Casey. Looks like you've done that before."

She held the bottle so the youngster could tug at it much like he would his mother if she hadn't rejected him. "My parents have a farm. This isn't so very different, and I want to do what I can to help you guys." Roy and Ed had worked tirelessly in the past weeks to cover the work of four men. "I know the family is grateful for your loyalty to the North Star."

Roy grinned in his easy way and shrugged. "When I came here looking for a job, I was pretty messed up. I had to leave home. My stepfather and I didn't get along. The McCords have treated me like family since the beginning. I know Justin can be a pain, but not everyone would have hired me."

"Why not?" She tipped the bottle a little higher. "You're a hard worker."

"My father came from the Wind River rez. My mother's white."

The matter-of-fact comment didn't surprise Casey

but made her think Roy had a hard time in his early life. Glancing sideway, she studied his handsome, chiseled profile—the raven-black hair he wore long and tied back, his eyes that were just as dark. *What led him to take a job at the North Star?* "Was Chance already gone when you started working here?"

Roy rubbed the calf's little fuzzy head. "Yep. He left after his wife and son died. The ranch needed help…and I knocked at the door. Bad time for Chance, good opportunity for me."

The calf drained the last of the milk from the bottle, and she let him butt against her. "Poor little fella. Wonder why his mama didn't want him?"

"It happens. Fortunately, not too often or we'd get no other work done." Roy put the calf in the straw-filled stall.

The baby Angus bawled and tried to follow him out. "Sorry, little man. You gotta stay here." He pushed him back inside.

A rush of sympathy for the orphan nagged at Casey. She reached through the slats to give the calf one last pat. "I can come out for another feeding when I get back from the airport. It's so sad he's in here all alone." She walked with Roy into the April morning and stood for a moment, gazing toward the mountains that rose stark against an opal-blue sky. She longed for spring to arrive, but a deep blue haze hung in the distance.

"How about I have Jamie feed the calf when he gets home from school?" Roy suggested. "And Ed or I can pick him up, so you don't have to hurry back. You guys take your time."

She nodded, thankful for Roy's help, but a prickle

of apprehension needled her. A sharp ache to reunite with Chance filled her heart, but after three weeks apart, a sense of uncertainty hovered, much like the haze that threatened to cover the mountains by nightfall. Sooner or later, she had to tell him.

Roy squinted into the sun. "It'll be fine, Ms. Casey, but don't wait too long. It's something a man would want to know."

She sighed. No sense in asking Roy how he knew her secret. Like Ed had said, Silver Wolf had a sense about things.

At the busy airport later, she stood next to the elk sculpture in the arrival area. *Thank goodness, the snow held off.* But she shivered a little and checked her phone for the time, then touched her fingers to the jade turtle pendant that hung around her neck. Any minute the plane should touch down. Any minute…

****

The plane dipped below the clouds and began the descent. Shortly, the small plane skimmed the runway alongside the Tetons and then taxied to a stop.

Releasing his seatbelt, Chance breathed a huge sigh of relief. Stiff from the hours in the cramped space, he straightened his legs, heard his knee pop, and reached behind his seat for the duffle bag. Now to get his feet on solid ground. Even before he had kinks in his back and a bum knee, he was never a big fan of flying. Once outside, he thanked Max again and repeated his promise to take him and Quinn to the rodeo this summer. "Do your best in school now." He shook the kid's hand. "You won't be sorry."

Quinn nodded. "I can't wait to visit your ranch. Sounds like a really great place."

Chance shifted the duffle bag over his shoulder and glanced toward the highway. "You're right, Quinn. The North Star is a great place." Which might be the only time in his life he'd admitted to that truth.

Inside the terminal, he saw Casey first, and his heart beat a little faster. In a few strides, he reached the woman who had, in so many ways, turned his life around. Without saying a word, he put an arm around her and pulled her close, kissing her forehead and just taking in the lovely essence of his wife. For an instant, he savored the sweet, elusive scent that always clung to Casey. "I've missed you. It's good to be home." He let her go to study her face. Something struck him then. The light in her eyes, the curve of her cheek. The way she smiled and yet did not. She looked different.

She patted his chest. "We're glad you're home. We all missed you."

Truth was, he didn't care about anybody else. He only wanted to hear Casey say how much she had missed him. How much it meant that they were together again. How she'd missed him keeping her warm at night.

She said nothing more on the walk to the parking lot but held out the truck keys.

Chance shook his head and went to the passenger side. "I'll let you do the honors, if you don't mind. My head's still a little woozy from the flight." He tossed the duffle in the back of the truck. A sense of déjà vu flashed in his mind of the day they'd first met at the Hitching Post, and she'd given him a ride to the ranch. Was Casey sorry she did that? If she hadn't, would he have just gone on down the road again? Never come home to the North Star at all?

On the highway, they passed the elk refuge, and Casey slowed the truck.

Chance had told her how the elk spent the winter here but, in the springtime, migrated back into the mountains for the summer. That drivers needed to watch for them crossing the road was just one thing he'd taught her about living in the valley.

She chattered on about the happenings at home—the spring roundup, the abandoned calf, Jamie's most improved math student award, and how she and Justin had worked on the book again. "I finally convinced him not to quit. I love reading that old journal. It's really a treasure. We're nearly halfway through what he plans to say in his book. We're calling it *North Star Legacy*. I can't wait until we publish it." Casey took her attention from the road for a moment and glanced at Chance. "Sorry, am I babbling? I'm sure you're tired after the trip."

"Let's stop." He pointed to a pull-off next to a marshy area. "I need to get out."

Casey eased the truck from the road and parked.

No other vehicles occupied the site today, but in another month, visitors to the parks would gather in every available empty spot like this one. They'd have more guests at the ranch, and he'd have fewer times to just enjoy the peace of the valley…and an hour alone with his wife.

"Come on. Let's take a walk." He clasped her hand and led her to the edge of the wetland.

Far beyond them, Sleeping Indian Mountain lay in eternal repose. Across the marsh, gnarled trees with still winter-bare branches drooped toward the water, and in the shallows two young moose dipped their heads to search for lunch. Silently, he watched and listened to the swishing of the moose in the water and the far-off whistle of a hawk. Nearby, a black-and-white magpie sat on a section of broken-down fence and eyed them. He'd missed all this.

"I love magpies," Casey admitted. "I know some people consider them a nuisance, but they have their place, just as every creature does."

Chance chuckled. He liked her philosophy and drew her over to sit on a fallen log. After a moment, he took off his hat and hung it on a branch sticking out from the dead cottonwood. He turned to Casey. "Sounds like you've all handled everything just fine while I was gone. For a woman who knew nothing about ranch life, you learned a lot in a short time and more than stepped up to the plate. But...am I wrong to say that something isn't right?"

Casey glanced away, focusing her gaze on the magpie.

A distance had grown between him and his wife, and a ripple of fear stuck in his belly, the fear of once again losing someone he loved. "Are we still okay?" He heard her quick intake of breath and waited for a reaction.

She swung her gaze back to his, and a small smile touched her mouth. "Of course, we're still okay, and I'm sorry if I seem...tired. I'll admit, it's been hard without you and Kyle, but we did all right. You can be proud of us."

The look in her gray eyes didn't convince him everything was fine. They glistened with unshed tears. He let it go for now and drew Casey close. This time, he kissed her as he'd ached to do for so many weeks.

Her sigh touched him and sent a surge of longing through him, so intense it made him wonder how he could ever live without her. Please don't let him ever have to find out.

At home, Chance followed Casey to the big house and thought back to the night they'd spent in the cabin. More than anything, he wished for its seclusion and some time alone. But that was a moment they would probably not share again, at least not for a while.

"Hello, Chance! Ms. Casey!" Ed stood just outside the barn and waved. "You want to come on down here? Blue Lady is nearly ready. Any minute now, we'll have us a new foal."

Casey hesitated for a second.

Chance saw how the excitement chased away the earlier shadows from her face. Before leaving for Denver, he'd often found her sitting with the mare, gaining the wild one's confidence, and perhaps overcoming some of her own fears. "Go on." He nodded toward the barn. "I'm sure Ed and Roy can use your calming influence."

She stepped away but halted. "You don't want to come?"

He glanced toward the barn and back at Casey. Eagerness to see the new baby glowed in her eyes. "I need to talk to Justin. You go on now. Blue Lady won't wait."

She bounced off to the barn.

Chance watched her go, a bittersweet pain stabbing his gut. In his absence, his wife had learned to live here without him.

Chapter 17

Casey stayed a long time in the barn. At the last minute, Blue Lady experienced a complication, and then, for a few moments, she feared they'd have another baby to feed by hand. But thanks to Roy's and Ed's efforts, the tiny red filly arrived, and the mare finally allowed her foal to nurse. Casey remained another hour to make sure all was well, then she and Jamie fed and comforted the lonely little calf, making certain he was warm and his stall clean.

"Must be the time of year for new babies, huh?" Jamie held the bottle for the hungry little critter. "Chance said he would come to the barn, but he had to talk on the phone to somebody. Somethin' about a prize bull."

Casey watched her son, proud of him for taking care of the little calf. "I'm sure it's business that Kyle usually handles, but now Chance has to do his job, too." The work would fall on Chance, as well as a ton of other decisions needing to be made. How would he handle the responsibility? More importantly, how would he handle what she had to tell him?

****

Chance roused when Casey crawled into bed later. "Roy said the mare had a little trouble. Is she okay now?"

"Blue Lady is fine." She settled beside him. "The

144

foal was coming out a little funny, but Roy helped them. Then Blue Lady just needed some convincing that feeding her baby is a part of her motherly duties. She finally figured it out."

"Good thing you were there." Unable to wait any longer, he turned and drew Casey close, nuzzling her throat and sliding his hands over her breasts and across her belly. The damn flannel pajamas. They usually made him laugh, but tonight, they were just in the way. He needed to feel Casey, her skin against his. He needed to know she still loved him.

Slipping free the buttons on the pajama top, he massaged her breasts in a gentle caress. They were always so soft and fit his hands perfectly, but were they somehow firmer? Did they overflow that space? He rubbed his thumbs over her nipples until they peaked and begged him to stroke and taste them. She moved closer in invitation, and he accepted. She moaned softly and ran her fingers through his hair and over his shoulders, fanning the flames until he ached to be inside her. He helped her remove the pajamas, her silky skin firing sparks of desire throughout his body. How he'd missed her these past weeks. Had she missed him?

Tonight, he found it hard to wait, but he never rushed their lovemaking, always wanting to make sure she found as much pleasure as he. He held back, stroking her and coaxing her to kiss him long and slow, while he teased her sweet spot and brought her to the edge. But then, he couldn't wait any longer and moved over her, reveling in the moment she let him inside.

Her velvety sweetness surrounded him, and her quick breaths kept time with his, but at the last moment, she pulled back a little, and he sensed this time she wanted to go slow and easy. Even if it tortured him, he would give her slow and easy and let her set the rhythm. He was used to Casey's sweet, unbridled passion and puzzled a moment. Why the hesitation? Was it the time apart? The memory of that damn video? He only hoped this reunion would put all doubts out of her mind forever. He drew out their climax as long as he could. When release finally came, he buried his face in her hair and breathed in the beguiling scent that belonged only to Casey.

Then he heard her quiet sigh and felt her tremble. She pushed and murmured "no" to any more kisses.

He moved away to give her the space she suddenly wanted but ached to know what had put this distance between them? He ran his hand over her tangled hair. "I love you, for always." He kissed her temple. "You know that, right?"

She nodded but didn't move closer. "Of course, I do," she whispered. "I love you, too. I guess I'm just…tired." She stayed on her side of the bed and reached for the flannel pajamas she'd moments ago tossed aside.

Did he do something wrong? Not give her enough time? Chance crossed one arm over his face and held back the nagging questions that only Casey could answer.

****

When Chance finally slept, Casey punched her pillow and lay beside him, wishing she could tell him how much she relished his warmth in the chilly house. She watched his chest rise and fall. Should she have told him tonight? Whispering her secret amid heated kisses would have spoiled the moment, but she could only hold onto the truth for so long. Had he felt the difference in her breasts that had blossomed? The slight roundness of her stomach? If so, he hadn't spoken it. He'd had one thing in mind, and Casey had released her worries to the enticement of sweet kisses turning hot and their fiery passion that always burned out of control. The weeks apart had not diminished her need for him, and sinking into the world where only the two of them existed chased away her fears. Yet, she held some hesitation. Some reluctance to just let go and enjoy the passion. The weeks apart had left a hint of doubt in her mind and a tiny fracture in their relationship. If only the fracture didn't grow.

She stroked her fingers over his chin with the perpetual five o'clock shadow. New lines creased the corners of his eyes. A few more gray hairs lay sprinkled within the dark ones. But at least in sleep, Chance's troubles fell away. If only the news of the baby wouldn't add to them. She rested her head against her pillow and rubbed a protective hand over her stomach. What lay ahead didn't matter. Chance had come home. As long as he was here, she could deal with anything.

****

Just as Roy predicted, the temperature dropped, and six inches of heavy snow covered the valley by morning.

Casey huddled at the kitchen table, wrapped in a long gray sweater, and clutched a mug of hot tea in her hands. Dragging herself out of bed was not high on her list of priorities, but she did it, grateful her stomach no longer rebelled. She didn't even need the crackers on her nightstand.

Chance had left at sunup, checking on cattle, and

147

Ed took Jamie to the bus stop. As soon as she finished another mug of tea, she would shrug into her warmest clothes and trudge to the barn for a calf feeding. She and Roy were talking about teaching the little guy to drink from a bucket soon.

Billie shuffled into the kitchen. "You don't look like you're loving this turn of events. But I can't say I blame you. My bones aren't caring for it much, either." She rubbed her hands one over the other.

Casey had often seen her father do the same thing after barn chores. She turned away from the dreary scene outside the window and set the kettle to boil again. "I've just about had it with winter. In Michigan, the orchards are blooming." She didn't mean to complain, but a twinge of homesickness tugged at her today. The tea kettle sent out its shrill whistle. She plunked a tea bag into the mug and poured the boiling water.

"And do you miss that?" Billie filled a mug with coffee from the pot Casey had started.

Sometimes. "Mostly, there isn't time to think about it, but…" Casey stirred milk into her tea. "I guess it really doesn't matter. This is my home now."

"It's a good home, and I'm glad you stayed." Billie watched Casey sip her tea. "Are you taking your vitamins? You know they're important."

Casey jerked her gaze away from the tea to Billie's all-knowing expression. Of course, Billie knew. Everybody on the whole darn ranch probably knew, except the one person who needed to know the most. She sighed. "Did Jeannie spill the beans?"

"Nope. Just isn't too hard to figure out. I never had children of my own, but I took care of Alicia when she was expecting, and Angela after her."

"Well, *I* don't need taking care of, thank you. I'm feeling much better, and yes to the vitamins. Now, I need to take my turn feeding our resident orphan. Then I'll check on Blue Lady and her baby." She downed half the tea and set the mug on the counter. "Leave this here, and I'll warm it later. I'm going to bundle up and get to the barn, but I'll come back to help you with lunch in an hour."

"Don't overdo it," Billie called after her.

I'm pregnant, not sick. She wanted to reply but didn't bother.

****

Riding fence lines through the snow, Chance found more than a few places that needed mending. The work took him the better part of the afternoon, and he didn't make it back until nearly suppertime. He led Smoky into the barn to unsaddle him.

Jamie stood at the stall where the new foal hid shyly behind the blue roan mare.

Chance stopped at the stall. "How's the newcomer doing?"

Mama horse eyed him warily and moved closer between the humans and her baby.

"Roy says she's doing really well, but I guess Blue Lady doesn't trust me too much. She doesn't want me to look at her baby."

Chance nodded and pulled off his worn leather gloves. "That's part of a mustang's nature. In the wild, if they feel threatened, the herd will surround the youngest. She's just being protective. Blue Lady is a good mama, even if she is young." He hesitated. "Does the filly have a name yet?"

149

Jamie shrugged. "I don't think so. Nobody has told me anyway."

"Then I think it's time you named her."

The kid chewed his bottom lip. "How come me?"

Sticking the gloves in his coat pocket, Chance shrugged. "Just thought you'd like to name her, if she's going to be yours."

Realization took a few seconds to dawn. Jamie's eyes grew wide. He stared at Chance. "You mean…? You mean…?"

"That she's yours to raise and train and someday ride. So, pick a name that means something to you and that you think suits her."

"I…wow. That's so cool. But does my mom know?" A frown puckered the boy's forehead.

No doubt Jamie had heard the discussions between Chance and Casey about the boy riding a cutting horse instead of the gentle Buckwheat.

He gave the kid a fake punch to the arm. "How about we tell her together? I'm sure we can get her to agree."

Jamie turned back to speak to the filly, who peeked out from behind her mother's flank. "You hear that? I can train you when you get older. Will you like that?"

The filly ignored the people looking on and nosed her mother's side.

"I guess it's her dinnertime." Jamie grinned at Chance.

"I think it's about time for our supper, too. How about you give me a hand with Smoky? You can brush him while I check his hooves." He continued to the Appaloosa's stall. Once he'd lifted the saddle and blanket from the Appy's back and parked them on a saddle block, he handed Jamie a brush. "You remember how I showed you to do this on Buckwheat?"

"Sure do." Jamie didn't hesitate to pull the brush over Smoky's dark gray coat.

Chance enjoyed the companionable silence that fell between him and the boy as they tended to the horse.

After a few moments, Jamie paused in the brushing. "I need to ask you something."

Hoof pick in hand, Chance straightened slowly to avoid aggravating the kink in his back. The serious look on the kid's face told him whatever Jamie wanted to ask was important. He tossed the hoof pick into the tack box. "Shoot."

Jamie started brushing Smoky again. "I asked my mom this, and she said I had to ask you."

Chance leaned against the gate to Smoky's stall and gave the boy his undivided attention. "So, what did you ask her?"

Jamie brushed a little faster. "I asked if…if it would be okay…if I…if I called you Dad, instead of Chance. I mean, my real dad died, and you had a little boy that died. Mom said his name was Scottie. So, I didn't know if maybe you would want me to call you…Dad. Or not."

A rush of emotion ripped through Chance. Taking off his hat, he ran his fingers around the brim. "That would mean a lot, Jamie. I'd be proud for you to call me Dad."

Jamie's gaze met his. Tears glistened in the boy's eyes.

Clearing his throat, Chance reached inside his coat and patted the shirt pocket where the picture still resided. Thank goodness, the photo wasn't in his pocket the day he went into the creek. Casey had taken it a few days before to have it covered in a plastic holder. He pulled the photo from his pocket and showed it to Jamie. "This is a picture of Scottie when he turned five, taken at his party. I think…you boys would have liked each other, and I'm pretty sure he'd be happy to know I have you to call my son."

The wide grin on the kid's face told him all he had to know. With Smoky brushed and munching on a flake of hay, Chance turned to the boy. "Got any math homework tonight?"

Jamie nodded. "I sure do, and boy, am I glad you're here to help me. Mom tries, but she just doesn't understand math, at all."

"Then let's get it done." Without further talking, Chance closed the barn and set out for the house with his stepson. The wind whipped across the ranch yard and swirled snow in their faces. Chance slipped an arm around the boy's small shoulders and drew him against his side. They'd taken another step in their relationship; one he hoped would bring them even closer. Now, if only he and Casey could settle whatever held them apart.

Chapter 18

Three days later, the snow melted, and sunshine spilled across the valley. After breakfast, Casey hurried to the barn for her calf-feeding shift. She left Jamie to help Billie with cleaning the kitchen. A rush of relief bubbled through her to get out of the house. The time she spent with the calf had become her favorite part of the day. She prepared his bottles and slipped into his stall, scratching the little guy's furry black head before giving him the milk replacement.

He latched on and slurped.

She laughed and held tight while he drained the bottle.

"He's one hungry little critter, that's for sure. Good thing he's got an attentive foster mom."

She glanced over her shoulder.

Chance leaned his elbows on the stall door and observed.

She didn't think he'd slept well since coming home. Beneath the shadow of his hat brim, he appeared more rested, but a few lines still lay etched deep around the corners of his eyes. "We had an orphan calf once on my dad's farm." She grabbed a second bottle and had to fight to get the empty one away from the calf. "My brother and I took turns all summer long feeding and keeping that little one alive. She grew into one of our best milk producers."

Chance opened the stall door and joined her inside.

She watched with affection as he crouched and ran his big rough hands so gently over the calf's small body. Not so different from how he'd stroked her last night. After the heat of passion was spent, she'd ached to tell him about their baby, but the words just wouldn't come out. She brushed her wayward thoughts away. "I was worried about this little one. It got so cold the other night. I know if his mother acted the way she should, he'd be outside with her, but still…"

"If you had your way, you'd probably bring him into the house," Chance joked.

"Well, he is just a baby, and an orphan one at that. I can't help it if I'm too soft-hearted."

He glanced at her and winked. "I wouldn't have you any other way."

She felt her face flush, and so he wouldn't see, she bent to check if the second bottle was empty yet. In the few days since he came home, they hadn't found time to talk much, except at night, and they didn't talk a lot then. Suddenly, her heart ached to go back to the way things were when they went for the sleigh ride under the stars. Chance had made her believe everything would always be wonderful between them. But so much had happened since that night.

He stood again, and his knee cracked. He winced.

Casey said nothing. He hated when she noticed.

In the next moment, Roy and Ed made their way to the stall. She could tell from their faces that something was up. *Isn't something always up around here?*

Chance exited the stall. "What is it, guys?"

"Well, we got some bad news and good news," Roy spoke first. The wrangler shifted his gaze to where

Casey stood beside the calf. "Which would you rather hear first?"

Chance laughed half-heartedly. "Always better to get the bad over with first."

Her husband looked like a man who couldn't take one more word of bad news. She waited for what Roy and Ed had to say.

Roy shifted his weight and took off his hat, slapping it against his leg. "We…lost a calf in the cold. Didn't think the mama was ready yet, so we left her in the south pasture. She must have dropped yesterday morning. I think the calf was maybe a little early, but we should have paid better attention. Sorry, boss. It was my responsibility."

No loss was ever good. How would he react to Roy's apology?

Chance nodded and was silent a moment. "So, are you telling me there's some good news in this?"

Exchanging a quick look with Roy, Ed stepped forward and motioned to the orphan calf. "We thought we'd see if the cow will accept this one in place of her own. We brought her into the pasture behind the barn. Had to get her away from her calf so we could take care of it, anyway. Roy says he knows what to do."

The two wranglers eyed each other and waited for Chance to speak.

He turned to Casey. "What do you think, foster mom? Think it'll work?"

The calf rubbed his head against her leg and let out a small "*ma-a-a.*" "It certainly can't hurt to try. At least he won't be in here all by himself. Of course, he just finished two bottles, so I'm not sure he'll be hungry yet."

Roy chuckled. "You ever seen a young boy who isn't always hungry all the time?"

The wranglers took the calf out to introduce him to his new mom. Casey almost went with them, but sudden fatigue reminded her she'd stayed awake late and rose early. She left the barn to make her way back to the house. She would miss caring for the little fella, but it was best if the cow accepted the calf. Pausing, she brushed a tear from her cheek. What would Mom say about this? *Casey, you shouldn't get so attached to an animal. They are here for a purpose, not for us to baby.* This wasn't the first time she'd gotten so attached to an animal. On the farm, they'd had baby chicks, and baby rabbits, and kittens, and…

"Hey, Casey, honey. Wait up," Chance called out.

She waited until he joined her.

"I know how much you enjoyed feeding that calf, but it really is better for him if the cow accepts him."

"I know, and it's fine." She shrugged. "I've got plenty of other work to keep me busy, especially since we open the cabins tomorrow. We have twenty reservations already."

"And I've got two wranglers arriving to start work." He stopped her from walking on, clasping her hand in his and drawing her close. "Life will get crazy. So, how about we take the afternoon off? Go for a drive?"

She tried to avoid his earnest gaze. "I should help Billie in the kitchen, and Jamie has homework to finish."

"The guys are going into town when they're done with the calf, and Justin and Jamie have a game of checkers planned for this afternoon. Roy said we can take Juanita. We'll be back in time for me to help the boy with his homework."

Fatigue still plagued her, and sneaking in a nap until it was time to fix dinner sounded lovely. She hesitated just a few seconds longer. "I…don't know…" His swift kiss chased away her doubts.

"C'mon," he murmured against her lips. "Who knows when we'll get time alone again except at night?"

She found herself smiling. "Let me wash off the calf slime and grab a jacket."

An hour later, they traveled north. Huge powder-puff clouds bounced over the Tetons, and the elk once again moving into the high country. Snow still covered the rugged mountains, but the valley sprang alive with a few early wildflowers poking through to greet the sun. Casey rested her head on the seat and listened to the hum of the tires on the highway. The breeze blowing on her face through the open window lulled her senses, and a soft country song played on the radio, reminding her of the lazy Sunday afternoons she'd always loved. *I want to hang onto this feeling as long as I can.* Her eyes drifted shut, and she imagined a day filled with only sunshine and cloud shadows on the mountains and nothing to do but…

Something woke her—a gentle touch brushing her hair from her forehead and a kiss pressed to her cheek.

"Hey, sleeping beauty. Are you going to nap all afternoon?"

She smiled and stretched before opening her eyes and looking around. He'd parked high atop a hill, in a place she didn't recognize. Stifling a yawn, she sat up and looked around. "Where are we?"

"Let's get out, and you can see." Chance came around and opened her door, taking her hand and tugging her out and toward a newly leafed aspen tree. He paused a moment and reached for something tied to a lower branch, a faded blue square of material like the bandanna he often wore while riding. Like a flag, the fabric fluttered in the cool wind sweeping across the hill. He pulled the bandanna free and motioned to a spot where they could stand and look out. Below the hill, a river wound through the valley, twisting and turning, but today not looking as swift and dangerous as the Gros Ventre and the Snake Rivers had in the past weeks of snow run-off.

From this vantage point, Casey saw a few ranches spread out, as well as the highway leading east. "It's like that place you took me to last summer, above the valley."

"The Buffalo River Valley. Amazing sight, isn't it? And that way"—he pointed behind them—"is Togwotee Pass and the Continental Divide."

The panorama could take one's breath away, and for a moment, the windy mountains captured hers, leaving her a little dizzy. Maybe it was just the heights. "It's a beautiful sight, but why are we here?" She passed a hand over her eyes and focused on the valley below.

Chance stepped away and gazed out over the scene, hands fisted on his hips. "I'm pretty sure this is the place I told you about, where I hid when I was a kid. I always wanted to escape if my folks wanted me to do something other than ride my horse. I used to think I'd imagined the spot, but it's real as ever."

"It's a long way from the North Star." The valley

below suddenly looked hazy. Casey forced herself to take a slow, deep breath.

"Yeah, that's why I came here. But I had another reason. Something about this place spoke to me. Like I was here in another time. Sounds crazy but—hey, honey, are you okay?"

I'm fine, she started to say, but the words stuck in her mouth. Then things turned fuzzy, and the ground rushed to meet her.

She awoke to Chance dabbing her face with the dampened bandanna. She pushed his hand away and struggled to sit. "Where'd you get water?" she croaked. Her mouth tasted dry as a creek bed in mid-summer.

"Canteen. In this country, we never go anywhere without water. Here, take a few sips, but don't overdo it." He held the canteen to her lips.

She took a drink and welcomed the cool water sliding down her throat.

He pulled it away and recapped it.

She tried to rise.

"Just take it easy." Sitting beside her, he shifted Casey to lean against him. He folded the bandanna and pressed it to her forehead. "Are you going to tell me what's going on?"

She made an effort to smile but stayed put within the circle of his arms. No sense falling in the dirt again. Leaning into Chance calmed her. "I'm sure I'll be fine in a minute or two." She rested her cheek against his soft cotton shirt.

"And why am I not buying that? Casey, whatever is wrong, I wish you'd just tell me. Ever since I came home, something hasn't felt right, and now this. What's happening?"

She couldn't hide the secret any longer and grasped his hand. "This is what's happening." She pressed his hand low against her belly. "It's nothing that won't be cured in about seven months." Worry about what he would say silenced any more words. She met his gaze and waited for his reaction.

His eyes darkened in their familiar way, as when he was angry or when they burned with passion. Then, like the sun that rose over the mountains and rushed into the valley, sudden realization stole over his face. "Are you sure?" His voice trembled, low and husky.

She simply nodded.

"How long have you known?" He rested his hand gently on her stomach.

"Since right after you went to Denver."

He shook his head. "You could've told me. I would've come home."

"I know," she admitted. "That's why I didn't. You needed to stay in Denver, with your brother, and I wanted telling you to be, you know, special? I didn't want to say it over the phone." She stared into his eyes that no longer appeared dark but reflected the sky above them. "Is it?" Might she see joy in her husband's face?

A slow smile touched his mouth. "You really are something, Mrs. McCord. And either you hide your secrets well, or I'm just an idiot."

She plucked at his shirtfront. "I wouldn't call you that. You've had a lot on your mind." She leaned up and touched his whiskery cheek. "I'm sorry I waited so long, but give me the truth. How do you feel about it?"

He said nothing for a moment, then lifted her hand and pressed the back of her fingers to his lips in an old-fashioned kiss. "Do you have any doubt in your mind how I feel?" He spoke against them. "I was scared as hell there was something wrong between us. That you were sorry you married me. Or worse yet, sick. A baby? Piece of cake. Just no more trips up a mountain in Juanita for you."

"But we didn't plan for this. It's so soon, and we've barely—"

He kissed her on the lips.

Casey closed her eyes and let the words slip away.

He broke off the kiss. "So, stop worrying. I want nothing more than to have a baby with you. What do you think she'll look like? Will she have your hair?" He lifted a length of the tangled strands. "It's always reminded me of a cougar's tawny fur. Or"—he tipped her face—"maybe your chin, that you jut out at me when you're being stubborn." His gaze locked with hers. "But I really hope she has your eyes. They are the grayest color. Do you know they are the first thing I noticed about you? Once I looked into them, I was a goner."

Even after all these months of marriage, Chance's way with words could still charm her. "Has anyone ever told you what a smooth-talking cowboy you are? And what makes you so sure this baby is a girl? We don't know that yet."

"I'm calling it, and I bet I'm right." He shook her hand. "I'll be the one to make the announcement the minute she's born."

At his words, a sudden chill rippled through Casey. Perhaps it was only the wind that gave her a shiver of apprehension, but she stared him straight in the face. "I'm holding you to that promise, Chance McCord."

Chapter 19

Early in May, Chance stood in the barn doorway and watched Kyle struggle to approach the barn. *He's not the same man I pulled out of Antler Creek.* The reality hit him upside the head. His kid brother with boyish curly hair, and who always wore snug, faded jeans, had changed. Dark jeans sagged low on his hips, and he sported a new cowboy hat over a fresh haircut. His pale face held a haggard look.

Still on crutches, Kyle hobbled along, with Marianne close at his side. In spite of Max's offer to fly them home, he and Marianne had insisted on renting a car and driving from Denver. They stopped at the first corral to watch Blue Lady nibble sprouts of grass and the red filly sprint about, kicking her tiny hooves in the spring sunshine.

Jamie ran out of the barn and waved. "Hi, Kyle! Hi, Marianne!"

Chance nudged him. "Go tell them I'll be right there." He had to take a minute and reconcile himself with the new image of his brother.

The boy hurried toward them and hugged Marianne.

"That's a fine-looking little filly." Marianne chatted with Jamie. "What do you call her?"

The kid puffed with pride and held out a hand to the filly that trotted over to the fence. "Her name is

April Dancer, because she was born in April, and she likes to kick her hooves like she's dancing." He rubbed the filly's scrubby mane. "She was born to Blue Lady." He nodded toward the mare. "But that happened while Kyle was gone."

"I missed all the excitement." Kyle glanced at the mare. "But not much has changed with the mama. Looks like she still trusts no one."

The mare stood off by herself and eyed them.

Chance straightened his shoulders, took a deep breath, and ambled over to greet his brother. "Welcome home." He put a hand on Kyle's shoulder and gave it a squeeze. "How was the drive?"

Kyle shifted on the crutches and grimaced. "Long, but Marianne's a terrific driver. She's taken good care of me." His grimace turned to a grin as he balanced on the crutches and reached for her hand. "Don't know what I would have done without her."

Since he'd last seen them, Chance sensed a change between the two. Had his kid brother also got his head straight about his girlfriend?

Holding Kyle's hand, Marianne turned to Chance. "We heard congratulations are in order, that you and Casey are expecting. You know Mom can't keep a secret."

He nodded. "Yeah, I'm sure the whole valley knows by now. Word travels on the wind around here."

"Well, I think it's wonderful." She stretched on her toes and kissed Chance on the cheek. "Just you take good care of her."

He met her earnest expression. "I intend to."

Blue Lady whinnied, and the filly took off on a run, doing little bucks across the pasture.

Marianne and Jamie both laughed.

Kyle frowned. "You think either of them will ever make a good trail horse? Can you even handle the mare yet?"

Chance shrugged, not wanting to talk about the mare's progress or lack of. Like himself, Blue Lady had come a long way since he'd loaded her into the trailer in Rock Springs, but they both still had lessons to learn. "Here's hoping. I've given the filly to Jamie to raise and train."

Marianne left Kyle's side and walked along the corral with Jamie, leaving the two brothers alone.

Chance noted the way Kyle's gaze lingered on Marianne and the soft sway of her hips. Amused, he shook his head. Wasn't he just as guilty of getting tangled in his feelings for Casey?

A moment of silence stretched between the brothers.

"You been to the house yet?" he finally asked. "Justin and Billie have been getting ready for your homecoming all day. They invited the Hansons over. Big dinner planned, and I think Billie even made your favorite chocolate cake."

Kyle tugged on the brim of his new hat. "Sounds pretty good. Think I'll head to the house now."

They'd almost lost Kyle. Having him home was a relief, but something was still off. Chance studied his kid brother's profile. "Everything okay, man?"

Kyle cast a glance around the ranch yard. "Sure. Just seems strange coming back after being gone. I…guess I can finally relate how it was for you."

"If there's anything I can do to help you—"

"I'm fine." Kyle steadied himself on the crutches.

"Tell Marianne I'll be eating chocolate cake. Life's short. Eat dessert first, right?" He turned and made his way slowly to the house.

Chance sensed a deeper meaning lurked behind his brother's words.

After dinner, Billie shooed everyone into the living room to wait for the dessert Kyle had already eaten.

Chance stayed behind in the kitchen to help Casey with the coffee. He carried the tray with the cups and immediately noticed Kyle's fidgeting. Something was definitely up with his brother. He even refused the coffee Casey offered.

Marianne and Kyle sat close together on the sofa. The crutches lay propped beside them. Kyle held fast to his girlfriend's hand and fisted his other one on his knee. Every now and then, he shook it and flexed his fingers.

Casey nudged Chance. "What's with those two? I can understand them being lovey-dovey, but from the minute they got here today, they've acted a little strange."

Chance glanced at his brother. He'd sensed at the barn that Kyle's journey home was far from over, but he had no answer and just shrugged.

Finishing her cake, Marianne cleared her throat and set her dessert plate on an end table. "Mom and D-Dad, and ev-verybody." Her voice quivered as she glanced around the room. "Kyle…Kyle and I have something to tell you. We hope…you'll all be okay with it." She trailed off and looked at Kyle.

He shifted on the sofa but finally drew himself up and faced Justin first. "We…what Marianne wants to tell you…all of you is that…we're married." His gaze flicked around the room. "We decided it was what we wanted to do, so…we did it. We got hitched. In Denver." He lifted her left hand to show them the simple gold band on Marianne's ring finger.

Chance chuckled silently. *Dang. So, they really did it*. Was that the reason for their behavior? To keep anyone from voicing their disapproval, he went to the couple and held out his hand. "Let me be the first to congratulate you. If any two people belong together, it's you. I'm damn glad you finally figured that out."

The stunned silence lasted about three seconds, and then everyone started talking.

Jeannie tearfully hugged Marianne and kissed Kyle on the cheek.

Morly pumped his hand.

Justin shook his head but finally slapped his son on the back and congratulated them both.

Chance let them all chatter and joined Casey in the kitchen.

"Bring me another can of coffee, please." She pointed toward the pantry. "And then tell me the truth. Did you know about this?"

He fetched the coffee. "Nope, but doesn't really surprise me. You knew a long time ago they had a thing for each other. I'm glad my kid brother finally found the nerve to ask Marianne."

Casey shrugged and measured the coffee into the filter. "Maybe she asked him. Knowing how you McCord men are, she probably had to."

"Knowing how you men are, she probably had to." He loved to tease her and folded his arms around her, crossing his hands above her slightly rounded belly. "Did I ever thank you for coming up the mountain after me? For not giving up on a lonely cowboy?"

She turned and kissed him. "I think you have. By giving me this." She rested her hand on the baby bump. "Did I tell you I felt her flutter? It's early, but I'm sure she's moving already."

He covered her hand with his own. "She's a wild one. I can just bet on it." Dipping his head, he shared another kiss with Casey while the coffee perked.

Later, sitting in one of the old redwood rockers, hat tipped low, Chance propped one booted foot on the porch railing and listened to the soft chirping of birds in the cottonwoods and the distant yipping of a coyote.

After tucking Jamie in, Casey yawned and went off to bed.

But he needed to sit and keep watch, while the ranch settled and waited for night to fall. Funny, he had a long-ago memory of his grandparents and then his parents sitting in these same rockers, watching as evening crept in, and the sun slipped behind the mountains. *Now here I am, in a place I never thought I'd be.*

Once the excitement died, the Hansons went home, and now even the wranglers in the bunkhouse were quiet. Kyle and Marianne remained in the house, and he'd left them alone to deal with the consequences of their actions. Justin wanted to know where the new couple would live, and Chance could tell, despite their smiles and well wishes, that Morly and Jeannie harbored hurt that their only child had done this. He understood. *Didn't I do the same thing? Brought a new bride home to the North Star and a surprised family?* Angela hadn't adjusted, though, and he ended up losing her when she finally fled. At least, Marianne and Kyle had the same background. They were both born and raised in the valley and knew each other since they were kids. Their marriage stood a good chance of making it.

The door behind him opened and closed quietly.

Marianne sat in the chair next to him and sighed.

He tipped his hat to see her face. Marianne was young, but she had a resilience about her, a determination he admired. "How are things going with my brother and Justin?"

She smiled a bit wistfully. "Your dad doesn't understand why we didn't get married here. He says we should have waited 'til Kyle is on his feet."

"Where is Kyle now? Is Justin giving him the third degree?"

"No. Your dad went off to bed. Kyle is bunking on the couch in Justin's study. He can't do the stairs at my parents' house. He can stay here for tonight."

"And you?"

The encroaching night held a chill. She wrapped her arms around herself. "I need to talk to my parents, and I'll come back in the morning. But...there's something I have to tell you. Please don't be upset, but maybe you can explain it to Justin. We thought he'd had enough for tonight."

Hearing the hesitation in her soft voice, Chance plunked both boots on the porch floor and leaned forward in the rocker to give her his attention.

"Kyle and I are not staying here. We leave for Spokane in two days. I still have my apartment, and I've taken a job teaching summer classes."

He pushed his hat back a little farther and rubbed his stubbly chin. "Why didn't you pass that information on to anyone else tonight?"

Marianne shivered. "I couldn't. It was enough to drop the bomb that we're married. I think my folks will be okay with our not living here, but it's you…and your family who will—"

"We'll manage," he assured her. *Won't be easy.* But he wouldn't say that. "Kyle still has a lot of healing to do."

"In more than just his body." Marianne moved back and forth in the rocker. "He wouldn't want me to tell you this. He doesn't want you to think he's weak, but Kyle's having nightmares…about the creek. Sometimes, even during the day, he gets…shaky. I think maybe he has Post Traumatic Stress Disorder? I've gotten in touch with a doctor in Spokane. I'll make sure Kyle receives the help he needs, but first, he needs to get away from here. Please understand." Her gaze implored him.

He understood plenty about bad dreams. They could make every waking hour a nightmare and turn life into a real horror show. He leaned back in the rocking chair. "You do whatever you need to and get my brother whole again. The North Star will be here when—should—you decide to come back." The ranch had been home to the McCords for well over a hundred years. Now Chance needed to make sure it would remain so in the future.

****

Finished brushing and braiding her hair, Casey opened the window a little wider. A sweet mountain breeze stirred in the night and whispered past her. Their bedroom was above the porch, and she heard a few snippets of the conversation between Chance and

169

Marianne—words like *we leave in two days*, *live in Spokane,* and *Kyle needs healing*. That Kyle and Marianne wouldn't choose to live at the North Star didn't surprise Casey, nor about the fact the younger woman would tell Chance first.

For a time last summer, she had thought Marianne was in love with Chance, but she'd soon learned it was the younger McCord who held, and would always hold, the girl's heart. Now Marianne was confiding in Chance, much like to the older brother she'd never had. Casey couldn't blame her. If anyone would understand, it was Chance.

How would Justin take to this latest turn of events? He'd looked forward to his younger son coming back to manage the ranch, and this was sure to disappoint him. Although, Chance had kept things running smoothly these past months. Chance, who the men now called boss, had taken over the reins in Kyle's absence. Justin did not accept change easily, and rounds of father and son arguing would erupt in the days ahead. She didn't look forward to that, but as she stood at the window, Casey believed Chance would accept the challenge. Even if his father didn't always believe in him, she did. *I just need to convince him of that.*

Chapter 20

"You look like you're feeling much better these days." Jeannie folded the last of the quilts and placed it with the others piled high on a table at the local community center's spring bazaar. The variety of patterns made for a colorful display in the booth.

Many hours of sewing over the winter had produced the lovely quilts. Casey had appreciated the time spent with other women, and that the proceeds from the quilt sales would help fund a local program for women and children in need. "I do feel better, and just in time to help with the bazaar. To be honest, I don't know how much longer I could've gone on so exhausted all the time, especially with the ranch getting ready for the summer season." She patted her growing baby bump and smiled when the tiny resident did somersaults. *Chance might be right about this child being a wild one.* "We have an ultrasound scheduled next week, though I'm not sure they need to tell us what we're having." She'd confided in Jeannie their certainty the baby was a girl.

"I can just see Chance with a little girl following him around. What a sight that will be." Jeannie fussed with the quilts that didn't need refolding.

The newlyweds had left nearly a month ago, but clearly, Jeannie was still distressed. What could she say to make things better? "Have you heard from

Marianne? Have she and Kyle settled in Spokane okay?"

Jeannie sniffed. "I…talked with her last week. She's busy teaching, and Kyle is seeing a therapist. They're happy, and I'm happy for them. It's just…"

Casey eased into a chair and pulled Jeannie's arm to make her sit. "You're sad you missed your only daughter's getting married," she finished the sentence.

Jeannie wiped away a few more tears and forced a smile. "Am I so transparent?"

"Just a good guess. I can relate. I'm sure part of my mother's problem with my marrying Chance is that she wasn't at the wedding, and we got married by a judge and not in church. Want to talk about it?"

Jeannie pulled a tissue from her purse and dabbed her eyes. "I always dreamed about helping Marianne shop for a wedding dress, picking out flowers, and watching Morly walk her down the aisle. I never once imagined she'd get married in a faraway place and not even tell us first." She sniffed again. "Don't get me wrong. I love Kyle. He and Mari are a perfect match. I know I'm just being selfish."

"Well, we all do crazy things when we're young and in love." *And sometimes when we're not so young and in love.*

A crowd of women descended on the table, and Casey rose to help one shopper unfold two of the quilts—a striking green pattern with calico squares and a red-and-blue log cabin print.

"We just built a new house, and I would love to have a gorgeous quilt for our bedroom," the woman gushed over the display. "But I don't know which to choose."

Casey glanced between the two quilts. "They're both beautiful, but I bet the green calico would look fabulous. It's my favorite."

The woman pulled out her wallet. "I'll take it."

When that sale led to three more in rapid succession, Jeannie chuckled. "You're a good salesperson." She lifted a corner of one quilt so she and Casey could refold it. "I'm glad you're here today."

"Me, too, and the money raised is all for a worthy cause. I love the idea of helping other women and children. I worked with kids at my library in Michigan, and we always had a great time."

Jeannie paused in the folding. "You miss it, don't you?"

Did she? She'd always enjoyed her work, and while most days she didn't think about it, sometimes... "I'd be lying if I said I didn't, but I have more than enough to keep me busy. I started a story and craft hour at the ranch for the kids. I brought some of my own books out of storage, and every afternoon, we sit on the porch in the shade, read a story, and make a craft. I had a program like that at the library. It keeps the kids busy and gives their parents a much-needed break. Jamie helps me, and sometimes, he gives cart rides with Buckwheat." She finished folding the quilt and placed it on the table. "Of course, life will change once the baby's here."

Jeannie busied herself straightening the remaining quilts. "How does Jamie feel about a new baby in the house?"

"He's excited about being a big brother and keeps promising me he'll help take care of her." The baby fluttered again, and Casey put her hand over the spot where tiny feet pummeled her. "I guess she knows I'm talking about her."

"Have you and Chance discussed any names yet?"

"We have. I rather like the idea of naming her after her grandmothers, but Alicia Arnette just doesn't sound right. Instead, I said, let's name her after their favorite flowers. So, it's Lily Rose. Lily Rose McCord. What do you think of that?"

"I think it's a beautiful name." Jeannie leaned over and hugged Casey. "I can't wait to meet Lily Rose."

More customers cut short their gabbing, and by the time the bazaar was over, they'd sold every quilt.

Outside, Casey walked with Jeannie to her truck. She fastened her seatbelt and tugged at the T-shirt that had become too snug of late. "I was wondering, are you free any day next week?"

Jeannie turned the key and started the engine. "We expect guests on Thursday, but I might have some free time early in the week. What do you have in mind?"

Casey adjusted the seatbelt to fit beneath her stomach. "I need to buy some craft supplies, but I would really like to shop for clothes that fit me. I know looking at maternity clothes is not the same as shopping for a wedding dress with your daughter, but I'd love the company. Maybe we could even go to Idaho Falls. I hear that's what folks around here mean when they say they're going to the city."

Jeannie's face brightened. "Sounds like a necessary excursion. We'll even plan on stopping for dinner and make it a regular girls' day out."

Relieved, Casey settled back in the truck. "I can't tell you how much I look forward to wearing jeans that don't squeeze me like I'm a plump tomato." She hesitated. "Jeannie, have I ever thanked you for being a good friend? For making me feel welcome here and for everything you've done."

"No need to." Jeannie shifted the truck into gear and pointed it toward the highway. "We women have to stick together. However, these days, I have an ulterior motive."

"That would be?"

"Having Lily Rose call me Aunt Jeannie."

"Of course she will." Casey gazed out the truck window and swallowed a twinge of regret. *But she might never know my family in Michigan.*

****

"Wyoming has two seasons." Chance had once told her. "July and winter." Having experienced one winter, thank goodness it was July. But today, Casey would've felt grateful for a breath of that other season. No mountain breeze stirred the still air on the porch, and a trickle of sweat inched down her forehead. She blew at the strands of hair that escaped her ponytail. A hot dry spell had parched the land over the past weeks, and thanks to fires in Montana, a smoky haze hung over the Tetons.

The porch provided a respite from the day's heat for an hour, but the kids, finished with their drawings, squirmed and grew restless.

"How about lemonade to cool us off?" She sent Jamie inside for the apples they'd sliced earlier. "Ask Aunt Billie for the cups, please."

She enlisted the older kids to help, and they encouraged the younger ones to gather the crayons. Casey displayed their construction paper drawings of mountains and stick cowboys and horses on a poster board for their "art show." She hung the last one and heard the kids calling out.

"Hi, Mr. McCord! Come see our pictures."

Chance climbed the steps. When he wasn't busy, he always took time to talk with the kids she'd rounded up for the day. The kids loved the fact he was a genuine cowboy.

A little red-haired girl of about four tugged on his shirt. "Where is your horse? I want to ride him."

Chance crouched to get eye level with the tiny spitfire. "Smoky's in the pasture. He worked all morning with me, and now he needs a nap."

"But I wanna ride him." She stamped her foot. "I'm a very good rider."

"I'm sure you are. Maybe Jamie will take you kids for a pony cart ride later with Buckwheat."

She folded her arms and pouted.

Chance winked at Casey.

She smiled. Obviously, the little girl was not happy with just a pony cart ride and gentle old Buckwheat. Was the scene giving them a glimpse into the near future?

"I'll bet she keeps her parents on their toes." He stood to study the children's drawings and took advantage of the moment to plant a quick kiss on Casey's heat-flushed cheek.

The two older girls giggled, and the wink he sent them only increased their whispers.

"What is it with girls?" He shook his head.

Casey gave him a teasing nudge. "Just their reaction to a really cute cowboy is my guess."

He leaned in to steal another kiss, giving the girls something else to snicker about.

"The parents are coming to collect their kids." She ducked under Chance's arm and tucked stray wisps of hair behind her ears to make herself presentable.

Jamie brought out the plate of apple slices and set it on the table. He touched her arm. "Mom, Aunt Billie says you should come inside. You have a phone call."

She paused. Who would call her on the ranch house phone this time of day? She glanced at Chance, but he just shrugged. A sudden shiver raced along her spine.

He nodded toward the door and turned to greet the first set of parents.

As she hurried into the house, Casey heard him remark about the little red-haired girl's determination to ride Smoky.

The phone receiver lay on the counter in the empty kitchen. Taking a deep breath, she picked it up, hoping to hear Mom say, *when are you coming home*? Instead, a masculine voice met her tentative hello.

"Sis, it's Jim."

Shards of icy fear raced through her body. *Mom! Daddy!* Her stomach clutched into a painful knot. She gripped the receiver and steeled herself. "What is it? What's wrong?"

Jim cleared his throat. "They found him. They found Matt. Divers recovered his plane, or what's left of it…and his remains."

The words hit her like a boulder. A sharp pain twisted her insides, and she grabbed her stomach. She thought that nightmare was over. *But maybe it's just begun.*

****

After the parents collected their kids, Chance went

looking for Casey. He found her curled on a bale of straw in the barn, crying quietly into her folded arms. He sat on the bale beside her, hands braced on his knees. "Casey, honey, what's wrong? What happened? Billie said your brother called. Is something wrong with your folks?"

She lifted her tear-streaked face. "N-no, they're okay. It's…oh, my god, Chance, they found the wreckage…of Matt's plane…and him." Her voice gave out as she collapsed on the bale.

The words sent a sharp arrow slicing through him, but even worse was seeing his wife in such a state. He gathered her in his arms, sat her on his lap, and held her while she sobbed. What the hell could he do to comfort her? What could he say? For a long time, he said nothing but just held her close and let her cry.

She finally shuddered and relaxed against him.

He brushed her hair back and kissed her wet eyes. "I'm so sorry. What can I do?"

She pushed away and wiped her hands across her face. "There's nothing you can do. Nothing anyone can do. I just have to deal with it."

"Let me take you to the house. Maybe you should rest."

She stood. "No. I need to tell Jamie. He must wonder what's wrong."

"Might be easier to hear it from me." He grasped Casey's hand.

"But I'm his mother." She tried to pull free.

He better figure out quickly how to handle this turn of events. Chance let her go but stood and lifted the tendrils of hair still stuck to her cheeks. "And I'm his father now. Please, let me do this." In the back of his mind, he recognized another turning point for their family…and their marriage. How they got through the next few days might test them all.

Chapter 21

"Is your going alone a good idea?" Chance watched Casey pull clothes from the closet and fold them into a suitcase. Since the phone call two days ago, he had said little but just listened while she made reservations to fly back to Michigan. If he'd learned anything in the ten months they were married, it was not to argue with his wife when she made up her mind. Which she most certainly had. But this time was different.

She scooped a few makeup items and a hairbrush from her dresser top. "I won't be alone. Jamie will be with me." She dumped the items into a plastic bag and stuffed it in the suitcase. "And I checked with the nurse practitioner. She assured me I should be fine, now that I'm in the second trimester. It's the best time to fly."

Some consolation. He sat on the edge of the bed and held back all the words he wanted to say. *Don't go, Casey. Don't do this to yourself. And to our baby.*

The call from her brother had struck like an unexpected bolt out of the blue and left its painful mark on her barely healed heart. She had allowed him to break the news to Jamie, who accepted the turn of events with more stoicism than he would have, even to assuring his mother he understood and wasn't upset. By the next morning, Chance knew she'd made a decision, and it was probably the right thing to do. But he didn't have to like it.

She closed the suitcase and grabbed the handle.

Chance leaned past her and pulled the suitcase toward him, placing it on the floor. He drew Casey between his knees and held both of her hands. Her eyes were dark today, dark as the gray rivers when they ran fast and deep. What lay ahead for her, and what would it take away from their marriage? "I want to tell you not to go."

Standing in front of him, she gazed into his face. "I have to. I owe Matt that much. His parents died when he was young, and he was an only child. His grandparents raised him, but they're gone, too. Somebody needs to be there for him. Somebody…who loved him." Her voice halted, and a soft sob swallowed any more words.

Did she love him more? The question haunted him, but he had to let her do this. He held her hands. "Yeah. You're right. If I could get away, I'd come with you."

She bowed her head over his, her long hair brushing his cheek. "It's better you don't. Some things we just need to face…alone."

He sighed and leaned his face against her rounded stomach where their child tumbled in her water ballet. Pressing a kiss to the tiny kicking foot, he still couldn't say the words dwelling in his heart. *Please come home, Casey.*

****

At the airport in Grand Rapids, Casey helped Jamie tug their suitcases from the baggage carousel. She turned to see Jim walking toward them through the terminal. He had put on a few pounds in the past year, and, as he came closer, she noticed he wore bifocals.

Seeing him, Casey breathed a tired sigh of relief. Her older brother was her rock in bad times.

He gave Casey a quick hug and tousled Jamie's hair before grabbing the suitcases. "How're you doing, Sis? Flights okay? We heard they've had fires out west."

"Not near us, thank goodness. Traveling was fine." *Even if exhausting.*

"I'm hungry, Mom," Jamie piped up. "You promised me we'd eat when we got here."

Jim ushered them out of the terminal and toward the parking lot. "Grandma's making dinner for us tonight, but how about we hit a fast-food joint for now?" He glanced at Casey.

Her brother knew how she felt about that, but at the moment, she didn't have the energy to protest.

"Can we, Mom? Please?" Jamie climbed into the backseat of the older SUV.

Jim stowed the luggage in the hatchback.

Casey slid into the passenger side. "I guess it'll be okay. Just so you don't spoil your dinner." Mom wouldn't like it if they didn't eat the meal she'd undoubtedly worked all day preparing. The entire trip, Casey had steeled herself for facing her parents. They knew about the baby, but would seeing her pregnant drive home the fact she'd married the cowboy from Wyoming?

A short time later, she sipped an iced tea at the fast-food restaurant and watched Jamie consume a burger and fries, courtesy of his uncle. She couldn't help but flinch. While carrying this baby, she'd become even more adamant about eating healthy.

"It won't hurt him." Jim sent his nephew a wink.

"How does your cowboy feel about your fussy food habits? I'm sure he's eaten his share of burgers traveling the rodeo circuit."

Casey thought about all the meals she and Billie had cooked for the McCord family and the ranch hands, as well as the guests. The mostly meat-and-potatoes kind. Her efforts to change their eating habits had fallen far short, even with Justin.

"Mom tries to make them eat healthy, but nobody on the ranch much listens." Jamie shoved fries in his mouth. "But she's a good cook. You should just ask the wranglers."

"Ranches, rodeos, wranglers—different world out west, isn't it?" Jim finished off his double cheeseburger.

She met her brother's steady gaze and read other unasked questions in his eyes. "It's his world. And now it's mine." Thank goodness, Jim didn't pursue the subject but instead talked about his favorite baseball team's prospects.

Jamie told his uncle about the red filly back in Wyoming. "I'll train her when she's old enough, but for now, she's still with her mama. That's Blue Lady. She was a wild mustang. We might get more mustangs. My dad can gentle them. He's really smart about horses."

At the word *dad*, Jim raised his eyebrows.

Casey pushed Jamie's milk carton toward him. "Finish your burger and drink your milk. We've still got an hour to drive to Grandma and Grandpa's house." The day of traveling was wearing on her. If only her family didn't say something to break through the thin veneer of stability covering her emotions.

Jamie ate and then carried their trays to the trash

can.

Jim leaned closer to Casey. "So, he calls the cowboy *dad* now?"

She steeled herself against making a sharp retort. "The cowboy's name is Chance," she reminded Jim. "And yes, the two of them discussed it, but it was Jamie's idea. He wanted…needed…to call Chance *dad*." Casey rose from the booth.

Jim stood and slipped a hand beneath her elbow to steady her. "Sure. I know. You and Jamie had a rough couple of years, and now this. Probably would've been better if they'd never found—"

"Don't say that!" She pulled away and choked down a sob. The mixed emotions swirling through her brain threatened to spill over. *No one understands how I feel. How this is tearing me apart.*

Jim stepped back. He ran a hand through his hair. "I just mean, it'd be easier for you, without having to go through this, especially in your condition."

She stopped and glared at Jim. He and his wife, Cindy, had been her emotional rocks when Matt died. She would never have gotten through the maze of sorrow without them. They'd helped her sell the house, move into an apartment, and deal with legal matters. She loved Jim dearly, but he had to know how his comment hurt. "Nothing has been easy since the day I knew Matt wasn't coming home." She slipped her purse back on her shoulder and headed for the ladies' room, needing to claim a moment of peace before they set out for the farm.

Chapter 22

Chance leaned on the saddle horn and squinted against the rising sun. He'd ridden out early to drive the herd of cattle into a different pasture and keep watch over them so the local wolf pack didn't steal any young calves. Kyle had tested the practice last year of staying with the herd in the daytime and bringing them in closer at night, and it worked. At first, the wranglers didn't like the idea, but Roy got on board and convinced the others it was worth the try. Chance gladly took the first shift. Early morning was the most peaceful time out here, anyway.

Not far away, Mariah lay atop a small rise, ever alert for any threat to the herd.

A few other early risers—jackrabbits and mule deer—made their way through the buffalo grass in search of breakfast. A brief storm last night had brought some much-needed rain, and the pungent scent of sagebrush drifted on the damp breeze. Chance angled Smoky toward the mountains and watched as the sky took on a pinkish hue. If only Casey was here with him to share the view! She would watch that amazing sky, and he would watch her, seeing the reflection in her gray eyes. They had watched the sunrise after the night in the cabin, and she told him the Tetons by morning was her favorite sight.

A sound off to his right drew Chance's attention.

Sitting straighter in the saddle, he scanned the pasture for any movement.

Mariah swung her watchful gaze in that direction, but the guard dog didn't rise.

She recognizes the sound. Soon, he did, too.

A rider on a black horse came loping toward them.

As the pair drew closer, he shook his head. His father had only recently gotten back in the saddle.

Justin pulled Coal up not far away.

"What are you doing out here?" Chance didn't expect nor want him out here working as the day grew hotter

Justin squinted against the sun. "Thought you could use another hand keeping an eye on the herd."

The old cowboy still sat his horse well and looked more like the rugged, handsome man Chance remembered from years gone by. *And I want him to stay that way.* "You didn't need to ride out here. Mariah and I have everything under control."

Justin pushed his hat back and settled his fierce blue gaze on him. "Well, I'm sure you do, but maybe I need to get out of that house."

Chance opened his mouth to say more.

"It's just too dang quiet with everybody gone," Justin cut him off. "And besides, I'm not dead yet. Don't put me in my grave 'til I am."

Chance clamped down on any more protests. "Point taken."

The old man rode closer to Smoky, and the two horses nickered. "How's this idea working out?"

Justin still believed in letting the cattle roam the open range and had voiced his opinion more than once. Chance didn't want to get into an argument about that now. "So far, so good."

"You seem to have gotten all the men on board, just by that smooth-talking of yours."

Getting a little huffy, aren't we? Chance chuckled. "It was more Silver Wolf's doing. He's got a way about him."

"Yeah, he's a hard-working wrangler. It was a good day when we hired him on."

They sat in companionable silence, with only an occasional hoof stomping and the song of a meadowlark to break the quiet morning air.

"How long do you think Casey and the boy will be gone?" Justin finally asked.

Chance's heart did a triple beat, but he shrugged. "She texted me last night. The service is set for next week. They had to wait for…the remains to be released."

"She doing okay?"

"So she says. Casey hasn't mentioned how her parents are coping, but it's got to be hard on them all."

"As well as the fact they just can't get a handle on why she married somebody they never even met."

"There is that, too." Agreeing made his stomach churn a little, but the truth was the truth.

The cattle shifted in the pasture, and they urged their horses to move around the herd, riding together side-by-side.

"There's something I've never told you." Justin shifted the reins in his gnarled hands. "You were quite small."

Chance waited for his father to go on. Lately, they were talking more, mostly out of necessity. Running the ranch and handling the guests required all-hands-on-deck, and Kyle's absence forced him and Justin to work together. This didn't sound like it had anything to do with business, though.

"I guess you were about Jamie's age. We...we were having some problems, your mother and I. When we met, Alicia was a very successful artist living in San Francisco. She left that to follow me here. Why I'll never know."

"You don't think love entered the picture?" *Why is he telling me this now?*

"Oh sure. We were very much in love, but sometimes...sometimes, I felt like I was her...hmmmm, trophy cowboy. She came here with stars in her eyes, but after a while, those stars dimmed. Then you came along, and things got better...for a few years. She tried to get involved in the ranch, but it wasn't in her heart. I couldn't blame her, but I had a lot of responsibility. We stopped talking much. One day, she left. Your mother just up and left. I don't think you remember any of it."

He remembered plenty about waking one morning to find his mother gone, with no explanation, and his father turned into a distant, work-obsessed man. How often had he run to Sam and Billie's cabin and cried in Billie's arms? She'd done her best to comfort a heartbroken little boy. He would never forget thinking his mother's leaving was somehow his fault for being such a rebellious kid. Billie had assured him he had nothing to do with his parents' problems. Strange how life had then repeated itself with his own first marriage, but with a more tragic resolution. "Doesn't matter if I remember or not." He reined Smoky beneath the shade of a cottonwood.

"I suppose not." Justin pulled off his battered gray

hat and squinted into the morning light.

His father's face appeared craggier and more marked by the painful memories. Chance leaned over, resting one arm on his saddle horn. "So, is that the only reason Mom left?" Maybe he had no right to ask, but suddenly he needed to know for certain what had almost destroyed their family so many years ago.

Justin let out a rattly sigh, and his gaze drifted off toward the mountains. "She found out there'd been someone else."

That was not what he expected to hear. Loneliness, the inability to fit in with ranch life, or the simple desire to return to California might have all made some kind of sense. But that another woman was involved came as a total surprise. "Were you still seeing her? This someone else?"

Justin whipped his head back. "Of course not!" He fixed Chance with an angry glare. "That was over long before I met your mother."

"Then what happened? I don't understand." Why would his mother, whom he thought had loved them and the North Star—as witnessed by the murals she'd painted on the house walls—leave because of something that took place in his father's past?

Justin's broad shoulders drooped. "She found a picture of us and couldn't understand why I'd kept it. She thought I loved the other someone more than her."

Did you? Chance bit back the question. What happened between his parents was none of his business, except for how it had affected him. And now, this many years later, they couldn't change anything.

"I finally went after Alicia to see if we could patch things up," Justin admitted.

"I guess you did," Chance quipped. "Kyle was born about a year later." He noted Justin's rueful grin.

"We worked things out, and we had a good life. Alicia was a remarkable woman. I still miss her, every single day."

Chance looked away and cleared his throat. "Yeah. Me, too."

Justin gazed out over the three hundred head of cattle grazing on the land. "You need to go after Casey. Lend your moral support and make sure she comes home."

The old man could read his mind after all. Chance heaved a deep sigh. "I had the same thought."

That evening, he walked the pine-needle strewn path to the cabin where Billie lived.

She sat on the little front stoop, wearing an old plaid robe in the after-sunset chill. She held a book in her hand but set it aside.

How many times in years past had he come here, looking for her and Sam's consolation, when he'd clashed with the people he loved best in the world? Too many to count. Now here he was again, needing the calm and sensible advice of Billie Murphy. He climbed the two steps.

"Have a seat." She patted the chair next to her.

He eased himself into it and stretched out his legs. Hours in the saddle and the stress of the day put a deep ache in his bones. So did the questions chasing around in his mind.

Billie took off her reading glasses. "We sure been busy around here, haven't we? But that's pretty much how summers go. You want some lemonade?"

He shook his head and leaned back, staring at the

tips of the old pine trees that flanked the cabin. "I thought today…about going to Michigan."

"And you want to know if it's a good idea."

Billie always was two steps ahead. "Is it?"

"Why do you want to go?"

He took a deep breath and let it out slowly. "I think they'll convince Casey to stay…and I can't live without her."

Billie folded her small hands over the faded robe. "How do you think she liked being here without you when you were in Denver? A stranger in a strange place. But Casey gave you that time, because she knew you needed it and without complaint. A real trouper, that girl, doing what needed doing and keeping a secret until you came back."

Casey had carried on when hardship entered her life, while he…he had just run away. Was he selfish for wanting to make sure she came back to the North Star? "Can I ask you something, Billie?"

"About Matt Girard?"

He couldn't help but wonder what kind of man Jamie's father was…and Casey's husband. "You were his aunt. Did you know him well?"

"Great-aunt. Matthew was my brother's grandchild. They raised him after his parents died overseas. When I came out here and met Sam, and we got married, we didn't leave Wyoming much, but we met Matt a few times over the years. Impressed me as a smart, very capable young man. Loved his family, but he had a bit of a reckless nature. He loved flying more than anything. Ironically, that love took him away from Casey forever. In spite of loving you, I think she still feels the loss."

Grief could be all-consuming. How well he knew. "I want to be there for her, but I'm not sure she wants to share this time. Casey said she needed to face this by herself. I think she wants to be alone with him…one more time."

"Doesn't mean a man can't look out for his wife and children and take care of them. But you need to realize maybe Casey didn't allow herself to grieve long enough for Matt."

"What do you mean?" He hadn't considered she was still feeling the loss of her first husband, even though several years had passed.

"She came out here, and you sort of overwhelmed her with your cowboy charm." She waved away his protest. "I know how that works, seeing how Sam Murphy did the same thing. Look, Casey needs you as much as you need her, but you both brought a lot of baggage into this marriage. It'll take some time to sort it all out. But from where I sit, doing that together is far better than doing it apart."

"So, you think I should go?" He turned his head to study the face of the woman who gave so much of herself. Whose opinions and counsel he valued above all others.

Billie squeezed his arm. "What you need to do is think about it. Think real hard. I know that's not part of your nature. Heaven knows you McCord men are a stubborn lot, and you like to act first. But sometimes you've got to do what's good for somebody else instead of just what's good for you."

He thought about her advice for a moment, then leaned over and kissed her soft cheek. "Thanks, Billie. You're the best." He rose and went down the steps.

"If you go, make sure it's because she needs you. Not because you need her." Billie's final words followed him.

The words played over in his mind as he left the cabin and walked slowly back to the big house. Before going inside, he stood beneath the vast night sky and watched the stars grow brighter. Somewhere glowed a star named after Casey. Her first husband had given her that for a wedding gift. A grand gesture this cowboy hadn't yet matched. Did Casey ever think about that? Now that she was back in the place where she'd lived with another man, lived a different life, did she wish she was still with him? Did she wish the child she carried was his? The stars couldn't give him any answers. Nobody or nothing could except Casey herself.

Chapter 23

Arnette Madison's kitchen reminded Casey of summers past, when they had worked together canning tomatoes, and green beans, and stuffing pickles into a big brown crock and covering them with fresh dill. Mom had twenty jars of beans lined up on the counter, and the huge kettle on the gas range waited for another batch. Whatever was ripening in the garden dictated what the jars held this time of year and went a long way in keeping her family well-fed over the winter. On a hot summer day, the teen-age Casey had always been anxious to escape her mother's kitchen.

She poured tea from a blue-knitted-cozy-covered pot and took the flowered cup to sit at the table. She hadn't slept well this past week. Staying in her childhood room proved a surreal experience. Waking to the raucous sound of a rooster crowing was even more of a dream-breaker. Most of all, she hated sleeping alone.

A check of her phone showed no reply to the text she'd sent Chance late last night. He was probably out with the cattle now and just hadn't bothered to look at his phone...or charge it. Or perhaps he'd caved to Justin's nagging and driven the cattle to the high country, staying at the cabin where they'd taken shelter in a mountain storm last summer. She was afraid of the storm and that the woodstove in the cabin might catch fire. Chance laughed it off and built a fire to take the chill off the air. Jamie fell asleep, and Chance kissed her. She fell in love with him that day. A few weeks later, she spent the night with him at that same cabin. Then he asked her to marry him.

A commotion stirred outside the door, and she snapped to attention.

Jamie traipsed in, followed by Mom. They carried baskets of more green beans and plenty of red, ripe tomatoes.

Barney, the old beagle, trailed behind them, no doubt hoping for a handout.

Jamie set his basket on the counter. "Here, Grandma, let me take those." He grabbed the wire handles and hefted her basket of tomatoes onto a nearby step stool.

Casey sighed. Her boy had grown so much stronger and more capable than the child she'd taken west a little over a year ago.

"Hi, Mom. I helped Grandma in the garden. She called you a sleepyhead, but I said that's okay. Baby Lily makes you tired."

As if she heard her name, Lily Rose woke and turned a somersault.

Casey rubbed her back and rose to check the garden's bounty. "These are beautiful tomatoes, Mom. You always grew the best of anyone else around here."

A well-built woman of medium height, Arnette kept her honey-brown hair short and free of gray, and she always wore lipstick. Even working in the garden this morning, in her trim denim capris and pink blouse, she looked ready for the cover of a farm magazine.

Relinquishing the basket to Jamie, she brushed her

well-manicured hands together. "Having my grandson here is a genuine pleasure. I can't believe he's gotten so tall and strong since we last saw him. And he's such a good helper." She bent to give Jamie a hug.

He ducked away and grabbed a cookie from a plate on the counter.

Mom tightened her lips and frowned. "Where are your manners, Jamie? You should ask first." She reached to move the plate.

The boy grabbed two more and dashed for the door. "I gotta find Grandpa," he yelled. "He said maybe we'd go fishing today." The screen door slammed, and he and Barney were gone.

Arnette shook her head. "I guess he doesn't want Grandma's hugs anymore, just my cookies. What are they teaching him on that ranch?"

Casey wanted to say, *it's not you. It's not the ranch. Jamie just isn't a little boy anymore.*

But, thank goodness, children were so resilient. She'd worried the trip might prove too difficult for the almost nine-year-old, but so far, he was taking everything in stride. *Too bad I can't say the same about myself.*

Turning to a cupboard, Arnette pulled out a colander. Setting it in the sink, she scooped green beans into it and started snapping them into a bowl on the counter.

"Let me help you." Casey went to the sink, needing to find some way to bridge the rift still simmering. Her mother's attitude only made things more strained. The friction grated on Casey's nerves like worn sandpaper until she couldn't stand it anymore. "I was always pretty quick at doing this." She grabbed a handful of beans and started breaking the ends off and snapping the beans in two.

"Don't snap them too small." Arnette peered over Casey's shoulder. "In fact, you don't need to do this. I'm quite used to handling it myself, and Cindy said she can come over later. She'll blanch and peel the tomatoes, so why don't you just go take it easy now?"

The sandpaper hit a raw spot, and a streak of hot stubbornness shot through Casey. Mom's criticism stung just a little too much this time. She snatched a handful of beans from the colander. "I don't need to take it easy, Mom. I'm not sick. I'm pregnant, and I can at least do this…to pass some time."

Arnette sniffed. "Suit yourself. You probably do a lot more work out in Wyoming, but you ought to take care of yourself, you know. You're older this time, and you need to be careful."

Casey slammed the handful of beans on the counter. "Mom! I'm fine, okay? I really am. So, could we please just snap beans?"

A few moments of awkward silence fell between them.

"Do you have something suitable to wear to the service?" Arnette's voice trembled a bit. "If not, we can go to the mall this afternoon and look for a nice maternity dress."

Better take the olive branch. "That would be nice, Mom. I'd like that."

For the next hour, they snapped beans, and Casey tried not to think about the real reason she'd come back to Michigan.

****

Chance stood on the wide front porch, straightened

his shoulders, and raked back his hair with his fingers. He took in the bright flower boxes that decorated the windows and a double swing that drifted lazily back and forth in the late afternoon breeze. Casey had grown up here and become the woman he knew. In a way, the house was not unlike the one at the North Star. Inhaling deeply, he blew out the breath and rapped his knuckles on the farmhouse door. While he waited for someone to answer, he turned and surveyed the gently rolling land that lay beyond the barn and outbuildings. A herd of black-and-white Holsteins grazed in a lush pasture, and an emerald-green cornfield waved under the summer sun. *They've had plenty of rain here.* Fire danger was high again when he left the ranch.

A dog barked, and the door creaked open.

He turned to see a petite but shapely woman in a dark dress and with wavy, short blonde hair facing him through the screen.

"Can I help you?"

He cleared his throat. "I hope so. Is this the Madison farm?"

The woman eyed him. She pushed an old dog back with her foot and opened the screen door, motioning for Chance to step inside. "You must be Casey's cowboy. I'm sorry. Was she expecting you?"

He entered the kitchen. "No, ma'am, I don't believe she is, and it's Chance. Chance McCord."

She studied him for a moment.

He stepped closer to the door. Her scrutiny was getting under his skin. He'd left his hat in the rental car and didn't have it to pull down over his eyes—his usual way to avoid someone checking him out and a part of his identity. In these parts, the hat just felt out of place.

As did he. He cleared his throat again. "Is she here?"

The blonde finally stopped staring and shook her head. "I'm Cindy Madison, her brother Jim's wife. They've gone back to the cemetery. Casey wanted to put out some garden flowers. They held the service for Matt today."

He knew that, and had arrived in time to go, but thought better of intruding on the private service and Casey's time with her family. "Yeah. How is…how is Casey doing?"

"It's been tough, but at least, they have some closure now, you know? That's a good thing." She hesitated a moment longer.

"Who was at the door?" A man's voice carried from beyond the kitchen.

Cindy Madison leaned toward Chance. "That would be my father-in-law, Lou, and trust me. His bark sounds mean, but he doesn't bite." She smiled and put a gentle hand on Chance's arm. "Come along, Mr. McCord. I think it's time you met the parents."

Chance braced himself and followed Cindy. How the next few minutes would go was anybody's guess, but for Casey's sake, he would do anything.

****

In her new black maternity dress, Casey knelt and placed the spray of deep-orange tiger lilies from her mother's garden over the freshly mounded earth. She spent a moment fussing with the waxy blossoms, then blew their dust from her fingers. She'd wanted to come back here alone, to think about things, mostly the words that still haunted her. The words she could never take back. Except maybe now she could, and then, maybe, put the past to rest.

Jim stood by his car alongside Jamie. He insisted on driving her, and Jamie begged to come along, but at least, they were giving her this much space.

Her hands stilled over the flowers. "It's been a while since we talked, hasn't it? And the last thing we said was—" She inhaled a deep, shaky breath, letting it out slowly. "I'm sorry, Matt. Sorry for the way I acted and that our last words to each other were hurtful. You were leaving again to go off flying, and it angered me. Flying always seemed more important than we were. I know now I was wrong. You loved us deeply, but maybe our love for you wasn't enough. Is that why you went flying? Were you looking for whatever was missing in your life? If so, I'm sorry for the anger I let come between us, for keeping you from living your dream, but most of all, I'm sorry we weren't enough." With the heel of one hand, she wiped away the tears slipping down her cheeks.

"Mom?" Jamie spoke behind her. "Are you okay?"

She turned and looked up. Jamie resembled Matt more every day, and he would always be a reminder of the man who was the first to claim her heart. "Sure. I just…needed to say goodbye." More tears welled in her eyes.

Jamie put out a hand and helped her stand. "Look." He nodded toward the car. "I told Dad it was all right to come over here, but I guess he's not sure."

Two vehicles sat parked in the cemetery drive now, and two men watched from a respectful distance. Casey sighed. How did she spare Jamie having to figure out what went on in the minds of adults? He was still a child but growing into a more intuitive person every day. She squeezed his shoulder. "It's okay."

Jamie waved Chance over.

He walked toward her, his knee faltering. He didn't wear his hat.

Casey read the lines of concern etched on her husband's handsome face. She turned away to hide her tears.

"Come here." The boy took his stepfather's hand and gestured to the new headstone. "I want to show you. This was my first dad. His name was Matthew J. Girard, and he flew airplanes. He was a good man, and he loved us. I…just…wanted you to know that."

Chance bowed his head toward the grave. "I'm sure he was a fine man, and that he loved you and your mom very much. You make him proud every day, Jamie."

His voice sounded low and sad, much like the day she stood with him on a faraway hill while he struggled to put his own pain to rest.

He curved an arm around Casey's shoulders.

She let him draw her close and pressed her face into his shirt, inhaling the scent she loved and that had traveled so far—reminding her of wild mountains and rushing rivers and open ranges. Bluebirds and magpies. Rangy moose. Majestic elk and mighty bison. A fierce longing rose in her heart, to see the blue lupine and the Indian paintbrush that spilled across the valley.

Jamie tugged on her sleeve. "Can we go back to Grandma's? I think she's got dinner ready."

Casey smiled through the tears. Food was always uppermost in her son's mind. She crouched once more, and kissing her fingertips, she touched the simple marker. "Go with God, Matt Girard." But she was certain he'd done that the moment his life ended in the cold and stormy waters of Lake Michigan.

****

That night, Chance closed the door to Casey's room and set his duffle bag on the floor near the small dresser. A bit of light cast shadows across the bed where she lay on her side. She looked so vulnerable in her flimsy summer nightgown with her hair spilling over her shoulders and her hands folded under one cheek. He ached to touch Casey and hold her, but the bed was a single. Too small for both of them, and she had enough trouble getting comfortable, anyway.

After returning from the cemetery, she barely ate any dinner and went to bed soon after. He sat with Jamie, bringing him up to date on what was happening with April Dancer, and then got the boy settled for the night. Now, after the long day of travel and the stress of meeting Casey's family, exhaustion tugged at his own body. The Madisons didn't have much to say to him, except for the sister-in-law, Cindy, who seemed the most accepting. That was fine. His only concern was for his wife and her well-being.

He glanced around the room, taking in the shelf with small trophies and a bulletin board that still held faded county fair ribbons. The poster of a boy band, popular maybe twenty years ago, hung on one wall. A fuzzy white sweater lay draped across a small pink, upholstered chair. The teenage Casey's room had not changed in all the years she'd been gone. Almost as if her family waited for her to come home someday…and stay. Surely, they never expected her to move a thousand miles away.

He moved the sweater and eased himself onto the chair to pull off his boots. Quietly, he set them aside.

The chair didn't accommodate him very well, but he'd slept in worse places. Leaning back, he unbuckled his belt, rested one arm over his face, and tried to relax. He almost succeeded. Then a soft whimper brought him to attention.

Casey stirred and murmured a name in her sleep.

His gut clutched into a tight lump. The name wasn't his.

Her eyes fluttered open, and her gaze darted around the room. She struggled to sit. "Where…am I?"

He leaned forward in the chair. "Casey, honey." He kept his voice low. "It's okay. You're at your folks' house. Remember?"

Coming more fully awake, she held back her hair and focused her eyes. "What are you doing over there? You can't sleep in that little chair."

He scrubbed his hands over his face. "Not a lot of options here. But I'm okay."

A cool breeze drifted in from the open window. She hugged her arms and shivered.

Chance rose and fetched the blanket at the end of the bed. "Lie down." He drew the cover over her. "Try to go back to sleep."

Casey grabbed his hand. "You, too."

Did she really want him? Or the person in her dream? "Your bed's a little small. You need—"

"You. I need you. Here." She moved over, lifted the blanket, and made room.

He shrugged out of his clothes and stretched out beside Casey, putting his arms around her and drawing her close. The elusive scent of her perfume— wildflowers and summer rain— drifted to him, and he tried hard not to respond.

She slid her hand across his chest and then down his stomach.

He held his breath.

She slipped her fingers beneath the band of his briefs and stroked him lightly.

He gulped. "Casey, honey. Please don't. It's been a while, you know."

"It has," she whispered. "I just need to touch you and make sure you're real. That we're real." She explored with her fingers and slipped one leg over his.

He enjoyed the caresses for a moment, but before this went too far, he grasped her hand and held it against his chest. "We are real. We always will be." He kissed her forehead and willed his body to behave. "Now, let's sleep."

She shivered. "No flannels. Keep me warm, cowboy." She snuggled into the curve of his shoulder and pressed her rounded belly against him.

A tiny foot kicked him in the ribs and made him smile. This baby would hold them together. He was certain. Chance stroked Casey's arm until he heard her breathing turn soft and even. He felt her sweet body relax, and his own heartbeat slowed its rhythm. No matter who filled her dream, she carried his child, and he was the one holding Casey tonight.

Chapter 24

Chance ventured into the kitchen and headed for the coffeemaker on the counter. Early morning sunlight filtered through the checkered curtains and warmed the room. The simple farmhouse was welcoming, even if the people who lived here were not. From outside, a rooster crowing joined the lowing of cows. The sound of the cows, at least, was music to his ears.

At the table, Lou Madison held a newspaper in front of his face.

Arnette stood at the stove, scrambling eggs in a cast-iron frying pan.

Chance stepped to the counter and glanced sideway at Casey's dad, who, with black-framed glasses perched on the end of his nose, seemed immersed in the paper. Neither of the Madisons acknowledged him. He took a mug from the counter and poured himself coffee, appreciating the aroma of the dark brew and needing its punch this morning. He sat across from Lou, cradling the mug and inhaling the rich scent. *Must be where Casey learned to make coffee.*

Casey's mother slid eggs onto a blue willow plate, added toast and two strips of bacon, and set it in front of her husband. "Put your paper down and eat your breakfast while it's hot. Lou." She pinned Chance with her piercing hazel-green gaze. "How do you like your eggs?"

He hesitated a moment, surprised she would ask. "Whatever's easiest."

Lou folded his newspaper, took off his glasses, and put them beside his plate. "Better give her an answer, or you'll get this stuff." He grabbed his fork and poked at what was obviously mostly egg white. "Only way they're edible is with a dousing of ketchup." He grabbed a bottle on the table, gave it a good whack, and dumped a glob onto the pale eggs.

Chance flashed Arnette a cheerful smile. "Over easy, please."

She turned back to the frying pan and cracked two eggs, this time real ones.

Lou shoveled a forkful of ketchup-covered eggs into his mouth and grimaced.

Chance dipped his head and held back a chuckle.

"Don't laugh. This is the price you pay for getting older." Lou pinched a thin bacon strip. "Turkey, can you believe it?"

Sounds familiar. Justin complained regularly that the thick steaks he'd always enjoyed were now a rarity.

"Would you eat stuff like this?" Lou took another stab at the ketchup-soaked glob.

Chance unfolded a napkin. "My father's had to change his diet since his heart attack and surgery last year. Casey tries to improve our habits, but I'm afraid she's not succeeding too well with the wranglers."

"Yeah, well, can't say I blame them. If they're working outside all day, they deserve a good rib-sticking meal." Lou pushed the rest of his eggs aside on his plate and finished the bacon and toast.

Chance quietly drank his coffee and wished Jamie would come downstairs to break some of the tension.

But the kid was still sound asleep when he'd checked.

Arnette set a plate in front of him and filled his mug.

He met her steady scrutiny. "Thank you, ma'am."

She held the coffeepot poised over her husband's cup. "You're welcome to call me Arnette. We don't stand on too much formality here." She refilled Lou's coffee.

Chance paused before digging into his breakfast. "I'll do that then. Thank you, Arnette."

"You're welcome." Her reply held a begrudging note, but she nodded and went back to the sink.

Lou shoved his plate aside and snuck an oatmeal cookie from the cow-shaped cookie jar on the table. He munched quietly for a moment. "Where's our Casey-girl? She still upstairs?"

"Yep." Chance swallowed. "With the baby coming, she gets tired. I told her to sleep in." An awkward silence followed his comment. Had Matt Girard faced the same disapproval? Somehow, he thought not.

"Well, let the poor girl sleep." Arnette huffed. "Heaven knows she's had a hard enough time this week, and in her condition, she needs all the rest she can get. She probably works too much on that ranch, anyway."

Chance set his fork down and counted to five. He wouldn't let Casey's parents win this round. They loved their daughter, but so did he. "Casey does as much or not as much as she wants. This summer, she's running a program for the kids who come to the ranch, and she helps Billie in the kitchen. She's not out chasing cows. I have wranglers who do that, but I suspect if that's what Casey wanted to do, then I couldn't stop her."

Surprisingly, he got a wink from Lou but only a grumpy harrumph from Arnette. He finished his breakfast.

Lou went back to eating his cookie.

His wife slapped the counter with a wet dishrag.

Shortly, Lou rose and reached for his ball cap hanging near the door.

Chance took their plates to the dishwasher and loaded them. He turned to the older man.

"How about you give me a tour of your farm this morning, Lou? That is, if you're feeling up to it."

Excitement lit Lou's gray eyes, and he pulled on the green-and-gold cap. "Up to it? Well, of course, I'm up to it."

"You better take the cart." Arnette dumped out the last of the coffee. "Too much walking and you'll be complaining by tonight."

"Cart, my eye." Lou grinned at Chance and jerked his head toward the door. "C'mon, son. Let's get outta here before I'm confined to quarters." He walked slowly and, with a definite limp, toward the door.

The farmer in Lou Madison will keep him going for as long as he can...and then some. Chance totally understood.

Outside, Lou stood on the porch, adjusting his cap. He grabbed a walking stick from behind a wooden rocker and tapped it against his side. "I'm supposed to have hip surgery in the fall. Not looking forward to that, but everything's wearing out. How about you, Chance? What's the story behind the hitch in your giddy-up? Too many hard landings?"

Chance chuckled at the old guy's observation. "You might say that. It's why I don't take those kinds of landings anymore, or at least not in the rodeo ring."

"Bet that was an interesting life, though. Is my daughter the reason you quit?"

Lou was nothing if not direct. He deserved a direct answer. "I quit before we met, but Casey is the reason I won't go back. Especially with the baby coming."

Lou studied him, then nodded. "I hope that's true. She needs somebody dependable."

"Yes, sir," Chance agreed.

"Well, now we got that settled, how about we take that tour? You got a hat? Gets pretty hot in the fields this time of year."

"I do, sir."

"Then get it on your head...and you can knock off the *sir* stuff. Like Arnette said, we don't stand on too much formality around here."

More than happy to oblige, Chance hurried to grab his hat. For more than an hour, he walked the perimeter of the fields and pastures with the dairy farmer.

Lou pointed out his best cows and recited how much milk they produced. "Jim comes early to oversee the milking in the big barn. He's modernized the process, and we've got a couple of hired hands. But back in the day, Arnette and I did most of the work ourselves."

Chance stayed close to the older man in case he fell. "My father did, too, on the ranch. It's a real issue now that he can't do as much." *How much is he doing while I'm gone?*

Lou stopped and smacked the stick against his hip.

A gesture of frustration and maybe pain? They should have taken the cart, but Chance would never say so.

"How many head of cattle do you run out there in Wyoming?" Lou gazed at his own herd.

"Three hundred right now."

He shook his head and lifted his cap to scratch his thinning hair. "What we got here must seem pretty small potatoes."

Facing him, Chance tipped his own hat back to let him see the respect he held for another man who lived close to the land. "Nothing is small potatoes when it's your living. Not by any means."

They ambled back at a slower pace.

Near the house, Jamie and Barney joined them. "Barney's getting kind of old, isn't he?" the boy observed. "We saw some rabbits by Grandma's garden, and he barked, but he didn't chase them like he used to."

"Happens to the best of us." Lou stopped and put a hand on his grandson's head. "Just like boys grow up too fast."

Jamie peered at him. "Does that mean you're getting old, Grandpa?"

Lou touched the tip of the walking stick to his forehead. "Not here where it counts, boy. You just remember that."

Jamie chewed his lip and thought about this for a few seconds. He turned to Chance. "Aunt Cindy said she'd take me and my cousins to a movie in town tonight, and maybe we'll stop for ice cream. Is it okay for me to go?"

Chance shrugged. "Fine by me, but you better ask Mom. You know she's the boss."

"Thanks, Dad. I gotta finish picking Grandma's tomatoes." He took off with the aging Barney running valiantly to keep pace.

"I see you've at least got that figured out. Always let the wife rule. Happy wife, happy life." Lou grinned and crinkled the corners of his gray eyes that were so much like his daughter's.

"Absolutely," Chance agreed. Keeping Casey happy and their marriage together was his main goal in life right now. He just had to keep figuring out how to do that.

****

The day's warmth lingered into the evening, and in the tall maples that shaded the front yard, a robin called for rain before calling it a day.

After dinner, Casey found Chance sitting on the porch alone. "Thirsty?" She handed him a glass of the sun tea she'd chilled earlier.

He took it and shifted over in the swing.

She sat and watched him empty half the foggy glass, then balance it on his knee. Busy with her family, she hadn't made an opportunity for them to talk much since he'd arrived, and last night, she'd been just too tired. Now she found it hard to know what to say. She dropped her gaze to his hands. More than anything, she wanted to hold them and rub his rough fingers against her face, but something held her back. "I heard Daddy gave you the grand tour today. How did that go?"

"It was good. Your dad and I have a lot in common, you know."

He sounds so positive. "I suppose so." She leaned her head back. "You're both hard-headed, and you don't always listen too well."

He lifted one brow. "Look who's talking."

She opened her mouth to protest but held the words

inside. Sunset colors streaked the sky and cast long shadows across the farm. Was the sun setting the sky above the mountains on fire tonight? She turned her head toward him. "Did you have a hard time finding this place?"

"Jeannie made sure I updated the maps app before I left." He tapped the phone in his shirt pocket. "Pretty handy feature, when you don't know where you're going."

She sighed. "I'm sorry I didn't ask you to come to Michigan. I guess that was me being stubborn. If I hurt you, it wasn't my intention." She felt relieved to say what had been on her mind since she left the North Star.

Chance drained the rest of the iced tea and set the glass aside. He made no move to touch her but leaned a little closer. "You had the right to face this however you wanted to."

Casey knit her fingers together above her baby bump. "I had…some things I needed to say and put the past to rest, and I needed to find a way to forgive myself."

He plucked at the sleeve of her shirt. "Did you? Find a way?"

"I'll always regret the last words I spoke to Matt." Maybe she needed someone else to forgive her.

He let out a deep sigh. "Yeah, last words have a way of haunting us, don't they?"

She suspected he knew the pain of that, too. "Why did you come here, Chance? Did you think I would stay?"

His jaw tensed. "That was a big part of it, but I also didn't want you to be hurt anymore. I thought maybe you needed someone who was nonjudgmental and wouldn't have any expectations of how you should feel."

"My parents have expectations, and I have a way of not living up to them." *It's always been that way.*

"They love you, Casey. They're good people."

She glanced up. His steady blue gaze sent a rush of warmth simmering through her, but she pushed the response away and frowned. "Are you taking their side now?" Did no one understand her feelings?

He nudged her shoulder. "No side. I just see me the way they do."

"I don't understand. How is that?"

He stretched one arm along the top of the swing, touching her hair where it spilled over her shoulder. "As the man who has kept their daughter and grandson far away."

His rough fingers playing with her hair sent a quiver across her shoulders. "I'm a grown woman, not their child."

He traced the curve of her cheek, letting his fingers linger. "I'm well aware of that, darlin'. But while you might be a woman to me, you will always be their child. And I'm just imagining how I'll feel some day, as the overprotective father of a daughter. By the way, how is our Lily Rose doing?"

The baby pummeled Casey with tiny feet. She gave Chance a wistful smile. Grasping his hand, she placed it over her rounded stomach to let him feel his child's reaction. "She's doing just fine, and she's very glad her daddy is here."

Chance kissed her then.

For the first time in days, Casey knew where her heart belonged.

They were still sitting in the swing when Cindy brought Jamie home.

The boy jumped from the car and waved goodbye to his cousins. In two leaps, he climbed the steps to the porch and saw Chance and Casey. He shuffled in front of them, wearing a frown. "Is everything settled now?"

"Of course it is, honey." Casey lifted her head from Chance's shoulder and reached over to rub away the smudge of chocolate that decorated Jamie's chin. "Why would you ask that?"

He shifted from one foot to the other. "Aunt Cindy said you guys had something you had to get settled. So, did you get it settled?"

Chance squeezed Casey's hand. "You bet, partner. We're all good."

Jamie considered this for about two seconds. "Can I have a snack before bedtime?"

Casey rolled her eyes. "Didn't you just have ice cream?"

"Yeah, but you know that don't fill me up much."

"One cookie and some milk, then get your PJs on. And don't forget to brush your teeth."

Jamie started for the door, paused, and looked back. "If everything is settled now, can we go home? I think April Dancer misses me."

Casey glanced at Chance and then back to Jamie. "Going home sounds like a fine idea."

Because home in the valley was where they all belonged.

****

In the early morning, Chance loaded luggage into the rental car and waited.

At the porch, Casey and Jamie said their goodbyes.

His wife hugged Lou and Arnette more than once, and both parents held her and the boy for a long time.

He leaned against the car, tipped his hat forward, and gave them a last bit of privacy. *Families.* They could bring so much joy…and cause so much grief. At one time, he'd thought staying out on the road would free him from obligations, but in the end, coming back to the North Star had finally given him peace of mind. Now, he couldn't help feeling the pain of two people who loved their child desperately and yet were willing to let her find her own happiness.

Casey's brother trudged from the barn, wiping an arm across his forehead. A thunderstorm the night before had left muggy air hanging like a wet blanket over the land. Jim stood beside the car, sweat beading on his flushed face and concern filling his eyes.

"Can I give you a hand…with anything?"

"Thanks, got it all done. Just giving them space." Chance nodded toward the house.

Jim glanced at the scene by the front steps. "Casey handled this all pretty well, I'd say. Better than I would have. My sister is a strong woman." He swung his gaze back to study Chance. "But I suppose you already know that."

Chance watched the scene playing out, how Casey straightened her shoulders after hugging her mom and dad. "I find it out more and more every day."

Jim nodded and ran a hand around the back of his neck. "I guess we were all prepared not to like you very much, but you have to understand how worried we were, not really knowing what Casey got herself into. She was still very vulnerable when she went out to Wyoming. We didn't want someone taking advantage of that."

Disappointment pricked at Chance. Did they really have such a low opinion of him? "Do you think that's what happened? Why we got married?"

Jim remained silent a moment. "What I think is that my sister loves you, and so does Jamie. If she's happy, then that's all that matters." He offered a handshake. "My only request is for you to take care of them."

Chance gripped Jim's hand. "I intend to do that." Nothing would come between Casey and him now.

Chapter 25

Chance brought a Great Pyrenees pup home at the beginning of August, and a few weeks later, the fat and furry Bear loved nothing more than to tease the long-suffering Mariah. He dashed across the ranch yard and growled at the older dog, tugging at her ears.

Mariah sent the pup sprawling with a swipe of her paw.

Bear yipped and rolled in the stubby grass.

Chance motioned Jamie toward the inside of the barn. "Put Bear in an empty stall for now, so he's out of the way. Ed's bringing new folks in soon, and I'll be busy. Make sure he's got clean water."

Jamie rescued the pup and carried him to the barn. "Bear won't stay out of trouble. He keeps bothering Mariah, and I think she's fed up." He bounced the puppy in his arms. "When's he going to learn not to pester her?"

Chance laughed. "What he needs to learn is to not act like a sissy. But he's just a baby yet. He's got plenty of time, and Mariah will teach him when he's ready."

"Hear that, Bear? You gotta be brave." Still chattering, Jamie carried the pup to settle him in the stall.

The last weeks of summer were winding down, but the guests and ranch work still kept them busy. Chance had a lot of work to finish today, but he glanced to where he'd noticed Casey earlier. His wife stood by the corral where Blue Lady and April Dancer grazed. She crossed her arms on the top fence rail, resting her chin.

What was she thinking? That the filly was growing like crazy and would soon be as tall as her mom? Or that the mare was still her elusive self? He'd started helping Jamie halter train Dancer, and they'd had some nice progression, but the mare was another story. Blue Lady still resisted most human contact and would wander away to the other end of the pasture if someone approached. Chance had all but given up on ever training her.

"Not sure what good that one is," Justin had commented when it became apparent the mare possessed an unbreakable wild streak. "Still don't know what made you bring her home."

"Casey wanted her" was the only reason Chance could give him, and after a time or two, the explanation seemed enough for Justin.

His wife wasn't ready to give up on the mare, and she came out almost daily to win over Blue Lady. She stood at the fence rail now, talking to the mustang. For someone who knew very little about horses, Casey had learned a lot in the past year.

Chance sauntered alongside her. "Someday Blue Lady will figure out we mean her no harm." He leaned down and pressed a kiss against Casey's cheek. "I think she's thankful you brought her here."

"I'm not sure of that." Casey shook her head. "I hoped, after her foal came, she'd understand we're not the enemy. But she still acts so distant. Like she's waiting for someone else or looking for another place. I think she's…lonely." She hesitated a moment. "I think of them a lot."

"Think of who?" He wasn't sure what she meant.

The mare stood at the far end of the corral, gazing at the mountains. As if listening to some faraway sound, she pricked her ears forward.

"The other horses. The ones in those corrals. Maybe that's what Blue Lady misses, someone she left behind."

Sadness still haunted his wife. Since returning from Michigan, she often acted withdrawn and melancholy. Was she, too, missing someone she'd left behind? He put an arm around her shoulders. "We can't save them all, but I know if you could, you would do that."

Casey sighed and leaned against him. "I keep hearing them hitting against that awful fence and knowing how much they want their freedom."

Nothing he could say. He knew what it meant to long for freedom.

"Roy said while you might own a mustang, they will never truly be yours. Do you think that's true of Blue Lady?"

"Roy's probably right, but after the filly is weaned, I'll work with the mare. Not making any promises, though."

She pressed her cheek against his shirtsleeve. "Thank you for bringing her home. I just couldn't bear to walk away. It would have broken my heart."

He caught the tremor in her voice. "Hey, you don't have to explain your reasoning. I've been known to fall in love with a few horses in my life."

Casey hugged his arm. "Did I ever tell you you're my hero, cowboy?"

He bent his head to kiss the woman who never

failed to make him realize how lucky he was. The first time they'd kissed was out here, behind the barn, in the fading summer twilight. They'd stood by this very corral, with him thinking he was ten kinds of a fool to get involved. Now, he blessed the day he did, because every day, he could enjoy a moment like this one.

"Shouldn't you take off your hat before you kiss a lady?" she murmured.

"I thought you might like this effect better." He grazed his lips over hers and drew her against him. This time, her sigh didn't sound so sad.

She slipped her arms around his middle. Allowing no distance between them, she kissed him back.

Tiny feet beat a muffled rhythm between them.

Chance laughed against Casey's lips. "Lily Rose, behave yourself," he admonished.

"She is relentless lately." Casey rested in his arms.

He leaned them both against the fence. Still concerned she wasn't feeling the best, he rubbed her back.

"Maybe you need to slow down a little. Let one of the girls take care of the kids." He'd hired two local high schoolers to clean the guest cabins in hopes it would lessen some of the work. But Casey insisted on holding her reading and craft time every afternoon.

"Like I told my mom, I'm having a baby. I'm not sick, and I will not lie around and do nothing."

"Okay, okay, I get the picture." He kissed her again and would have lingered longer, but Mariah's barking drew them apart. "Ed's back from the airport. Max Pierson and his son, Quinn, are with this group."

Casey slipped away and watched the van Chance had bought this summer roll into the drive.

Reluctantly, he let her go, hoping later they'd have a little more time alone. The pressures of the ranch lately had kept them both too exhausted to do more than fall into bed at night.

Jamie tore out of the barn and ran toward the new arrivals.

Behind him, the puppy caused a ruckus at being left alone.

He was sorry the precious stolen moment had ended, but Chance accompanied Jamie to greet the newcomers. Not long after, he glimpsed Casey carrying Bear into the house.

The chubby puppy nestled his head on her shoulder.

Maybe the pup would keep a smile on her face.

****

The next evening, Casey sat on the porch steps and watched everyone get ready for the ride into town. She'd decided to avoid the crowds and remain at the ranch.

"You sure you don't want to come along? Looks like everybody is going tonight, even Billie and Justin." While he waited for the guests to gather for the trip into Jackson for the rodeo, Chance turned to her. "Ed is driving the van, and the other wranglers are going on their own. But you can ride with Jamie and me."

She snuggled the puppy close. "I'll just stay here with Bear. You all go on and have a good time. Make sure Jamie behaves himself."

The kid raced out the door and ran for the truck. He threw a "Bye, Mom" over his shoulder.

"Hey, come back and give your mom a hug," Chance called out.

Jamie skidded to a stop, stirring a small cloud of dust at his feet. He dragged his boots back to the porch and gave Casey a quick hug, then ran off again.

"He's getting to that age," she mused. "No public displays of affection allowed."

Chance sat beside her. "Fortunately, I don't have a problem with it." He leaned over, kissed her, and rumpled Bear's furry ears. "You sure you don't mind staying here alone?"

"I'll be fine, and Jeannie said something about stopping by. She has some baby things for us."

"Ah, yeah." He rubbed his chin. "Guess we should do some shopping soon. Maybe a trip to Idaho Falls is in order?"

Casey brightened. "That'd be great. We need to look at cribs and baby clothes and…" She saw the guests strolling to the house and cut her conversation short. She watched the three families and their kids climb into the van. *They are a noisy bunch. So glad I'm staying here.*

Max and his son were the last to join them. "You're not going?" Max adjusted his brand-new cowboy hat, tipping it a little rakishly over his brow. "Sounds like a fun time."

Max and Quinn were both affable enough, even if Max did like to pour on the charm with the ladies. He'd worked hard at charming Billie to make Eggs Benedict for breakfast. She had promptly turned the request over to Casey, declaring her cooking skills didn't go that far.

"I'm staying here to hold down the fort. Rodeos aren't my thing, but you all have fun." She grabbed Bear so he wouldn't scamper after the children and noticed how Quinn stood by Chance. The look of admiration on the young guy's face plainly showed he considered a former rodeo champ a hero. He'd dogged her husband's every step since they arrived.

"Are you riding tonight, Chance?" Quinn asked.

Chance glanced at Casey and shook his head. "Nope. Told you once, I'm all done with that."

"But you ought to."

"Come on, Quinn, don't bother the man. You heard what he said." Max steered his son toward the van. "Let's get loaded up, or they'll leave without us."

Casey watched everyone go and sighed in relief. Sometimes, all she really wanted was a moment of silence. Before long, Lily Rose would begin her nightly tumbling exercises that left her exhausted. *How can I possibly have three months to go?* Mid-November couldn't come soon enough.

With Bear tagging along, she went back into the house. A call from Jeannie told her their neighbor wouldn't stop by until the next day, so Casey searched for the book she'd been reading. Stretching out on the sofa, she propped the book on her belly and settled in for a nice relaxing evening. Before reading two pages, she closed the book. How were things going at the rodeo? Jamie, no doubt, was having a great time. But what about Chance? Did watching the riders bring back old memories? Did he still wish he was one of them?

Chapter 26

The sun slipped behind the mountains, and the lights at the rodeo grounds blinked on. Inside the arena, a calf-roping event sent riders in hot pursuit of bawling calves, and the crowd cheered. The noise, as usual, was deafening.

Chance walked behind the chutes, and it all came back—the smell of animal sweat and dirt, along with the well-remembered rush of adrenaline. Even after all this time, his heartbeat slammed into overdrive at the memories.

He'd arranged for Max and Quinn to get a close look at the action behind the scenes. He hoped to let the kid know that, while the sport might be exciting, rodeo was not pretty. The men and women who took part were their own breed, and for a time, he'd been one of them. Constantly seeking the next thrill, he'd moved from county to county. Had the moments of glory made up for the long nights alone?

Jamie ran ahead and walked with the Piersons. He had come to the rodeo a few times over the summer, first with the Hansons, and then with Billie and Justin. Now, he filled Max and Quinn in on what was happening.

Chance stopped by an empty chute to watch some of the action, but from where he could keep an eye on the three. Granting the boy this freedom away from

Casey would give him more confidence. She'd gotten better in the past month, allowing Jamie to ride Ranger, Kyle's well-trained buckskin. She still had an overprotective nature, but that was Casey. Soon, she'd have the baby to fuss over. By his own admission, Chance already felt overprotective when he thought about having a daughter. If a few years ago someone had told him he'd feel this way, he'd have laughed in their face.

A couple of dust-covered, rough-looking cowboys jostled by him.

One turned to look back. "Hey, man. Hey, Chance. Is that really you?"

He recognized the guys as other bronc riders he'd known in Cody and Cheyenne and a few other places. The one, his name was Paolo, clapped him on the shoulder.

"Well, I'll be, if it ain't the man that never went less than eight seconds. You ridin' tonight? Didn't see your name on the—"

"Nah." He inclined his head. "No riding for me. Just here with a group from the ranch."

The other cowboy—was his name Brice?—sauntered back to offer his hand.

Chance shook it firmly. The two cowboys had helped him through some miserable nights on the road.

"We heard you were back in Jackson Hole but didn't know for sure." Brice leaned away and spat out tobacco juice. "What's goin' on nowadays?"

He met the guys' curious stares. *Might as well be honest.* "I busted my knee a while back. Pretty much ended my rodeo days. So, I came here. You know the old saying, 'home is where, when you go there, they have to take you in.' " He glanced around them to keep track of Max and the boys.

"I recall you and your old man didn't see eye to eye. That get any better?"

Brice was always the talkative one, and that hadn't changed. Chance shrugged. "We're working on it. My brother got hitched and left the ranch a few months ago, so it's pretty much Justin and me running the show now. We are…we're doing okay."

"Well, that's good to hear. So, how's it feel being back here tonight?" Brice asked.

"Probably getting a taste of the old times," Paolo offered. "I mean, once rodeo is in your blood, you never lose the urge to climb on a wild horse and let 'er buck."

"Chance was kind enough to arrange a tour behind the scenes." Max Pierson broke in. Having walked back toward them, he stood beside Chance and took in the two cowboys. "My boy thinks this sort of life is what he'd like to have. Chance is giving him a good look."

Quinn and Jamie wandered the line of chutes, hanging on one of them to get a better look at what it was like to wait inside for the gate to open.

Chance watched them. "The kid should know, rodeo life is not all it's made out to be. Not all glory all the time. Sometimes, there's loneliness…and pain." Was he talking to them or himself? He'd learned the truth about the time he started walking down a long stretch of lonely highway. A hard-won truth, and one he needed reminding of every now and then. Shaking the thoughts away, he swung back to the action in the arena. "I think they're about to bring on the bronc riders." He waved to Quinn and Jamie.

The boy came tearing back. "Hey, Dad, you think Quinn and me can be on a kids' tag team? Somebody said we can still sign up."

Brice and Paolo both stared at the boy and then at Chance.

He saw unasked questions pop from the cowboys. They knew about the loss of Scottie and Angela. He put his hands on Jamie's shoulders, drawing the boy toward him. "Guys, this is my son, Jamie. His mom, Casey, and I got married last year, and we're expecting a baby in the fall. Jamie, these are some friends of mine, Paolo and Brice."

The boy gave them the once-over. "Hi, do you ride broncs like my dad? Are you riding tonight?"

"Well, I'll be," Brice murmured.

Paolo stepped forward and gave the boy a playful punch on the shoulder. "Glad to meet you, Jamie. Yep, we're bronc riders, but your dad was the best. He said he doesn't ride anymore."

Jamie peered backward at Chance. "I wish I could see him ride, but he kinda made a promise to my mom that he wouldn't."

Thanks, kid. But better that he was honest. "That's a fact. With a ranch to run and a new baby on the way, I can't afford to blow out my knee again." *Or any other body part.*

"We tried to talk him into it," Quinn piped up, as he joined the group. "I searched Chance online. Best all-around cowboy at Cheyenne and Amarillo, best—"

"They know all that," Chance cut in. "We better go claim our seats before somebody else does. Good seeing you guys." He shook hands with Paolo and Brice again. "We'll be in the stands, so give us a good ride."

"You won't think about it?" Quinn nudged Jamie. "Even if your kid wants you to ride?"

Giving a last glance at his one-time buddies, as they prepared to climb into the chutes, Chance turned Jamie away. "A promise is a promise and needs to be kept. You remember that, it'll make your life a whole lot better."

With that bit of advice, Chance hurried the Piersons and Jamie along, away from the chutes and the sudden pull of their attraction.

****

Casey woke with a start. She moved her feet and touched Bear, where he lay curled at the foot of the sofa, still blissfully asleep. Careful not to wake him, she shifted her legs over the side of the sofa and sat up. What had pulled her from the deep sleep she'd fallen into?

Around them, the big house slumbered in silence, save for the ticking of the clock on the mantel.

She glanced at the clock. Almost ten. Everybody should be home soon, but for the moment, an uneasy calmness hung in the air. Stretching her back against a cramp, she wandered down the hallway to the kitchen and glanced out the open window above the sink.

The moonless night cast no shadows, but lightning flickered above the mountains. A roll of thunder rumbled across the valley.

Sliding the window closed, she turned to set the kettle to boil. Another sound drew her attention. *Barking.* Mariah's barking. The old dog usually stayed on the porch at night, but she sounded farther away. What had disturbed her? Casey switched on the porch light and stepped outside the kitchen door just as the wind picked up, blowing from the mountains and across the pastures.

The first spatter of raindrops hit the dusty ground. Another streak of lightning snaked across the sky, illuminating the barn and corral where they kept the mare and filly.

Mariah stood near the corral, still barking.

But at what? Casey jumped at the puppy, sniffing her feet. Bear had followed her. She scooped him into her arms and carried him back inside. "You need to stay here," she scolded and tucked him into his puppy crate. Back at the door, she peered into the darkness again, and when lightning lit the sky with a streak that reached from one horizon to the other, she saw it—the open gate to the corral. The gate to Blue Lady's and Dancer's corral swung back and forth in the wind. Casey's heart thumped hard in her chest. Had they already escaped?

****

Chance paced at the edge of the empty chutes and watched the storm. In the last hour, the mounting clouds had raced north and spared the rodeo grounds, but the announcer handed out the awards late, and everyone wanted to stay until the end. He'd let Jamie hang out with some local kids, but as he waited for everybody to gather for the ride back to the North Star, he muttered a curse of impatience. Lightning flashed, and distant thunder rumbled. He had a bad feeling.

"Hey, Chance, you got a minute?"

He jerked around to see a young guy with a big camera hustling through the crowd toward him. Damn, not what he needed right now. He held up a hand to ward him off. "Sorry, buddy, I need to—"

"Pete Sanders here. I only have a couple of

questions. Okay if I take your pic?" He didn't wait for an answer but clicked away. "You're Chance McCord, right? Heard you were a big shot in the rodeo world. Mind giving me a statement?"

"About what?" Chance glanced behind him. Where was everybody?

"I just heard some cowboys talking in the chutes. They said you might be thinking of making a comeback. Care to comment?"

Now who the hell had spread that rumor? Brice and Paolo? *Thanks, guys.* He waved Pete Sanders aside. "I don't." Maybe, at one time in his life, he'd been glad to get recognized and had eaten up the media attention. But he didn't feel the need for validation anymore.

The guy flashed him a name badge for a digital news site that covered happenings in the valley. Casey had mentioned the name occasionally, and that maybe they should advertise the guest cabins on the site.

Pete whipped out his phone and tapped a few notes. "Aw, c'mon, just give me something I can take back to the keyboard. Something a little punchy."

I'll give you something punchy. Instead, he tipped his hat back and put on his best cowboy swagger. "You know, Pete, I'm not sure who you've been talking to, but here's my statement. My rodeo days are over. I'm only here tonight to bring ranch guests for the event. So, no story. Nothing exciting. Is that enough of a statement?"

Pete lifted his camera. "Okay, but could you at least step over by the chutes and let me take a photo? Just a quick one."

He would have protested, but the guy wasn't going away. Stepping closer to the fence behind him, Chance leaned one arm on the top rail and nodded toward Pete. "Shoot. One."

Pete clicked three times and moved around to get another angle.

Chance brushed past him, clapping him on the shoulder. "That's enough. I have people to round up. You have a good night." Just past the chutes, he saw lightning snake across the sky to the north. The storm still hung in that direction. He glanced around at the dissipating crowd and spotted Roy laughing and joking around with a bunch of cowboys and barrel-racer cowgirls. Chance motioned him over. "Sorry to spoil the party, but I need you to head back right now. Casey's alone, and I don't like the looks of that storm. By the time we get everybody gathered and loaded, it'll be another hour."

"Sure thing, boss-man." Roy waved at his friends and headed for Juanita.

Chance blew out a hard breath. Depending on the wrangler to look after his wife might not be the best idea, but at the moment, he had little choice. *Now to find the rest of the group.*

****

Rain ticked harder on the windows. Casey slid her bare feet into a pair of boots, found a slicker in the mudroom, and flung it around her shoulders. She jammed her arms into the too-long sleeves and turned off the flame under the kettle. Flashlight in hand, she started out for the corral. The sky lit up again, and she struggled to quell the fear thrumming through her veins. *Please be there! Please, Blue Lady, don't have run away.*

As she raced across the ranch yard, the rain stung

her face like tiny needles. Reaching the gate, she grabbed ahold to stop it from swinging wildly in the wind. She beamed the flashlight around the corral, and her stomach sank. The corral appeared empty, but then a movement near the barn caught her attention, and she swung the light in that corner. She saw the filly hovering near the door and uttered a sigh of immense relief. With Mariah at her side, Casey hurried toward Dancer. "It's okay, baby. You're safe now." She tried to remain calm, yet spoke loud enough to be heard above the din of the storm. "Let's get you inside." She feared the filly might shy away, but thank goodness, Dancer followed her and the big dog.

Casey stuck the flashlight under her arm and used both hands to slide the door open.

Without further encouragement, Dancer ran inside.

"You'll be fine, but I need to find your mama." She closed the door again and turned to touch Mariah's furry head. "Where is she? Can you find Blue Lady?"

Mariah galloped outside the corral.

Casey followed. *Please, Blue Lady, be somewhere close by.* Rain slanted and rushed across the land in dark sheets. She could see nothing beyond the barns and corrals. Venturing any farther was a foolish idea, and the crack of a branch falling somewhere confirmed the decision. She called to Mariah. *I'll just check on the filly and head back to the house.* Two steps from the barn, a sudden pain gripped her belly. Her knees buckled.

Clutching her stomach, Casey gasped and leaned against the door…and waited for the pain to pass. *No, don't let this happen.* After a moment, her stomach relaxed, and she took a deep, relaxing breath. When a light beamed across the ranch yard, she looked to see the headlights of a vehicle. *Not the van or truck, but Roy and Juanita.*

He parked by the barn.

The lightning flashed, and she saw him get out. "Roy, over here!"

In a quick sprint, he flew over the fence. "Ms. Casey, what in the heck are you doing out here? Are you okay?" He slipped his arm around her and steadied her against a sudden gust of wind.

"I-I think so, but come inside the barn and check April Dancer. The mare…Blue Lady is gone. The gate came unlatched, and she got out. I put the filly in the stall and went to find her mother—" Another pain ripped across her belly and cut her off. She sagged against Roy.

With no hesitation, he lifted her in his arms and, with one foot, slid the door to the stall open. Carrying her inside and past the filly, to where several bales of straw sat in the corner, he gently lowered her. "Ms. Casey, what's happening? What's going on?"

Casey sat still until the pain passed, then lifted her gaze to Roy's. Fear filled his dark eyes. She rubbed her stomach and felt some of the tightness lessen. She'd had contractions like this for weeks before Jamie was born, but she was months away from her due date. "I'm not sure. I walked outside the corral a little way, and then I got…stomach pains." She inhaled a deep breath and let it out slowly. "Just give me a minute. But please, go check on Dancer and make sure she's okay."

Roy hesitated but then did as she asked. In a few minutes, he came back and crouched beside her. "She is fine. Now, how about you? I better get you to the house."

"But what about Blue Lady? She's out in this terrible storm." The thought chilled her bones. Anything could happen in this wild country, where people fell into creeks and almost drowned.

"Trust me. That mare can take care of herself." Roy shifted closer and tucked her wet hair over her shoulder. "You can't worry about her, Ms. Casey."

Casey pulled herself together and salvaged a bit of dignity. "Where is everyone else? Why are you home before the others?"

Roy stood and rubbed his hands on his jeans. "The boss was worried about you and sent me ahead." He held out one hand to Casey. "Let's try to make it to the house before he gets here. Can you walk?"

She grabbed his offered hand and let him help her. He slipped one arm around her, and they set out in the rain that still lashed in a relentless torrent. Once inside, Casey shed the slicker and went for towels. "Here, dry yourself off." She handed one to Roy and motioned for him to sit at the long table. After hanging the wet slicker out of sight in the mudroom, she put the kettle to boil.

Roy tapped his fingers on the table and watched her move around the kitchen. "Shouldn't you sit down...or something?"

When another pain built, Casey closed her eyes and imagined flowers and summer meadows. In a few seconds, the pain subsided.

"Do we need to call somebody?" Roy's usually calm voice shook.

"Actually..." Casey opened her eyes. "I think the pains are lessening. This one wasn't so bad." Poor Roy.

His expression was so full of concern. She sat at the table and made an effort to smile. "You can make me tea, though."

By the time headlights beamed down the driveway, the storm had abated, and she'd had no more pains for nearly an hour. "Please promise me you won't tell anyone about this," she whispered. "Especially not Chance. He doesn't need to know."

Roy opened his mouth.

"Promise me!"

He ran a hand over his face. "Sure, Ms. Casey."

Justin and Billie entered the kitchen with Jamie in tow.

Jamie ran to Casey. "Mom, are you okay? You don't look so good." The boy grabbed her arm.

Casey squeezed his shoulder. "I'm fine. But where's your dad?"

"He's making sure everyone gets back to their cabin," Billie said. "Are you sure you're all right?" She touched Casey's forehead with her cool fingers, then smoothed her damp hair and glared at Roy. "What's happened?"

Casey darted Roy a quick glance. "Nothing. Everything is fine." Putting anything over on Billie was pretty much impossible, but she had to try. She pushed herself away from the table and moved slowly to start the coffeemaker. Just so the pains didn't start again. She busied herself putting out cups and making hot chocolate for Jamie. She heard Justin grumble about the weather and Billie shush him while the puppy whined in his crate. Her hands shook a little, but she turned to Jamie. "Bear probably needs to go out, but you better put him on a leash." They didn't need another animal to go missing. "Stay close to the house."

Jamie hurried out the door. A few moments later, he hustled back inside, holding Bear in his arms.

Chance walked into the kitchen behind them. Immediately, he stopped and surveyed the room.

Did he sense the tension?

"What's going on?" he demanded, snatching his hat and wiping his forearm across his face. His unsettling midnight gaze flashed straight to Casey.

She couldn't keep everything secret. "Blue Lady…is gone. The wind blew the gate open somehow."

Justin harrumphed and shook his silvery head. "Wouldn't surprise me if she didn't open it herself. That mare has looked to get away ever since you brought her here. You just let yourself in for heartbreak, trying to tame a mustang like that."

Chance stepped between his father and Casey and faced her. He lifted a brow. "How do you know this? Did you see her get out?"

She saw his jaw tighten, while lines deepened at the corners of his eyes. She bit her lip. What should she say?

"The gate was open when I got here," Roy spoke. "I put the filly in the barn, but the mare had escaped. I would've gone looking for her—"

"But I wouldn't let him. The storm was bad, and we didn't need anyone else going into a creek." A surge of exhaustion drained Casey, and she gripped the edge of the counter. *If only I could just get away from here.* The sudden thought frightened her. Did she really mean that?

Justin shook his head and turned to walk away.

Billie clutched Casey's arm. "That's enough. You best head to bed now. I think you've had enough excitement." She glared at the men in the room.

Justin wheeled toward Chance. "You should never have brought that horse here. Now your wife's upset, and that's the last thing she needs in her condition."

Casey clenched her hands. If one more person mentioned her *condition*, she might scream. But she didn't want more friction between father and son, just when they were getting along better, and especially not over this. "Remember, it was my idea to bring Blue Lady here. So please, just stop."

Roy turned from Chance and Justin. "First thing in the morning, I'll look for her, Ms. Casey. She might still think wild, but she'll want to come back to her young one. I bet she won't have gone far."

"Thank you, Roy," she whispered and lifted her chin. A rush of gratitude filled her for the wrangler who had befriended her more than once. "I guess if anyone can find Blue Lady, it's you."

Once upstairs, Casey shivered and stripped off her damp clothes. She slipped into her flannel pajamas and crawled into bed and thought about what she'd said. Before leaving the kitchen, she'd caught a glimpse of Chance's tense face. He hadn't looked happy. Had she just created another rift?

****

Three days later, Roy rode in, leading Blue Lady.

While setting up the afternoon story and craft hour on the porch, Casey saw the blue roan trotting behind Roy and Scout. Gasping, she dropped everything and made a beeline for the corral.

Jamie clamored atop the fence. "Hey, Roy, thanks

237

for bringing my mom's horse home."

April Dancer ran to her mother and nuzzled her side. Poor Dancer had spent the three days calling out in piteous whinnies.

The cries about broke Casey's heart, and she couldn't help swiping away a few tears at the reunion of Blue Lady and her filly.

Roy closed and latched the gate, giving it a push to check the security. He wrapped the lead rope around his arm.

"Where did you find her?" Casey rubbed the heel of her hand across her cheek.

"She was down in a narrow draw, near the river. She didn't give me much of a fight. Think maybe she was glad I found her."

Casey pulled a tissue from her jeans pocket and wiped her nose. Then impulsively, she hugged the wrangler. "Thank you, Roy. I guess no one else thinks Blue Lady is worth the trouble, but I'm glad you do."

He patted her back one-handed, then stepped aside and slapped the rope against his thigh. "No trouble. I could hardly listen to that filly crying for her mama much longer, anyway."

Casey saw the dark flush on his cheeks. She'd embarrassed him, the last thing she'd ever want to do. "I'm sorry." She pushed back her hair, her hand trembling. "I'm just relieved you found her."

"Look, Mom, she's dancing again." Jamie pointed to the filly, who kicked her hooves and dashed around the corral.

Dancer might be happy, but Blue Lady observed her offspring's joy with a somber shadow lingering in her sable brown eyes.

Sympathy welled inside Casey. *After nearly a year, she still misses her life in the wild.* "Do you think she'll ever know this is her home?"

Roy shrugged and looked away. "Hard to know. She's still a mustang and as wild as they come. She might never be yours, but she was willing to come back. That's a start."

"I hope so." With a bittersweet sigh, Casey gazed at the horses. Then she spotted Bear gamboling across the pasture and poked Jamie. "You better go get him. Don't let that rascal inside the fence. Blue Lady doesn't care for the dogs too much."

Jamie jumped down and chased after the pup.

After a few seconds, Roy faced Casey and ran his gaze over her. "You feeling okay these days?"

She tucked the tissue in her pocket and managed a small smile. "I am, and after today, I feel even better. Thank you for not saying anything the other night."

He nodded, then suddenly glanced over her head. "Hey, boss. I brought the mare back. Now I'll get on to that work you told me about this morning." He tipped his hat to Casey and took off to mount up on Scout.

She watched him ride away, with Scout kicking Wyoming dust behind them. They should all be thankful for Roy's loyalty to the ranch. She turned to Chance, who stood beside her now. "Isn't it great Roy found her? He said she gave him no trouble."

"Yeah, so I see." He rubbed a hand over his shadowed chin. "Does that mean you have a new hero now?"

Her stomach jumped at his unexpected question. She glanced up. Why would he say that? Was he teasing, or did she detect an odd note in his voice? "Are you upset because Roy went after Blue Lady? Because finding her took him away from his work?"

Chance flicked his gaze away. "I would've found the mare. You didn't have to ask Roy."

"I didn't ask. He did it as a favor…to me."

"Whatever you say."

Last summer, before they married, Chance had told her Roy had a thing for her. She'd refused to believe that crazy notion then; she didn't believe it now. But maybe Chance still did. A hot wind blew across the ranch, drying her throat. Lately, the wind blew every day, and sometimes, the steady gusts grated on her already frayed nerves. How did anyone learn to live with the relentless Wyoming wind? Casey rubbed the grit from her eyes and wet her lips. "Whatever you're thinking, whatever's in your head, it's not true. You know me better, or at least you should."

His dark-blue gaze slid back and pinned her with its intensity. "What's happening to us, Casey? Ever since we came back from Michigan, something's been missing. Aren't you happy here?"

The question stung. She took a moment to regroup. She'd done her best to adjust to ranch life and had helped hold everything together while he and Kyle were gone. She'd returned to Wyoming after burying her first husband. Was that not enough? "I'm not sure why you would think that. Do I not live up to your expec…tations?" She choked on the last word and, wheeling about, fled toward the house.

He caught her and pulled her close. "Dammit, Casey, you know that's not true. I've never had any expectations. I just want this to work…for us."

His raw voice reached inside her and rubbed

against nerves already taut with worry over their relationship. But they had two children; somehow, they had to make this marriage work. "So do I. But do you remember last winter…that…video?"

He loosened his arms. "I thought we decided not to talk about it."

"And we haven't." Although, much as she tried, she couldn't banish the memory. "Because it really meant nothing. But if you can't give me the same trust, I'm not sure what to do." She swallowed a sob swelling in her throat.

"I'm sorry. After what happened with Angie and Kyle, I can't—"

He'd once believed his first wife and brother had had an affair. Not true, but the nightmare still haunted Chance. She stepped away. "The past needs to stay there, Chance. We can't keep dragging it back into our lives and let bad memories consume us. And you need to consider this. Who am I sleeping with? Whose child am I carrying? If that isn't answer enough, then I don't know what is. A woman's allowed more than one hero, but only one will hold her heart. You ought to know who holds mine." As Casey made her way to the house, she dealt with the painful truth. *He has the power to break it.*

Chapter 27

Fall drifted into the valley, and the willows along the river turned to gold. Summer warmth still lingered, but nights brought a taste of the long winter ahead.

Wrapped in a heavy sweater, Casey took her mug of tea to the porch to watch the sun disappear behind the mountains. After pink skies in the mornings, this was her favorite time of day—when the last light shimmered in golden beams and then faded away into an infinitely dark sky with the fine view of a million stars.

She leaned against the porch railing and waited for Chance. The last few weeks, he'd been busy with the fall roundup and she with getting Jamie back in school. They hadn't talked any more about the incident that led to the distance between them. His comment about Roy being her hero still stung, but she set her feelings aside for the sake of their family. Today, she saw something else that twisted the knife in her heart a little more—an online newspaper story and photo that showed Chance at the rodeo this summer, gazing at the chutes with the caption, *Local Champ Debating a Return?* as the catchy headline. The article detailed his history of traveling the circuit, as well as the many accolades he won in those ten years. Reading the story put Casey in a funk all day, and even now she couldn't shake the question dwelling in her mind. *Does he want to go back?* Despite the promise he made the day they married, did Chance still long to hit the rodeo circuit again? Did she dare ask him? She thought back to the night of the sleigh ride, the fierce cold, the northern lights, and the warm cabin. What she wouldn't give for one hour of that intimacy.

He had taken one last group of trail riders for a trip into the high country. They'd only ridden in an hour ago. He was still in the barn, putting out hay and filling water buckets. Always the last to turn in at night and the first to rise in the morning, he worked hard. Did he harbor regrets about coming home to the valley? He never intended to stay, of that she was certain, but she'd changed his plans. They'd believed their love could surmount any difficulties. A year later, Casey wasn't so sure. But she had to find a way to bridge the gap before the rift widened.

He crossed the yard.

She noticed the hitch in his stride. His bum knee bothered him a lot in the colder weather. But even so, his cowboy swagger made her heart beat a little faster. If he hurt, he never complained, but after a day spent in the saddle, for sure he felt the stress deep in his bones.

Mariah sauntered alongside him, vigilant and ready to lend support if her master needed it. But, her pace, too, had slowed. She made it up the steps, and the furry old dog wagged her tail and ambled over to Casey.

As much as her growing belly would allow, she bent to pet Mariah.

Chance spotted her on the porch. "What're you doing out here? It's getting cold."

"Just waiting for my favorite cowboy." She pushed herself away from the porch railing. The desire to be near this man she loved and to touch him overwhelmed the fears and anxiety. She ached to share her thoughts about the turning of the season, the anticipation of changes to come, and counting the days until Lily Rose arrived. How did she make him aware of her feelings? The question had put a note of melancholy in her heart, even before she read the article. She needed to share all this with the man who had brought her to this life. But what if none of that mattered to Chance? What if the itch to get out on the road still needed scratching? She raised a hand and touched his stubbly cheek. "How was the trail ride? You look tired."

He took off his hat and dropped it on a nearby chair. "One of the horses went lame, but we got him home. Ed's tending to him. We saw a few elk, and a grizzly crossed our path. That took some maneuvering to keep everybody calm and find another way home."

No wonder they got back late. So many dangers, but a year into their marriage, she'd learned to accept worry as a way of life. She slipped one arm around him and gave in to the need to lean in. Thank goodness, he'd come home safe again.

"I probably don't smell too good."

"Have I ever complained? I'm a farm girl, remember. Horses, cows, saddle leather—I rather like the combination."

With a soft chuckle, he pressed a kiss to the top of her head. "Let me get cleaned up. Then meet me in front of the fire."

"I left some supper on the stove. I'll heat it." That earned her another kiss and hug.

"You know the way to my heart."

She gave him a playful shove. "Go on then, and I'll meet you in the kitchen in twenty minutes." Once again, her fears took a back seat to everyday life.

Later, Casey eased onto the sofa in front of the flickering fireplace and stuck a pillow behind her back to ease the dull ache.

Chance settled beside her. "Have you talked to your parents lately?"

"Mom called yesterday. Daddy had hip surgery earlier this week. He's doing well, and, of course, he can't wait to get back to work. At least, she has my brother to help keep him in line, or he'd be out on the tractor way too soon. He's just about as stubborn as they come."

"Having met Lou, I can see how that's true, and also how much you take after him."

Casey jutted her chin out. "If I wasn't so stubborn, we wouldn't be sitting here right now with a baby on the way."

"You got me there. I guess I'm thankful for your stubbornness, and for your dad's handing the trait down."

A twinge in her back forced Casey to shift on the sofa and find a more comfortable spot. But at eight months, that probably wouldn't happen. Lily Rose hardly ever slept. *Maybe she's just eager to be born and make her mark in this world.*

"Here, turn around." He settled his hands on her shoulders and massaged them gently.

She rolled her head from side to side and let some of the day's tension slip away.

"Now, lean back." He moved onto his side and scooched farther on the cushions, leaving a space for her to stretch out beside him.

"I'm not sure there's room for three of us."

"Sure, there is." He snuggled Casey against him and placed a hand over her stomach.

Did he feel his daughter's nightly aerobics?

As a log fell, the fire snapped and sent a small shower of sparks whirling.

Casey relaxed, relishing the warmth of his strong arms around her. Maybe this was all they needed to heal the rift. "I heard Justin talking to Kyle today," she remembered to tell Chance. "Sounds like he's doing better. He and Marianne are moving into a bigger apartment, and he has a job now, at a local farm store. I think they're happy."

"Good to know. He and Marianne getting hitched was the best thing that could've happened to my brother."

Casey thought a moment. "Do you think they'll ever come back to the North Star?"

"Hard to say. Sometimes, things happen in your life that change you so much, you can never go back."

That was so true…for them, too. She turned her head. "But you did." She loved the sleepy look in his eyes and the sexy smile that touched his mouth.

"Very glad of it, too."

Closing her eyes, she waited for his kiss and settled in for its long, slow sweetness. Maybe the gap would close here. Maybe, she could forget all her worrisome fears and just let it all go.

He teased her lips, brushing his across them. Casey sighed and ran a hand through his hair, pulling him closer. *This.* This could mend the hurt. He ended the kiss much too soon.

"We're good yet, right? The baby, I mean. We've still got some time?" He pressed his face against hers.

Reluctant to move, she kept her eyes closed, wanting to hold on to the moment. But she heard the concern in his voice. "Mmm hmm. Four weeks. Why do you ask?"

"I need to make another run to Rock Springs before a big snow rolls in."

The loneliness of those holding pens, the relentless wind, and the haunting sound of the clanging gate all came rushing back. She wanted to save more of those horses, too, but was this a good time? "Why do you have to go now?"

"The agent got in touch with me. They've got three geldings with three strikes."

Three strikes meant the horses had been offered for sale three separate times but with no interest to adopt. What might be the mustangs' fate was anyone's guess. She understood his wanting to rescue them—she wanted him to—but a small flicker of fear rippled inside at the thought of him leaving the ranch. She searched her husband's gaze. He and Roy spent countless hours working with the mustangs. Their friendship seemed anchored in that work. The payoff being that, in time, the horses would take their place on the ranch. Chance could guide more guests on trail rides, which would add to the ranch's coffers. She didn't want to jeopardize the plan with her worries. "Will they ship them somewhere else?"

"Don't know for sure where they'll go, but there's always a chance the end result won't be good."

"Can't you send Roy?" Casey regretted the words the minute they left her mouth.

Chance pulled away, as much as the sofa would allow. "I'd rather do it myself. Besides, I want him here. Somebody needs to keep an eye on Justin. He's better at it than me."

He and Justin had bickered lately about a number of things. Casey often heard their tense words in the early morning hours and knew the disagreements kept Chance on edge. Maybe getting away for a day would do him good. But something inside her head said *no*. "But should you go alone? There's a storm on the other side of the mountains. What if—"

He heaved a sigh. "Casey, honey, you've got to stop worrying about everything. I'll leave before sunup and be back tomorrow night. It'll be fine."

She wanted to believe that was true, but some small doubt lurked in the corner of her mind, and she couldn't wish the worry away.

****

Dawn barely lit the morning sky. Gazing out the kitchen window, Casey waited for the soft pink color, but only a deep blue haze hung over the mountains. She finished wrapping a sandwich and added two chocolate chip cookies to the lunch bag. "Storm's still brewing. Do you think it will snow by nightfall?" She tried to keep her voice even, but a shiver crept over her in the cold house.

"I'll get ahead of the front." Chance settled his hat on his head and buttoned his fleece-lined coat. "Won't take me long to make the trip. I've done it enough times now."

She handed him the paper bag and a thermos of coffee.

He took them and studied her for a moment. "Why don't you go back to bed 'til Jamie gets up?"

Casey shrugged. She hadn't slept much last night;

she wouldn't sleep now. More than anything, she wanted to say *don't go. Something might happen.* But in the late-night hours, she'd decided not to say anymore. Wrapping her arms around her stomach, she followed him to the door.

A bracing wind swept in when he opened it. "Casey…I…" He slid one hand along her cheek.

She lifted her face for a kiss.

He only pressed one to her temple. Then he left.

A few moments later, the truck and trailer rumbled down the long drive. With a deep sigh, Casey watched the taillights disappear into the shadows. The thought *come back in time* ran through her mind. *But in time for what?*

Chapter 28

At the holding pens in Rock Springs, Chance climbed into the truck and slammed the door. He reached inside his coat and pulled his phone from his flannel shirt pocket to check the weather app. Nothing had changed since he'd left the ranch. He could only hope the storm on the other side of the mountains stayed put. Weather reports were sketchy about which way the snow would go, but a bitter wind had already cut across the barren buttes surrounding the pens. As he'd loaded the mustangs, he'd tucked his chin into his collar. He needed to get on the highway and ahead of the front. With three horses in the trailer, he had little choice.

He filled the travel mug with the barely tepid coffee left in the thermos and wolfed down the ham sandwich. He appreciated his wife's determination he eat something besides gas station food. Hard to get used to after years of living on his own. But he had to admit, knowing someone cared that much about his sorry self felt good. Maybe she fussed a little too much, but he was damn lucky to find a woman as caring as Casey. He shouldn't have made light of her concerns last night. After the serious bumps their marriage had endured this past year, she had a right to her doubts and worries. Something he should have learned the first time around with Angie. He hadn't listened to his first wife. One reason why she left the ranch. A nagging voice in the back of his head told him to hustle home and listen to Casey.

Finishing the last bite of sandwich, he washed it down with a few gulps of the lukewarm coffee and started the truck. As he pulled away from the holding pens and headed north, he noted the sky to the west had turned a darker shade of gray. The weather front was moving in swifter than he'd hoped. Could he still get ahead of it? He muttered a curse and stepped on the gas.

But twenty miles out of Rock Springs, snow began to fall.

****

"Have you heard from that man yet?" Billie bustled around the kitchen while she prepared dinner. "I hope he waits and gets on the road tomorrow."

"He planned on coming home tonight." Casey struggled to slam the door shut against a fierce gust of wind and motioned for Jamie to take off his boots. She stuffed gloves and stocking caps in their coat pockets and hung the parkas on the hooks by the door. The cold had cut through even their outerwear. She rubbed her icy hands together. "The temperature is really dropping fast. I hope Roy put Blue Lady and Dancer into the barn. I don't need them escaping on a night like this."

"Just don't you be going out there to check on them."

Startled, Casey stared at Billie.

"Yes, I know that's what you did during that summer storm, and no, Roy didn't tell me." She kept whipping potatoes.

No use denying the truth to Billie. The woman had an uncanny knack for just knowing things. Casey ushered Jamie through the kitchen and sent him to change out of his school clothes. She wandered into the living room and checked her phone for messages. None. Well, not surprising. A lot of long empty spaces, with no signal, stretched between here and Rock Springs. *But does that mean Chance is driving in this weather?*

She pushed aside the curtains and stared out at the snowy early twilight. Darkness was falling early. Too much like the night Chance and Kyle ended up in the flooded creek. Too much like the night when another man didn't come home.

She hugged her stomach.

Lily Rose was quiet tonight and only gave a lazy stretch now and then.

Fatigue tugged at Casey, but sleeping was out of the question until she saw the truck headlights in the drive. Turning away from the window, she spotted a phone charger lying on the coffee table and sighed. *His phone won't work soon.*

"Why isn't Dad home yet?" Jamie spoke from the doorway. "I thought I heard his truck."

Casey went to his side and pushed rumpled hair from his forehead. "It's a long trip to Rock Springs and back. With the bad weather, maybe he'll spend the night."

He tried to wiggle away. "But he'd let you know, wouldn't he?"

Not wanting Jamie to see her worry, she hugged him. "You know signals can get lost in the mountains. I'm sure we'll hear something soon. Come on, let's help Aunt Billie get dinner on the table."

Heading for the kitchen, she rubbed at the muscles in her back where, in the last hour, the ache had grown

252

stronger. She was a little worried about the pain, but nothing could happen until Chance came home. *Nothing*. She wouldn't allow their baby to arrive unless he was at her side.

****

Chance couldn't see a thing. A solid curtain of snow blew across the highway, blinding his view on all sides. How long since he'd left Rock Springs? The clock in the old truck ran slow. He slipped his phone from his shirt pocket and clicked the screen. Great. Out of juice and he forgot the charger. Casey would give him hell for that. He slowed the truck to a crawl and gripped the steering wheel against the blasts of wind. Was there any other fool on the highway? Hard to tell with visibility so poor. Down here in the Wind River Mountains, he really was in no-man's-land.

Peering into the swirling white maelstrom, he wrapped his fingers around the steering wheel and fought to stay on the road. But when an especially powerful gust caught him unaware, he felt the trailer slide. This wasn't good. He turned the wheel into the slide, and the truck straightened briefly. But winding down the mountain, the road beneath the tires turned to glass. He couldn't stop a sudden jerk to the left. The vehicle crossed the lanes and careened into the snow banking in the ditches. The driver's side door slammed against an immovable rock, and the airbag deployed. A resounding boom rattled his head, just as the voice he remembered from the day he and Kyle almost drowned in the creek whispered in his ear. *Hang on, son. This won't end here.*

****

A few hours after dinner, Casey sat at the long

table in the kitchen, clutching a mug of tea. Everyone else had turned in early, but sleep was the last thing on her mind. Fear, thick and unrelenting, clung to her skin and crawled across her scalp. She hated the waiting. Why hadn't she insisted Chance postpone this trip? She closed her eyes and searched for a bit of hope, but only a desolate sense of loneliness gripped her. A light rap on the door jerked her away from that yawning hole.

The door opened slightly, and Roy poked his head inside. "Ms. Casey, sorry to bother you. Just checking to make sure you're all okay. Boss-man told me—"

"It's okay, Roy, please come inside." She motioned for him to sit.

He hesitated a moment, then closed the door behind him and shook snow from his hat and shoulders, but he didn't sit.

"There's still coffee, if you want some."

He pulled off his leather gloves and poured a cup, then leaned against the counter, watching her with those dark eyes. "No word I take it?"

A sudden lump swelled in Casey's throat, and she could only shake her head.

Roy nodded and drank the coffee. "I've got everything battened down. Ed's making one last barn check. I put Blue Lady and the filly inside."

"Th-thank you," she managed past the lump. Swallowing the last of the tepid tea, she glanced at Roy. From her first day at the ranch, she'd depended on him, as a friend and a confidant, in figuring out how to live in this vast and dangerous country. "I should have told him not to go," she finally spoke. "But it was important he rescue those horses before they disappeared into some terrible place."

"You can't take the blame for what Chance does or how he does it." Roy stared into the cup. "When he gets a bug about something, he's going to do what he wants."

"Now you sound like Justin." Casey shifted on the bench. The ache that had plagued her all day sent stabbing fingers across her back. She lifted her chin and took a breath. "He still doesn't understand Chance. There is always some friction between them, and I don't know if they'll ever get along."

"Could be they won't." He met Casey's gaze across the room. "The bigger question is can you live with that? Looks to me the responsibility of the ranch will rest on Chance. Kyle isn't coming back anytime soon, if ever."

She didn't want to believe what he said. "How do you know that? Maybe after Kyle heals, he'll want to return. He loves this place."

"Not as much as you all seem to think. Before Chance ever came home last year, Kyle and I had some talks. He wanted to leave then, but there was no way Justin could handle the work, and Kyle knew that. He couldn't just walk out the door like his brother did and never look back."

Casey had realized long ago Roy possessed wisdom beyond his years. "Chance said sometimes things happen that change you so much, you can never go back." After what Kyle went through, she couldn't blame him for needing to escape. "I guess my biggest fear is how long 'til Chance wants to escape?" There, she'd finally voiced the fear that haunted her.

Roy drank the rest of the coffee and set the cup on the counter. "That won't happen, Ms. Casey. Chance has too much here that's important now. You and Jamie, working with the horses, and soon, this little one. Only something out of his control will keep him away."

Casey tipped her head and met his dark gaze. "The North Star gained a fine man when you hired on. I hope you'll always be here. I'm not sure what we'd do without you." She saw a shadow reflected in his eyes, almost a glimmer of sadness. What sort of emotion walked in Roy Silver Wolf's soul?

"I best get back to the bunkhouse, but you call me if you need me." He started for the door.

Casey rose. A sudden rip of pain took her breath away, and then a flood of wet warmth slid between her legs. She couldn't stifle a gasp.

Roy rushed to her side, catching her arm beneath the elbow and helping her sit. "C-Casey?" he choked on her name.

Dread washed through her, and she reached out to grip his firm hand. "Sorry, Silver Wolf." She tried to swallow her fear. "This isn't good. You better get Billie."

Chapter 29

Reaching one hand to his forehead, Chance found his hat gone and a lump rapidly swelling above his brow. Unrelenting cold seeped into his bones and numbed his extremities. Except for his head. His head hurt like someone had beaten him with a giant claw hammer. He leaned on the driver's side door and struggled to put together the last few moments before the truck slid off the road…along with the trailer. *The trailer!*

The horses sent out calls of distress and kicked at the trailer's sides.

Were they injured? He put a shoulder to the door, but it didn't give. He leaned across the seat toward the passenger door, but his head throbbed and his stomach lurched. Concussion? Hard landings had given him a few of those, and he knew the signs. He waited a few seconds for the nausea to pass. A light flickered in his eyes. Was that part of the head injury? No, the light flashed from outside and shone around inside the truck cab.

"Check those horses, Cory," a man barked. "Then give me a hand here. The door's jammed." He pounded on the passenger door. "Hey, buddy, hang on. We'll get you out of there."

The vibration of an engine sounded close by. Chance glimpsed another vehicle pull alongside the truck.

"Need help?" someone yelled.

"Yeah, pull ahead and come around this side. We need to open the passenger door."

Three yanks later, a gush of icy wind and snow blasted into the cab and slapped Chance in the face. The cold jolted him awake, and he lunged for the open door. Somebody grabbed his arm, so he didn't pitch headfirst into a snowbank. He leaned over, hands on his knees, and waited for the dizziness to pass. A grip on his shoulder steadied him.

"We're getting another trailer out here for the horses. They look to be okay. What about you, man?"

He opened his mouth to reply, then heard another voice. One that struck him like a punch to the solar plexus. He straightened to face the man with the white hair and drooping mustache.

"I called our ranch. Jack said he'd be here soon as he can with the trailer. Cory, why don't you stay with the horses while we get this fella some help…"

Through the falling snow, Chance saw the older man's jaw drop.

Lane Harris glared at him. "What're you doing in these parts again?"

Chance rubbed the side of his aching head. "Hello to you, too, Lane. And I'm doing exactly…what it looks like I'm doing." Of all times to meet with the old man again, why now?

Lane waved his arms at the snow-covered road. "Well, looks like a stupid fool thing if you ask me. You always haul horses in a blizzard?"

"Wasn't planning on it. Thought I'd stay ahead of the storm. But it didn't work out that way." He coughed, and pain flashed through his head.

"Doesn't surprise me none. You never did use your head," Lane grumbled.

The last thing Chance wanted was to have a go-around with a man who had little use for him. His only concern was for the three mustangs. He moved toward the trailer but stumbled.

Lane grabbed his arm and handed him his hat. "You best get in my truck. You don't look so good."

"I'm fine. Just need to stay upright." *Don't tell me what to do, old man.*

"Which maybe won't happen here real soon. Don't be a fool, McCord. Come on, I'm taking you to the D and L. Delia can check you out."

His vision blurred. Chance passed a hand across his eyes. "Delia hates me more than you do. She'd probably rather I was dead."

Lane snorted a short laugh. "I can't deny that, but she's doctored enough wranglers. She'll take a look at you."

In the back of his foggy brain, he remembered his first wife's mother. How she'd blamed him, how they'd both blamed him, for the accident that took their daughter's and grandson's lives. He was the last person they wanted to see.

A guy pulling a trailer stopped his truck nearby. The snow had let up some, but the night still laid cold and black around them. The driver jumped out and joined the kid called Cory at the back of the trailer.

Lane tugged Chance's arm. "This break in the storm won't last. We better get moving."

"The horses—"

"They'll haul them to my place. We can shelter

'em for the night."

All things considered, he didn't have much choice. His head throbbed like an ax split his skull in two, and the cold numbed the rest of his body clean through. Maybe this was some sort of weird justice. That he should have to rely on the two people in the world who hated him more than they could ever express. Chance followed Lane to his truck. Once inside, he rested his head against the back of the seat. How would he ever get home?

****

Lying on the sofa, Casey struggled to rise above the pain. Had an hour passed since she talked with Roy? She suppressed a moan and listened to the clock ticking on the mantle. She focused her gaze on the hands. *Nearly eleven o'clock.*

"Just try to relax, sweetie." Jeannie's soothing voice sounded close by. "Take some deep breaths. Help is on the way."

Deep breaths, yeah, like that would help. She had a knife stuck in her back. When the contraction passed, she struggled on the sofa. "Can't breathe. I need to sit."

Jeannie stuck a pillow behind her and offered some crushed ice on a spoon.

Casey pushed it away.

"You need to keep hydrated," Jeannie insisted. "Just take a little."

Casey obliged and let the cool liquid trickle down her parched throat. The ice revived her a little. She glanced around the shadowy living room. "Where's Roy?"

"He's out waiting for the paramedics. We thought it best to call them to take you to the hospital. You gave that young man quite a scare."

But he'd held her hand while she waited for the pain to subside. He'd been her lifeline at the moment. "He's…always here for me."

Jeannie lifted another spoonful of ice. "Yes, well, I think this time he wishes he was anywhere else but here."

Casey accepted a bit of the ice and swallowed. "Is Jamie okay? Is he still asleep? Where's Billie? I told Roy to get her. But how did you—?"

"Hush now." Jeannie patted her shoulder. "Justin called me. You've got that man half-scared to death. He's been trying to contact Chance, but he's not answering his phone."

"It's dead. He left the charger home." *He never listens to me*. Casey met Jeannie's concerned gaze. Her eyes filled with tears. "I knew he wouldn't be here."

Jeannie set the cup of ice on the end table. "He's a stubborn man, just like the rest of them."

"But part of this is my own fault, and I'm afraid he'll blame me." She shifted her position and stretched her legs the length of the sofa. "I should have told him not to go."

Jeannie raised her eyebrows. "How is this your fault? Sometimes, this is just the way things go. Our most important business is to take you and Lily Rose to the hospital. I'm pretty sure that little girl won't wait for her daddy to get home. Now, try to rest."

Tears leaked from the corners of Casey's eyes. She sank against the pillow and rubbed her stomach. *Please let my baby be all right.*

Billie entered the room, clutching Jamie by the hand. "He heard the commotion and insisted on seeing you."

Jamie broke free and ran into the room. "Mom! What's happening?" He knelt by the sofa. "Are you okay? Is Lily Rose?"

Casey read the fear in his eyes and pulled him close for a fierce hug.

"Your mom will be fine," Jeannie rubbed the boy's back. "Your sister has decided to put in an early appearance is all. We'll be off to the hospital in Jackson as soon as the paramedics get here."

Casey held her son's face in both her hands. "You need to stay with Billie and Justin, okay? I love you." She kissed his forehead.

Jamie swiped at his eyes with the heel of his hand. "Where is Dad? Why hasn't he come home yet?"

When another contraction built, Casey bit her lip.

Billie tried to draw the boy away.

Jamie still hesitated leaving. "Where do you think he is, Mom?"

"He'll be here…as soon as he can," she managed. "Remember, he told us he'll always come back."

"Let your mom rest now," Billie whispered and led the boy from the room.

She refused to let the pain monster have her and breathed along with Jeannie until the contraction passed.

Then Roy entered the room and leaned over to gently brush her hair back from her face. "The rescue guys are here now, Ms. Casey. Don't worry. Everything'll be fine."

She was tired of hearing that, but Roy's calm, sensible words gave her some solace. She grabbed his hand. "Please, Roy, just find Chance. Lily and I need him."

"Yes…m-ma'am." Roy's voice broke a little. "Yes, ma'am, I will."

****

When he entered the Harris's ranch house kitchen, Chance heard Delia Harris gasp. As he wavered in the doorway, he watched her careworn face crumple into a frown and her slender body tense.

But then, she moved quickly and pushed him to sit on a kitchen chair. "Take off your hat," she barked.

No sense arguing with the woman, but when he felt her fingers probe the bruised flesh, he winced, and his stomach rolled. He tried to move away.

"Sit still and let me take a look." She clicked on a flashlight and peered into his eyes. "You should probably go to the hospital, but we can't get there in this weather. You're just lucky Lane and Cory happened upon your truck in the ditch."

Chance swiped a hand over his face and fought off the waves of dizziness still surging through his head. "You don't have to tell me that."

"I guess I also don't have to say it doesn't seem wise to trailer horses in this storm."

"Nope, don't have to tell me that, either. Like I told Lane, I wanted to get ahead of the snow. I had hoped to make the Tetons by morning."

Delia went to the counter and poured coffee into a gray stoneware mug. She brought the mug back and pressed it into his hands. "See if you can keep that down. I've seen more than my share of concussions on this ranch, and I'm pretty sure that's what's going on. You better stay awake."

"I have no intention of sleeping. I need to make it

home." He stared at his former mother-in-law and forced himself to take a gulp of the coffee. She had the look of many western women—slim and strong, her silver-streaked brown hair pulled back in a single braid—but her face bore deep etches from the wind and sun…and the sorrow. If only her daughter could have had her mother's strength.

"What's there?" she demanded.

"He's married again." Lane shrugged out of his fleece-lined coat. "Some gal who's not even from Wyoming this time."

Their animosity crackled in the room, but at least, they weren't tossing him into the snow.

She pulled out a chair and sat. "Tell me about her."

"Excuse me?" What did she want him to say?

Delia leaned forward and rested her elbows on the table. "Tell me about your new wife. Is she anything like Angie?"

The question took him aback. He swigged more coffee, grimacing at its bitterness. "Not at all. She's…Casey is…" He searched for the right words. "Everything I never thought I deserved."

"And Angie wasn't?"

He pressed two fingers to his eyes. He didn't need this conversation right now. Didn't need to feel their resentment, but he couldn't escape. "Angie and I were too young. We didn't know what we were doing, getting married, and having a baby."

She slapped the table. "So that's your excuse?"

The woman wouldn't let up, and nothing he could say would make these two people believe him or understand the truth. They'd loved their daughter, as had he, but they didn't know the rest. They didn't know or want to admit the girl they'd raised had some mighty big problems. Problems he didn't know how to handle, even though he'd loved her. "I don't have any excuses for what happened between Angie and me. It just happened, and we've all had to live with the consequences. I lost my wife and son. You think that was easy? You think I haven't spent the last seven years of my life wondering what I did wrong?"

"She said you were signing up for another rodeo gig. That's what Angie told us before she left the ranch."

Chance bowed his head for a moment. That lie had followed him long enough. He glanced up. "I wasn't. I wouldn't have done that to Angie. Remember, she left me."

Delia's eyes shone with unshed tears. She stood and walked over to the stove, where a kettle of soup simmered. She stirred with a wooden spoon and reached into a cupboard for bowls. Ladling soup into them, she set one bowl on the table for Lane and another in front of Chance. "Since you're stuck here 'til morning, you might as well eat something." She sniffed.

Even after all these years, losing her child was as painful as the loss of his. Something a parent never got over. Chance felt their pain as much as his own. He glanced around. "Can I make a phone call?"

Delia nodded toward a room off the kitchen. "It's on the desk."

His head spinning, he shuffled to the small office where piles of papers sat alongside a single file cabinet and an older computer. An ancient rotary phone sat on the desk. He paused and got his thoughts straight before calling the North Star.

"Where in the blazes are you?" Justin asked.

His father's voice roared over the phone line and sounded much the same as when he'd yelled at the boy Chance for some transgression. He sucked in a breath. "The road turned to ice, and the truck slid, and…" He dragged a hand over his face and gave up explaining. "Can I just talk to Casey, please?"

"Well, you could if she was here, but they've taken her off to the hospital in Jackson. Looks like the baby is on the way."

The bomb hit him squarely between the eyes and jolted him out of any brain fog left over from the concussion. "But it's too soon." A tidal wave of fear swept through him.

"Guess your baby doesn't know that. Jeannie's with her. When do you plan on getting home?"

He gripped the phone in his hand. "By morning. I'll be there by morning." One way or another, he would get home. He had to be there for Casey.

****

How can this be happening? Just when the promise of a new life had bloomed, how could it all come crashing in so fast? Casey lay in the hospital bed and struggled to listen to the obstetrician.

"We need to airlift you to Denver, to St. Margaret's Women's Center. We've slowed the labor for now, but your baby will need to deliver. Her heartbeat is strong, but at four weeks early, she will do best in a neo-natal intensive care unit. As soon as the storm lets up, we'll have you onboard the medivac helicopter. In the meantime, hang in there, Mrs. McCord."

Casey held back a sudden urge to cry. "But my

husband's not here…"

The doctor pinned Casey with her sharp glare. "And he's where?"

"Somewhere between here and Rock Springs." Jeannie stood bedside with a cloth in her hand.

"We can't wait for him." The doctor turned on her heel and left the room.

Casey took a deep breath and forced herself to relax. She was so tired, but scary questions raced through her mind. What if Chance didn't make it home? What if he left her to raise two children alone? *No, this will not happen! Not this time. Not again.* She lifted her chin in defiance of what life might have in store.

"We'll get him there." Jeannie dabbed Casey's forehead with the damp cloth. "Morly and Roy are on the phone now, calling the Highway Patrol and ranches between here and Rock Springs. And I'm coming with you. I won't leave your side."

Casey just nodded. By the time the snow stopped and the helicopter was ready, she'd accepted the responsibility to protect her precious daughter and herself. Chance would make it home…sometime. She believed that. But he wouldn't be here to see his baby girl born. She touched the jade turtle pendant and summoned the courage to face what lay ahead. Would they all make it home again?

Chapter 30

Roy propped one booted foot against the bottom fence rail and leaned in. The sun barely peeked above the horizon, but already, the sky glowed with that rare pink light. The glimmer reflected in the snow until the entire land shimmered, as if immersed in some ethereal mist. Soon, he and Scout would go out to check the cattle. He'd already looked in on Blue Lady and her filly and the others in the barn, filled water buckets, and put out hay. Now, for this moment, he had to just stand here and let the events of the night lift away.

For the first time in years, he was afraid. Afraid of losing what he didn't and could never have, but still feeling the pain of that loss. Denying feelings. Yeah, he was good at that. He'd denied himself feelings since he was just a kid, but this feeling had dug deep into his soul and might never let him have any peace. Someone whispering behind him made him turn.

With his parka hanging open and hair sticking up in tufts, Jamie stood in the snow. His hand rested on Bear sitting at his side.

Roy read the same fear in the boy's eyes. "Hey, what're you doing out here?" His voice echoed in the frosty morning air.

"Aunt Billie told me to take Bear out. She let him sleep in my room last night."

Some guard dog. Roy motioned for the boy to

come closer.

Jamie stood at the fence with him and watched the sun rise over the North Star. "I wish my dad was here. He should be here. My mom shouldn't be alone again."

He looked at the kid in surprise. "How old are you?"

"Nine."

Smart kid. "He'll be back soon. He called from a ranch near Pinedale. He had to hole up there during the storm last night. But he's okay. He and your mom will be together soon."

Jamie narrowed his eyes. "You care about my mom, don't you?"

Where is that coming from? "Sure, she's a fine lady. Of course, I care." Roy saw a knowing look fill the nine-year-old's face.

"No, I mean, you like her."

The observation wasn't just an offhand remark but an emotion that rose from a place deep inside the boy. Roy had to respect whatever the boy thought. "Sometimes, sometimes we have feelings for someone, here." He put his clenched fist against his heart. "You know? And they're good feelings, but that's as far as they go, and all they'll ever be. Do you understand?"

The boy slowly nodded but gave him the side-eye. "I've seen you and my mom talking."

"Your mom and dad, they're like this." Roy held up two crossed fingers. "Only got eyes for each other. It'll never be different." He waited a few seconds for that to sink in. "You want to help me feed the horses? I have more hay to put out."

"Yeah. I'll take Bear to the house." Jamie trudged back through the snow, with Bear bounding after him.

"Put a hat on," Roy called out. "It's cold out here." Had he calmed the boy's worries? He hoped so. Now, if he could only settle his own.

****

At the moment, Casey decided nothing was worse than being transported in a helicopter. Except the fact she was in Denver, far away from home, and everything that could go wrong was.

"It's called placenta previa." Jeannie repeated what the high-risk obstetrician had said moments ago. "The condition can be dangerous for both mother and baby. So, they're taking you in for an emergency C-section. Do you understand that, sweetie?"

Against the starched white pillow, Casey nodded and focused on the painting on the wall behind Jeannie. Wildflowers. Red, like Indian paintbrush, and blue, like the lupine. She'd seen those flowers the day Chance brought her up the mountain, and she'd first told him about the baby. She rubbed her rounded stomach. Their daughter had been strangely still all day and throughout the night. *Please be all right, Lily Rose.*

Now, dawn peeped through the hospital window. The snow had stopped, and in her mind, she saw the sun rising and sending light across the valley to shine on the mountains she loved. Almost as much as she loved the man who had kept her in the West. Was the sky turning that shimmering pink hue over the valley? The Tetons by morning. Would she see them again? Would she one day show them to her daughter?

Casey took a deep breath and tried to draw on the inner strength and hope that had always seen her through the tough times. But this time, hope hovered too far out of reach.

****

Lane Harris climbed into his truck and stuck the key into the ignition. He stared across the seat at Chance. "Your wife and baby all right?"

Chance gazed across the range that lay covered in snow this morning. "I don't know…what's happening." He struggled to get the words past the strangling fear. In one of Lane's pastures, the horses he'd just rescued enjoyed their new freedom, galloping together, and kicking snow behind them. Maybe he should've remained wild and lived far away from people whom he only ever seemed to hurt. Maybe, when he saw Casey on the mountain that summer, he should have sent her away. He would've spared her all this grief. She would've gone home to Michigan and met a better man who could give her so much more.

"Cory will get your truck and trailer hauled in. He already went to see about it."

"The horses—"

"Leave 'em here for now. We've got our own small herd of mustangs. Every year, we add a few more. Keeps Delia busy finding folks to adopt them. It gives her some happiness."

"That's good." Chance glanced at Lane. "Thank you for doing this. It's more than I could expect from you and Delia."

Lane just nodded and started the vehicle.

Soon, they were rolling north, staying behind the snowplows that sent sprays of white flying. They didn't talk much but just listened to the highway reports on the radio.

Hours later, and a few miles from Jackson, Lane sniffed and cleared his throat. "I know you suffered the loss same as us. You didn't deserve it. Angela was…a troubled girl. Delia would never accept the truth. We thought things might get better for her at college. Then she met you."

Chance stared out the side window and understood the old man's pain. "I never wanted to hurt her." The sad truth—one he couldn't change—would always haunt him.

"I believe that now. But some pain never heals. Never goes away. You can only go on and find a new normal. That's what a grief counselor told us."

"Going on is the only way to live with loss." His own counselors were less astute, but they'd taught him similar rules.

At the hospital entrance, Lane glanced across the seat. "I hope your wife and baby will be fine. Delia said to tell you she'll pray for them."

Lane might think they'd moved on, but a deep sadness still lingered in the older man's eyes.

Chance suspected the sadness would never go away. He slid from the truck and winced. Every muscle ached from the jarring he took in the accident. *Almost like getting thrown from a horse.*

At the door, he met the well-groomed Max Pierson. As always, Max made Chance feel like a secondhand ranch hand. "Max, what are you doing here?"

The pilot zipped his flight jacket and clapped Chance on the shoulder. "Morly called me. I'm here to fly you to Denver. They airlifted Casey early this morning. C'mon, let's get to the airport."

Too stunned to speak, Chance followed Max while a hard truth drummed into his brain. He'd failed Casey…again. And this time, she might not grant him forgiveness. *She doesn't deserve this. I don't deserve her. What will happen to us?* What reality awaited him in Denver?

Chapter 31

The hospital doors at St. Margaret's opened like yawning jaws. Chance checked at the visitor's desk to get a pass and directions to the maternity floor. He'd borrowed Max's phone charger on the plane and texted Jeannie, but she hadn't replied. Well, cell reception wasn't the best inside these buildings.

As he made his way down the empty corridor, he heard his boot steps echoing. When he stepped inside an elevator and punched a button, the jolt of it moving brought home where he was and why. He closed his eyes to absorb the truth and squelch the panic.

Jeannie met him at the door to the NICU and gave him a quick hug. "Thank goodness for Max. He was a godsend to get you here."

"I…what's happening, Jeannie? What do I need to know?" He steeled himself for whatever she might say.

She took his hand and drew him toward the nursery window.

A nurse in blue scrubs with pink teddy bears tended to a crying infant in a warming crib.

"You have your Lily Rose," Jeannie whispered. "And she's beautiful."

In a rush of emotion, Chance took off his hat and stepped closer to the window.

The nurse smiled and lifted the baby.

Wisps of blonde hair curled across Lily's head, and

she raised a tiny fist. He couldn't turn away, but then his chest tightened. "Is she…is she all right?"

Jeannie patted his shoulder. "She's very healthy, just small. She's breathing on her own, but they'll keep her until she gains a pound or two."

He couldn't quite wrap his head around the reality. A daughter. He and Casey had a little girl. *Casey.* His stomach clenched. "What about…what about my wife?" Jeannie's hesitation brought his attention from the nursery window. The look in her eyes told him what he'd feared the most. An icy chill gripped him. "Jeannie?"

She breathed a long sigh. "There were some complications, Chance. Casey…had a pretty rough time. They did an emergency C-section, but they couldn't stop the bleeding. They had to remove her uterus. She's still not awake."

He felt the blood drain from his face. They would never have more kids? Casey loved kids. They'd talked about having another baby. *I shouldn't have left her. I shouldn't have…* He flattened a steadying hand against the window. Once again, life spun out of control, tearing him between wanting to stay here with his child…and needing to be with the woman who meant more than life itself.

Someone else stepped to the window. "Hang in there, cowboy. She'll be okay, but it'll take a while."

He glanced sideway. Christina Truelove, the nurse he'd met when Kyle was in Denver, stood beside him.

"Your baby has the best care. Go to your wife," Jeannie said quietly.

Christina led him down another corridor before stopping.

Outside the room, he braced himself.

"She's been through a lot, and now, she just needs to know you're here." She gave him a small push into the room.

Another nurse leaned over the bed, taking vitals.

"This is Mr. McCord," Christina said. "How about we leave them alone?" She waited until the nurse finished her duties, and then shut the door behind them.

Chance stood in the middle of the room. A blood pressure cuff on Casey's arm puffed and ticked down numbers. Another machine beeped. Sounds in a hospital were so strange. They intimidated and threatened and made him feel helpless. He approached the bed where Casey lay silent, so unlike the warm, passionate woman he knew so well.

Tossing his hat on a nearby table, he pulled a chair close to the bed and looked away from the needle in her slender hand. He hated the bruises, the way her lips looked cracked and dry, and how her beautiful gray eyes lay hidden behind darkened lids. He touched her tawny strands of tangled hair and smoothed them across her shoulders.

She stirred but didn't awaken.

He touched her pale cheek. "Casey, honey, can you hear me?"

No response.

"I'm sorry…I wasn't here. Sorry you had to go through this." He lifted her hand without the needle, kissed it, and pressed it against his face. Her skin felt cool and lifeless. "Please wake up, Casey. I…need you to wake up. Don't make me go through the rest of my life without you."

She still lay silent.

Chance leaned over and kissed both her eyelids, then sat again and rested his forehead against her side. For a long time, he counted each breath she took and willed Casey to say his name. When he felt featherlight fingers skim over his hair, he lifted his head.

"Our baby…is she…?" she rasped in a hoarse whisper.

He met her misty gaze. His heart thumped hard. "Our Lily Rose is fine. She's fine, and she's beautiful, just like her mama." He grasped her hand and kissed it, vowing he'd spend the rest of his life making this up to Casey.

She gave him the grace of a small smile and stroked his stubbly jaw. "I was…worried about you, Chance. I'm so glad you're here…even if you are…a scruffy cowboy."

At the sound of what he hoped was absolution, he let out a breath, bowed his head, and tucked his face against Casey's side so she wouldn't see his tears.

Sitting in the hospital café later, he considered the blessings of second chances and how a man like himself had found the love he and Casey shared. For years, he had a hard time believing his life could be better, but today, he realized life was all about second chances.

Christina Truelove approached and sat at the other side of the table.

He glanced up. "You get around, don't you?"

She smiled. "There was an opening here at St. Margaret's, and I thought maybe I should work with new mothers and their babies rather than people with broken bones." She waited a few seconds. "How is your brother doing these days?"

"Okay. Having some issues, but he and Marianne are married and live in Spokane."

"What is this?" Christina moved closer and touched the lump on his head. "Were you knocking some sense into yourself?"

He grimaced from the leftover pain and jerked away. "It's nothing. Just a reminder of the past."

"I'm sorry. I didn't mean to make light of it." Christina sat silent for a moment. "Your wife is a tough gal, but seriously, how are *you* doing?"

He shrugged. "Just sitting here thinking about the years I spent alone."

"You're not alone now."

He wrapped his hands around his coffee cup and leaned forward. "Yeah, but it scares the hell out of me. I failed Casey. I could have lost her, and I wonder if things will ever be the same between us. He took a quick swig of the brew, needing a jolt of caffeine.

"Your wife is a heck of woman, and I think love will find a way."

Christina Truelove had a demeanor that took him back to another time, and he had the feeling again that he knew this woman. But from where? He studied her face.

"I've felt it, too. She waved away his scrutiny. "From the minute I saw you last spring. The feeling needled at me, then suddenly, one day, I figured it out. My husband, Jacob Truelove, was driving the truck that Angela's car slid into."

His heart plummeted into his stomach. How many times could the past come crashing back to haunt the present? He remembered a man who wasn't at fault, but who jackknifed his semi-trailer in a sudden snowstorm.

Not so different from what he'd done with the horse trailer. Except that a young wife and mother crashed her car into Jacob, taking her life and that of her little boy. The accident left three shattered families behind.

He didn't want to think about those sad memories, but, by some twist of fate, in two days he'd come up against the other people who were most affected by that incident years ago. "Not a link we like to think we share."

"Yet, there's a reason we've met again." Her blue eyes glistened.

"And have you figured out what that is?"

Christina folded her hands on the table. "Not yet, but we'll know someday. I'm sure of it."

"Your husband lived, but he was injured." He didn't want to think about that tragedy, but once again, ugly truth stared him in the face.

"Jacob was setting up flares outside his truck. The car hit him first. He's still in a wheelchair."

So many consequences because of the actions of two people. If only Angela and I hadn't fought that morning. If only I hadn't gone off with Justin to see about some damn cattle, leaving Angie alone. If only I didn't do the same thing to Casey.

A few moments passed in silence.

Christina touched his arm. "Have you held your baby yet?"

The thought terrified him. "I didn't know I could. She's so small."

"You're the daddy. Of course, you can." She tugged on his sleeve. "Come on. Let's get you scrubbed and suited up."

He barely fit in the nursery rocking chair, but the

tiny bundle placed in his arms fit perfectly in the crook of his elbow. His baby's wisps of hair, fine as corn silk, swirled around her puckered little face with an impudent chin. "Just like your mama's." He touched Lily's baby-soft cheek with a tentative finger and marveled at the perfect child he and Casey had made.

His daughter screwed up her little pink mouth and let out a healthy wail.

"Lily Rose," Chance spoke the way he remembered speaking to another baby in a different time. "Welcome to the world, baby girl."

She opened her blue eyes wide and focused on his face. In that moment, a bond as strong as the Wyoming wind formed between father and daughter. When he watched Lily's miniature fist close around his finger, Chance lost his heart forever.

****

Casey tugged a brush through her tangled hair until all the snarls were gone, then gathered the limp strands into a ponytail. The antiseptic smell of the hospital hung in the room and did nothing to calm her unsettled stomach. She sighed and set the brush on the bedside table. Two days had passed since Lily's birth, and these simple actions still exhausted her. She shifted position in the hospital bed, careful not to jar her ravaged insides. Considering what she'd gone through—the bumpy helicopter ride and the scary rush into surgery—it was no wonder she ached from head to toe. The truth the doctor had explained this morning only made the ache worse. That she wouldn't have any more children stuck like a thorn in her heart. Did Chance know? He was gone when she awoke. She needed to ask how Jamie was doing back at the North Star. He looked so worried the night she went into labor. Did he understand what happened?

The last forty-eight hours were a blur, but she remembered hearing her baby's cry and having a quick glimpse of her pink-faced little girl's indignation at being thrust into a cold world. *Lily Rose.* Being so woozy from anesthesia, Casey recalled nothing after that. Now, despite her own discomfort, she longed to hold her daughter in her arms. Chance said he'd held Lily that first day and that she was beautiful and doing just fine. *Chance.* He'd spent the last two nights sleeping in a chair beside her bed, the nurse Christina had said. So, where the heck did he go? Now that she was awake, they needed to talk…about what happened…and the surgery. She pressed a hand against her fluttering stomach and winced at the pain from the stitches. But the piercing ache in her heart hurt worse.

Familiar whistling in the hall drew her attention. Casey glanced toward the doorway. She smoothed the ponytail lying over her shoulder and straightened her hospital gown.

Chance strolled into the room, holding one hand behind his back. Seeing her sitting up, he swept off his hat and quickened his pace. "Casey, honey, how're you feeling?" He dropped his hat onto the table and stood at her bedside, still keeping one hand hidden. "Christina said they had you up."

Casey groaned. The short walk she'd taken with the nurse had been an exercise in utter determination. "Yes, they said I have to start moving. But did you see Lily this morning?"

"I did, and she was screaming her lungs out while they gave her a bath. That little girl has sure got a voice."

I want to do that! I want to take care of my baby! Suddenly, she burst into tears and buried her face in her hands. Why had everything gone so haywire? What did she do wrong?

"Aww, Casey, honey, don't cry." Chance dragged the chair near and sat. "Lily is doing great. She'll be ready to go home any day. She's our daughter. You know she's strong."

"But…but I want to hold her. I'm her mother." *And my milk is coming in, and my breasts are sore.* "We need each other."

"I'll take you to see Lily. The doc just wanted you to get a little strength—"

Feeling weak and useless, she lost control and sobbed harder. "This is it for me. For us. I can't have any more—"

"I know that hurts you. But we'll be okay. We have Jamie and Lily. They are enough." Chance gently drew her hands from her face. "Look at me now."

She blinked through tears and met his steady gaze. His eyes were so blue. *Like the sky above the mountains right before a storm.* That was the same thought she had the first time she ever looked into his eyes. A few more silvery strands streaked his neatly trimmed dark hair. She scanned his face. He was clean-shaven today. She let out a shaky sigh. "Are you trying to impress me?" She rested her face against his work-roughened hands.

Smiling, he rubbed a thumb across her cheek. "What I'm trying to do, Casey McCord, is say that you are the love of my life. Nothing will ever change how I feel. *Nothing.*" He leaned over and kissed her.

Casey sank into the kiss and stroked his smooth jaw, inhaling the spicy scent of aftershave. She wanted to let the painful truth go, but her heart still ached. She drew away. "I wanted to give you a son…after Lily. To take over the North Star someday."

He shook his head and straightened in the chair. "I'm a lucky man. I have two sons. Scottie isn't with me, but Jamie is. Now, we have a daughter. As feisty as Lily Rose is, she'll be the one to take over the ranch. And, I have a wonderful wife. A man couldn't ask for anything more." He cleared his throat and reached for something on the floor. "The lady in the floral shop said these mean *I love you*." He placed a green-tissue-paper-wrapped spray of red roses across her lap. "If you ever had any doubt."

Casey managed a smile and lifted the roses to smell their sweet petals. She snuffled away more tears. "I have no doubt. But what you said about sons…thank you for accepting Jamie as yours."

Chance brushed a hand across his mouth and glanced away. "You know that boy means the world. Always will." At the sound of voices in the hallway, he pushed himself from the chair. "Speaking of sons, I've got a surprise."

In the next moment, Jeannie entered the room with Jamie in tow.

Seeing him, Casey almost broke into tears again. She and Jamie hadn't been apart this long in forever.

With a whoop, he ran toward her.

Chance grabbed his arm and held him back. "Take it easy on your mom, son. She's feeling a little sore today."

"It's okay." Trembling, Casey set the roses aside

and reached for Jamie. "Give me a gentle hug." Thank goodness her boy didn't have a problem with showing affection today. Just feeling his sturdy arms around her neck gave her heart a lift.

"I'm so glad you're okay." He pressed his head against her shoulder for a quick embrace. "Billie said you got to go in a helicopter. Did you like it? I've been helping Roy with the horses. Oh, and we saw Lily. She's pretty small, but Jeannie said she's growing already." He turned to Chance. "Can we take Mom to see her?"

Bracing a hand over her stomach, Casey winced and held back a laugh at Jamie's chatter. Leave it to her boy to lighten her mood.

A nurse in bright-pink scrubs pushed a wheelchair into the room. "Here is your ride, Mrs. McCord. We thought it better if you had a little assist."

In the nursery, she guided Lily to her breast and held the tiny hand fisted against her taut skin. She felt her milk let down, and relief flooded her body. "She's a hearty eater, anyway." She glanced at Chance, who sat beside them and watched his child tugging in earnest. "I guess she's a McCord through and through."

He touched Lily's soft hair with one finger. "You're both…pretty amazing." He choked a little over the words but lifted his gaze to meet Casey's. "And you're beautiful."

She blew out a breath. "Considering I'm sitting here in a hospital gown with my hair a mess, and my breasts leaking, I'm not sure that's true, but thanks for the compliment, cowboy." Seeing his sexy grin warmed her heart. "You look pretty good yourself." She noticed Jamie and Jeannie no longer stood at the nursery window. "I guess he's bored with his sister already."

Chance shrugged. "They went to the café for lunch. You know the kid's always hungry."

Casey smiled and leaned her head against the rocker, hoping the best things in her life never changed.

Chapter 32

The cold of the December evening didn't reach into the barn at the North Star, and the warmth from the animals lent a cozy air. Chance finished filling water buckets before heading up to the house for Christmas Eve dinner.

Jamie had set out flakes of hay for Blue Lady and Dancer in their stall and waited for Chance to finish his chores. "I bet they're happy you let them stay together." He motioned toward the mare and the filly nosing at their hay.

Chance closed and latched the door to Smoky's stall. "In the wild, mares often keep their young ones with them, even after they're weaned."

Jamie rested his arms on the stall's top rail. "Do you think the first Christmas Eve was like this, Dad?"

"How's that?" He checked on the Belgians and the others that shared the barn.

"Did it smell like horses and hay and sweet feed?"

He contemplated the boy's observation. "Guess we can't be sure, but it's a good way to imagine it." He closed the bins of feed and joined Jamie at the mare's stall. "You ready to head up to the house? Billie made something special for us tonight, so we better not hang out too long."

Jamie nodded but still stared at the mare. "Do you think Blue Lady is happy here? Does she remember what it was like to be wild?"

"You're just full of questions tonight, aren't you?" Jamie was an inquisitive kid, but he ruffled his hair.

The boy tipped his head and looked up at Chance. "Mom says she might always miss being able to run free. That's kinda sad, isn't it?"

Chance entered the stall and held out a hand to the horses. "Despite all her issues, Blue Lady has come a long way." *As we all have in the past year.*

Dancer came to him with no hesitation.

The mare finally ambled over and accepted the gift of an apple he'd brought in earlier.

"I guess maybe she finally trusts you, huh?"

"I think she still likes Mom the best, but some things just take time." He untangled the mare's forelock and scratched her head. "Sometimes, the life we want isn't what's given to us, and we have to find the silver lining. Sometimes, we find out that it's better after all. Isn't that right, girl?"

Blue Lady only responded by crunching the apple.

Footsteps echoed in the center aisle of the barn, and soon, Roy joined them.

"Hey, Roy, Blue Lady let my dad give her an apple. She finally likes us, I think," Jamie said.

Roy grinned. "Maybe she finally got smart."

Chance left the stall and closed the door tight. "You and Ed got plans tonight? You're welcome to join us." The two wranglers had often been his lifelines in this year of change. He hoped the bonus checks he'd given them earlier today showed his appreciation.

"Thanks, but Ed's going into town to see his girl."

"And you?"

Roy straightened his shoulders. "I'm headed to

Lander to see my mom. We haven't spent Christmas together in a long time, and she asked me to come home. My stepfather has business elsewhere, so he won't be around. Then I'm going to see my dad's family at the Wind River." He handed a gift bag with two wrapped presents to Jamie. "Just a little something for you and Lily Rose, from Ed and me. Merry Christmas."

Jamie's eyes shone. "Thanks, Roy! I'll open the one for Lily. She can't do that just yet."

"Won't be long I bet before she can, though. She's a scrapper, I hear."

"Yep, she likes to keep us all awake at night." Jamie glanced at Roy. "You sure you don't wanna have some dinner? My mom said you should come in."

Chance watched a shadow chase across Roy's face. "Speaking of dinner, we better get going. You head to the house and put that gift under the tree." He steered Jamie toward the big door. He waited until the boy left, then turned to Roy. "I probably don't say this enough, but thank you for sticking with us. And…thank you for looking out for Casey when the baby came. Not sure how we'd manage if you didn't come back."

Roy met his steady gaze. "Crossed my mind that maybe it's time to move on but probably won't happen yet. I just need to make some connections with my family on both sides."

If anyone understood that thinking, Chance did. He pulled off his gloves and held out a hand toward Roy. The wrangler's firm and heartfelt handshake told him all he had to know. "Give your mother our best. Take the time you need. The North Star will be here when you get back."

Chance closed the barn, and the two men walked into the December twilight.

Roy climbed into Juanita and drove away.

Chance could only hope the wrangler would indeed return but understood full well why he might not.

The sun had disappeared, but a glimmer of light still glowed over the Tetons. Tonight, the sky would be clear. Maybe he and Casey could come outside later for a few moments of stargazing and to look for the star that was named after her.

On the porch, both dogs lay together. Bear had finally calmed down for the night, feeling secure and safe beside the ever-watchful Mariah.

Chance stooped to give them each an ear scratch. Inside the big old cedar house, the tantalizing aroma of baked pies and perking coffee greeted him. The kitchen was warm and inviting, but the light from beyond that room drew him. Hanging his hat and coat on the hooks by the door, he pulled off his boots at the bootjack and felt the relief of a day's work done.

He paused just outside the living room and took in the scene that provided the comfort he never thought he'd find. Watching Billie and Justin bicker over their game of checkers and Jamie rearrange the nativity scene under the shining Christmas tree brought solace to his soul. But most of all, seeing Casey in her rocking chair, snuggling and humming softly to their baby, told Chance he was home. "How is our Miss Lily?" He knelt beside Casey and blew on his hand before touching the baby's wisps of corn silk hair. "Think she'll give us a few hours of sleep tonight?" *Or a little time for kissing…and maybe more?*

Casey gazed at the baby girl, who was spunky from

the beginning. "I told her Santa won't come if she's awake, but I'm not sure she cares." She looked past Chance. "Where are the guys? Didn't you invite them in? We have so much food."

He shrugged. "I did, but they've got young guy plans. Ed has a lady friend in Jackson now, and Roy went to see his mother. He said he needed some family time."

She just nodded, and then she grabbed his shirt and tugged him close, kissing him full on the mouth.

His lips were still cold, but hers tasted sweet and brought an instant warmth to his heart. He slipped a hand into her hair and stroked the back of her neck.

She leaned into him. "Do you have plans for later, cowboy?"

"Not that I know of. What did you have in mind?"

"Hmmm, maybe a little stargazing. And a little more of this." She kissed him again.

"I always have time for this." He buried his face in her hair, savoring the softness of Casey. In the background, he heard Billie laugh and Justin grumble that he'd lost another game of checkers.

Then Jamie started singing a Christmas carol.

Between them, Lily Rose wiggled and let out a squawk.

Casey gave a wistful sigh. "I think we've got our hands full here. Our lives will never be the same."

In the soft glow of the Christmas tree lights, Chance knew he wouldn't have his life any other way.

Chapter 33

The early morning light Casey loved turned the sky pink and the valley below to a golden hue. In the distance, the jagged peaks of the Grand Tetons, topped with early summer snow, reflected the colors.

With Lily Rose in her front carrier, Casey ventured to the edge of the overlook. Wildflowers, just beginning to peek from their slumber, spilled down the side of the ridge. In the valley, the Buffalo River still ran fast from spring runoff. A cool wind rushed through the pines and sent a sigh rippling through their branches. She pulled the baby's knit hat over her curly hair.

She and Chance came to this spot often to escape the ranch, much as he had escaped here as a boy. Casey liked to point out the flowers, and the mountains, and the occasional moose or bison they could see from this vantage point. She wanted her daughter to grow up knowing about her home. Once, they saw a pair of eagles fly overhead. "This valley wasn't always my home," she confided to the eight-month-old. "But it's home now and always will be, and now it's yours."

Lily babbled and held out a chubby arm, pointing to where Chance and Jamie poked around by the grove of aspens. She kicked her feet and squealed in delight.

She was a daddy's girl and never failed to smile in his presence. Casey understood.

"Hey, Mom. Come here," Jamie called.

She wandered over to see what held Chance's and Jamie's attention.

Chance crouched and examined something on the ground.

Casey stood behind him. "What is it?"

"We found some rocks, Mom." Jamie waved her closer. "Have a look."

They could find plenty of rocks around here. Why were these so different? She peered over Jamie's shoulder. Two flat stones lay embedded in the dirt with only the tops showing.

Lily cooed at her father and vied for his attention, but for the moment, the stones held Chance's interest.

"What's so special about them?" Casey asked.

"Bear was digging over here, so we came to see why." Jamie knelt beside Chance.

Chance brushed his hand across the exposed surface and uncovered etchings on the stone.

"Looks like some kind of writing," Jamie said. "I think it says, hmmmm, maybe Garret?"

"And Martha," Chance finished. "Look here." He cleaned off more of the stone.

Jamie and Casey leaned closer.

"It says McCord." Jamie jerked his face up. "But why?"

Chance rested his hands on the stones for a minute. Then, he pushed himself slowly to stand. "Garett and Martha. I remember my grandparents talking about them. They came here in the late 1800s and settled in the valley."

"They're the people from Justin's old journal." Casey stared wide-eyed. "The ones I helped him write about in North Star Legacy. Do you think…?"

Chance met her gaze. "They're buried here. The years they died might be etched on the stones, too, but that's worn off."

"How amazing you found them. After all this time. But why were they buried here?" Since coming to Wyoming, she'd often compared herself to Martha, who had dealt with a harsh land but stayed because of the man she loved.

"My guess is they liked this spot and wanted the overlook to be their final resting place. I understand why." He ducked under the aspen boughs and went to stand at the edge of the ridge.

Casey left him alone to reflect on the discovery. She turned as Bear ran off after a chipmunk, with Jamie in pursuit. "Don't go far," she called out. "The bears are awake now." A moment later, she joined Chance.

He stared at the mountains beyond them. "Maybe it's why I always felt drawn to this place. From the time I could saddle up and ride out on my own, this is where I felt a connection to the valley and the mountains…and to the past."

"Daddeee, daddee, daddee," Lily chanted in her baby talk.

Chance wiped the dirt from his hands and finally gave Lily the attention she was seeking. She grabbed hold of his finger and tried to chew on it.

When Casey would have protested, she bit her tongue. A little dirt wouldn't hurt Lily. She touched Chance's arm. "I'm glad you found the stones. I think it's a sign the valley will always be our home." His easy grin, the one that had enticed her to stay in Wyoming in the first place, warmed her heart. That smile would forever keep her here.

He put his arms around her and Lily.

Casey leaned in and rested her head against his shoulder. As always, she felt safe encircled in his embrace.

"Wherever you are is my home," Chance whispered in her ear. "You and Lily and Jamie." He kissed her cheek and hugged her and Lily close. "You're all I'll ever need."

Lily babbled and kicked her feet in her cowboy booties. With a chubby finger, she pointed toward the sky.

Casey followed her daughter's gesture and nudged Chance. "Look, there they are."

Above the valley, two eagles soared and caught a wind current. Together, the raptors made a graceful journey through the bright Wyoming sky.

Perhaps in the autumn, they would see their eaglets flying.

Author's Note

After many trips to the rugged and beautiful state of Wyoming, I feel I know the state well. My son lived there for ten years and has been an invaluable source of information. I tried to stay true to the terrain, but for the sake of my story, I might have changed some details. The truth is, in Wyoming, one travels fifty miles to go five, and a lot of empty spaces exist. But the sky above the Tetons truly does glow pink at sunrise.

A word about the author…

Lucy Naylor Kubash has had a lifelong love of reading and has been writing for as long as she can remember. She is published in short fiction and novel length contemporary romance, as well as nonfiction, having written a column called the Pet Corner for over twenty years. She is a member of Michigan Romance Writers, Romance Writers Online, and Women Writing the West. She loves anything to do with the American West and traveling there whenever possible. When not writing, she likes to spend time with her family and pets. Read more about Lucy and her books at www.lucynaylorkubash.com

Other Titles by this Author
Chance's Return, North Star Legacy #1
The Haunting of Laurel Cove
Will O' the Wisp